I WILL ALWAYS FIND YOU

JEFE CARTEL BOOK 1

WILLOW SANDERS

Enjoy!

xox

Willow Sanders

Tag me on insta

@author willow sanders

I Will Always Find You
Willow Sanders
Copyright 2017 Willow Sanders
Digital ISBN: B079JSLQ36
Paperback ISBN: 978-1986419307
Editing: RJ Locksley

❀ Created with Vellum

Cover Design by Becca Rose Designs
www.beccalittle.com
info@beccalittle.com

WARNING:

This book is a _romance novel._

It contains romantic elements (read: sex. Lots of sex).

It uses dirty words—both of the four letter variety, and of the
"_How do we refer to his package in another way without saying penis._"
variety.

If you're like 'hell yeah- bring it' --- your story awaits.
All others don't say I didn't warn you.

Camille

W ho shatters a figurine? A cheap, porcelain figurine of a little girl, mid-pirouette in a tutu and pigtails? A stupid piece of shit my mom got for less than a dollar at some kind of stop-and-save store. The little girl's pigtails, which at one time had been dark brown, looked just like my own hair. That was of course before I had learned the benefits of a good highlight or a properly executed ombre. With age the little ballerina's paint had chipped and faded, she now looked more like a Dalmatian than a dancer. Her dress and toes used to have pink rosettes along the hem of the skirt and at the point of the toes, but over the years those too had chipped and fallen off in the never-ending shuffle of being packed and unpacked to move to another city.

Each time my mother had decided to move, that little ballerina was the first thing she packed. She took great care to wrap it in whatever sales paper was lying about when seemingly on a whim she decided that Oklahoma City sounded so much nicer than Dallas, or that Los Angeles had lost its luster, *lets give Miami a try*. Wherever we ended up, that little ballerina was the first thing she would unpack from the few boxes that fit in her ramshackle Geo Metro. In every shithole apartment we lived in, that ballerina occupied the place of pride in every one.

And now it was gone. Totally obliterated. A blizzard of snowy plaster across the cheap tiles of my fireplace surround. It wasn't the only thing that they destroyed. *They* being the assholes who broke into my condo and ransacked the place.

I wasn't wealthy by any definition. My tiny one bedroom condo in southeast Kansas City wasn't going to be featured on the cover of *Better Homes and Gardens* anytime soon. It was my house though. Mine. I owned it. It was my roots. Roots I had spent two years scrimping and saving, living off Ramen and Mac and Cheese to have enough money to buy it.

I tried not to mourn the teal throw pillows I had gotten on sale at Homegoods for eleven dollars. They had coordinated so well with my now torn-to-pieces gray sofa, and the shredded-to-bits peacock inspired curtains. The pantry had been filled with food which was now an amalgamation of flavored and shaped littered across my kitchen floor. So much wasted food. So many people hungry people could be fed from what was now crunching beneath the shoes of the officers trudging through my condo.

"Ma'am."

I'm twenty-nine. Way too young to be called Ma'am.

"Cammie." I offered.

"Do you have anywhere that you can stay tonight Cammie? Whoever did this; they did a number on your door. I don't think it's safe for you to be sleeping here with a busted door."

I was late coming home today. *Today* being the beginning of August, with opening day only a few weeks away. Which for me, working in the Communications department for the Kansas City Chiefs, meant late nights attempting to catch up on the never-ending list of tasks that I couldn't ever seem to find the time to dig out from under. This was the reason why, at ten o'clock at night, I was just discovering the mess that was now my condo.

"I can call one of my friends."

I pulled out my phone and blindly scrolled through the host of numbers in my phone, mentally taking stock of whom in there was *friendly* enough to host me for the evening. As I scrolled, Danny's face appeared on my screen. Apparently, the shock of walking into a house in shambles made you forget that you had a boyfriend who might be able to come help.

"Danny."

"Cam, are you okay? You sound funny."

"Can you come to my house?" I asked, my voice sounding far away even to my own ears. "Someone broke in and the police are here. They say I need to stay somewhere else for the night."

A graduate student at Mizzou, Danny would have his Master's in Exercise Phisiology in spring. We met while he was interning with the team the summer previous.

"Babe." I prepared for the rebuff before he even began. "I'm all the way out in Columbia. Can't one of your friends come and help you?"

Mizzou *was* ninety minutes away. Deep down though, I imagined some kind of white knight moment. The type where he asked repeatedly if I was okay screamed into the phone that he was coming, and in the background, you could hear screeching tires and honking horns.

A headache started to build behind my eyes, causing my vision to go cloudy. There was no reason to continue a phone call that wasn't going anywhere.

"You're right," I told him, not wanting to continue a pointless conversation. "I'll see if someone local can help."

Here's the problem with being a latchkey kid with a transient mother. The types of friendships that other people have? Where you meet your friends in Pre-K and you're inseparable till college, those friendships I didn't have. I had no one whose wedding I would stand up in, or buy the white picket fence house across the street from, or plan to get pregnant with.

When you had to say goodbye to people every six months to a year, it made it hard to want to connect. That was of course if I even got a goodbye. Most of the time I would home from school on a Friday none-the-wiser to the fact that in a few short hours we'd be vacated from whatever place we called home, and be on our way to the next city. Where the process would repeat.

Office Harris, according to his name badge, looked like he was on his last notch of patience waiting for me to settle on my temporary quarters so he could move on to the next ill-fated person experiencing some kind of tragedy that night. I was too ashamed to admit that despite a Rolodex full of people in my cell phone, none of them were really the *ride or die* type. I couldn't find a single person who I could, in good conscience, bother at near midnight on a work/school night.

"Hi Jenny?" It's me, Cammie." I announced to the pretend person on the other end of the phone. "Look, I'm sorry to call so late, but my house got broken in to."

I continued to my imagined best friend, who was now shouting her non-existent concerns and shock into the phone.

"No, honest, I'm fine. I wasn't home when it happened. You know--preseason and all. Yeah, I know."

I replied back to pretend Jenny who was chastising me for working so many hours.

"They did get the house pretty bad. The police don't think it's safe for me to stay here tonight."

I placed Officer Harris in my periphery. He combed the perimeter of my condo having seemingly decided I no longer needed a babysitter.

"You're a lifesaver, Jenny." I told pretend best friend, "I'll be there in about a half hour."

More assurances to my safety were mumbled into the phone. I'm certain this sell job was Oscar-worthy. I imagined if I truly had the type of friends that I could turn to in a crisis what they would actually be saying in a situation like this. *Oh my God! Are you okay? That is so scary. I'm so glad you're okay! Come over as soon as you can.* I nodded a few more times; promising to come post haste, before ending my imaginary call.

I shoved as many outfits I could into my Vera Bradley weekender, in addition to the few 'valuables' I possessed. Incidentally, none had been taken. Of course a pair of diamond earrings I wore for most of my childhood, and the pearl necklace my mom gave me for graduation probably didn't count as "valuable."

The officers promised to keep me updated on the findings, handing me a police report that I could file with the insurance company, and wished me luck on 'everything.' As if some general-ized statement of good wishes could erase the fact that my house looked like it had suffered through some kind of apocalypse. Like a banal 'good luck' could erase the fact that I currently sat in my Kia in front of the local Marriott to get a room for the night.

Now, let's get one thing straight. I'm not that girl. The melo-dramatic one who laments every bump in the road as if it were some kind of curse bestowed upon her. Like misfortune was her birthright. Honestly, though, I was beginning to feel that way. Sure there are plenty of people in the world who don't have two parents. Foster kids, for one. Kids, who lose both parents tragically in a car crash, like the Lifetime movies always show. Or, people like me who was raised by a single parent, and then they pass away.

Times like this though? When the only person I have to depend upon is myself? Where there is no one to call and bemoan my misfortune. No one's house to run to and sob out my crisis, and let someone else share in the burden. Sometimes, like now, I did wonder *Why me?*

Since self-pity got me nowhere, though, I only allowed myself five minutes--ten max--to wallow in the hand I had been dealt. By the time I had pulled into the hotel I had already pep-talked myself back from the abyss. It could be much worse. I had a house. That I owned. Even if it was in a state of disrepair at the moment. I had a job. One that, thankfully, paid me well enough that I didn't have to worry about putting an overnight hotel stay on my credit card.

Sure, I didn't have parents to run to. Or really, anyone whose door I could knock on and collapse into tears in fear of my safety or over the injustice of being violated in such a way. But I was alive. I was unharmed. There was nothing in that apartment that couldn't be replaced. Regardless of how long it took me to do it.

After texting Danny to let him know I'd found a place to stay, I collapsed into the reasonably comfortable bed and sleep claimed me soon after.

"YOU FOUND ME!" the young girl squealed, trying to wiggle from beneath the hands that encased her. They were large hands. Adorned with every jewel imaginable. Bruised at the knuckles, and full of blood caked scabs. Despite the gruesome appearance of the hands that held her, she was not afraid.

"Siempre voy a encontrarte."

The man with the hands told her. I will always find you.

Camille

My sleep had been fitful at best. The stress of the break-in must be messing with my head. Why else would I dream about creepy Spanish speaking men? The dream was fairly benign. Just some interaction with a young girl and a man with creepy looking hands, but it completely unsettled me.

First, I didn't speak a lick of Spanish. I took French in High School. In the dream, though, I understood every single word. Second, while in the context of a hide and seek game, the man's promise to always find me left me feeling uneasy, not warm and fuzzy. It played on an unending track inside my head. The mountain of tasks I needed to complete couldn't drown out the soundtrack of his promise.

"Jesus Cam, you look like hell. Are you feeling okay?"

Jasmine, one of my coworkers, sidled up next to me in the break room. An exclamation point between the dichotomy between us, her long hair lay in a complex braid, and as usual, her make up was so perfect she could host a You-Tube tutorial.

She is the closest thing to a work friend. We eat lunch together most days. Sometimes in meetings, we exchange eye rolls over something our boss said. She is the only one whose after work texts would sometimes morph from work to *OMG what is Kim Kardashian thinking with that blonde hair?*

"Mina," she hated being called Jasmine. Something about Disney princesses. "Don't you know you're supposed to say something like 'you look tired' or equally vanilla so as not to insult someone when you sincerely mean they look like shit?"

Already on my third cup of coffee, and not even ten yet. It was gonna be a helluva day.

"Why pussyfoot around the obvious. The bags under your eyes are the size of suitcases. Late night?"

I ran a hand through my tangled hair. Hotel shampoo did not agree with me.

"Well, I worked till ten." I hedged.

Just because we were work friends, I didn't need to give her a front seat to my life, the soap opera.

"Yeah--but we're always here until ten. You don't usually come in the next day looking this. Did that man-child keep you up all night?"

Not many people knew about Danny and me. Technically he had only been an intern, and for a very short time, but regardless it felt very *Jerry Springer*. Since Mina and I shared a cubicle wall, it hadn't taken her long to suss out our relationship.

It's not that big of a deal. My contribution to the company certainly didn't rank high on the corporate flow chart.

"Danny is back at school. He started his last trimester, so it's been a few weeks since we've seen each other."

"Cammie?"

Our conversation abruptly halted with the appearance of our receptionist, Sasha. She was someone in the "friendly" column but not quite "friends."

Sasha poked her head into the break room, "there's an Officer Parker here to see you?"

If the floor swallowed me up, I'd be okay with it. I struggled to face the imperious glances they both directed my way. Honestly, my life was a trashy talk show. I couldn't make it out of the kitchen fast enough, with Sasha hot on my heels shooting off rapid-fire questions as to why a cop was looking for me.

"Should I call the team lawyer? Or what about Mr. Urtz? Should I call him at least?"

As if I needed my boss or the company lawyer knowing my business. I surpassed embarrassed and summited mount mortified. Though it entertained me she thought I was important enough to be sought out by police on company matters.

The officer stood as soon as he saw us around the corner. He extended his free hand, the other occupied with holding his hat.

"Ms. Saint, I'm sorry to bother you at work. We have a few more questions we needed to ask you for these reports. Can we chat for a few minutes?"

Sasha shooed us into the conference room. I hoped she caught my mouthed thank you as I shut the door. It tickled me that the cop bothered to ask me if he could 'have a minute' of my time. As if I could say no. He was a cop. There had to be a rule stating cops who show up at your place of business causing the collective company to rubberneck past the glass-walled room the two of you occupied, that as a tax-paying citizen, you were not allowed to refuse to be questioned. Regardless of the level of mortification. Or how inconvenient it was.

"This is a pretty sweet gig." The cop tried making idle chit-chat.

They were probably taught in cop school to feign interest in anything related to your interviewee to make them feel less on edge.

"How often do you get face time with Mr. Hunt?" His focus bounced all over the room and past the glass door. It happened a lot with people not used to being in the conference room of a football team. Typically it would charm me more than bother me, but the less time I was on display for everyone in the office, the better.

"I work in the Communications Department," I clarified,

trying not to roll my eyes. The owner of the company didn't typically seek me or my opinions out.

"I handle press junkets, assist in some of the events, answer fan inquiries. There isn't much I do which requires interaction with ownership."

That had sounded much bitchier than intended.

"Yes, it's a pretty sweet gig."

I slapped a smile I didn't feel across my face. I could only hope it would win me some points. Just in case there were resident files cops kept, I didn't want him to write 'raging bitch' in it. You know--in the off chance, I was ever pulled over for speeding.

"I'm not an executive," I further explained. "I'm quite certain he doesn't know my name. He didn't anyway, until now."

The last bit I tried, unsuccessfully to suppress under my breath, based on the cop's smirk.

"You're not in trouble Ms. Saint. We're just trying to piece together a timeline from last night."

"Like I told the officers last night. I got home around 10:30. I left work yesterday morning around 7:45 so there's a huge span of time for something to happen, really."

"Understood." The officer flipped through his notebook referencing the information, I'm assuming, the officer from last night had provided.

"Are you aware of any other types of suspicious activity in your complex?"

My laughter was an accident. Truly. As I said earlier, I work for a football team. My work is awesome but it's also incredibly time-consuming. My nights are late. My mornings are early. In between is a whirlwind. Don't get me wrong. I work for a football team. How many people can say that? Not many. It's the sweetest gig, but also, the busiest.

During football season, I never arrived home before ten. When I physically left work at that time, I still had two or so hours of work to do when I got home. The offseason was significantly fewer hours, but neighborhood watches and the PTA or whatever the hell neighborly types joined--not my cuppa.

"Sir you're the cop. You know more about suspicious activity in my complex than I do."

At least he chuckled. Of course, it didn't make me feel any more at ease. I was in a fishbowl. With a cop. And the entire office gawked from the other side of the glass.

"Touché Ms. Saint. I'm curious. From what I can tell, you live in a respectable neighborhood. There hasn't been so much as a D and D from your area in at least a year. How about any arguments lately? Or do you owe anyone money? Maybe you lost a wallet? Or someone overheard you talking about a big ticket item you purchased?"

Hmm. How odd. Thinking back on the night before, I did a general inventory of my condo. I don't think anything was taken. Lots of things were broken. My entire condo was turned upside down. But, I don't think anything was actually *missing*.

"You know, sir. I don't think anything was stolen. Then again, after my statement was taken, I left. I need to go and take an actual, physical inventory to know for sure."

"What about a dispute? Would someone wreck your apartment because of a dispute you were having?"

"Officer--"

"Parker." He finished.

"Officer Parker. Sir. I have a boyfriend who attends Mizzou. I rarely see him. Not really many friends. Around here, I mean. All my acquaintances are from work, and I can't imagine any of the people here had any issues with me."

Officer Parker stood, tucking his notebook into the front flap of his shirt, and pulling out a business card.

"Peter Parker? Your name is Peter Parker?"

His pale skin pinkened all the way up to his clean-shaven head.

"My dad is a big comic book fan."

He sheepishly ran his hand across the back of his neck.

"Since childhood, because of his last name, he said he always wanted a Peter in the family."

Relieved to finally be finished with the interview and no longer the main event in the circus for the passers-by I showed him to the front office. It made no sense. He came all the way downtown for two questions. The office kept some goodie bags in the front hall closet, which we gave to visitors. Based on the reaction Peter gave me when I handed him one, I quickly sussed out why he had made the trek into the city to see me.

Was it so hard to pick up the damn phone? Now I had the pleasure of answering questions from every nosy nelly in my office.

THE BURNING SENSATION between my shoulder blades yanked me from underneath my task-focused haze. It was almost eight o'clock. A push to my iPhone's home button confirmed I'd been sitting in the same position, intently focused on what I had been doing, for almost six hours.

Working late didn't bother me. Sure, I had next to no social life. My boyfriend was ninety minutes away, clearly our plans didn't occur nightly. At the moment I was stuck in a hotel, anyway. What was there to look forward to? Fast food and pay-per-view?

As if summoned by the mere thought of him, Danny's face appeared on the screen.

"Did they catch the asshole who did it?"

"Hi, babe. No." I sighed, trying to balance my purse and laptop bag, while also cradling the phone between my shoulder and ear as I made my way outside to my car.

"It just happened last night. Plus I don't think they put an APB out for small time break-ins. I'm lucky I got a police report. Thankfully, I'll be able to recoup some of the damages from my homeowner's insurance."

It had been one of the first things I had done. An adjuster was on his way out the following morning to assess the damages. Once I filled out a few forms, and his assessment corroborated what I had claimed, I could expect my check a by the end of the week.

"So, I'm not coming out this weekend." Danny cut into my explanation. "I have an eight-week intensive, and I need my Saturdays for research."

While disappointing news, rationally I knew something like this was bound to happen. I couldn't be upset. Since the day we met, I knew he was a student. My heart, however, did not want to get on board with the sensible argument my head was making. It wanted Danny to come to Kansas City for the weekend, especially since I had to winnow away the hours in a boring hotel. I wanted Danny to be vested in my well-being. Primarily because my house had gotten broken in to.

"I understand."

I needed to stop buying such big bags. My stupid keys always got lost at the bottom somewhere. And it was always at the least convenient time.

"I feel like I haven't seen you in ages." I continued, still unsuccessful in my key search.

"Wait." The idea struck and I couldn't believe it never came previously. "What if I come and visit you?"

It should have been my first suggestion. Sure it would take some maneuvering with my workload and schedule. And it was almost a two-hour drive. But what were a few later than usual nights and a two-hour drive if it meant we'd have the whole weekend together?

"If I could manage to leave here at almost a normal time, I could be in Columbia by late dinner!"

I loved my idea the more I talked about it. And the more I talked about it the more excited I got.

"I can keep myself entertained while you do you work in the Library on Saturday. In fact, I know I'll have leftover work I need to do. We could work in the library together--"

"Babe." The tone of his voice broadcast what I already knew

was coming, even without him cutting me off before I fully boarded the excitement train.

"You know I would love it if you were here."

There was a but coming. I steeled myself against the but. The but was going to disappoint me.

"I'm buried up to my eyeballs Cam. It wouldn't be any fun. My work keeps piling up. I don't know if I'm going to have enough time to call you, let alone host you. Why don't we plan on you coming to visit when I'm not stressing out about whether I've taken on more than I can handle. Okay? Cammie? Come on babe... don't give me the silent treatment."

VAUGHN

I'm too old for this shit. There have been too many sleepless nights. An infinite number of hours spent working while the world is tucked into bed, oblivious to the dangers out there. I spend those nights poring over case files, hunched over some dimly lit desk, eating takeout from some greasy spoon in whatever yokel town they stashed me in. In my thirty-eight year existence, I've done more than my share.

Missoula. Bismarck. Sandoval. New Orleans. Paducah. They are all the same. Bled together, even. I couldn't tell you what made Bismarck different from New Orleans, or Paducah. New town. New shit hole hotel, and hole in the wall diner.

This case? It is my golden unicorn. Until I tucked it in and put it to bed, I couldn't sleep. Or sit still. Or focus on anything else. Two years. It was my goal. I want this thing delivered to the powers that be, tied up in a pretty bow, in two years. I'd be forty then. I wanted to walk away from this life. I put my time in. It felt longer than nearly twenty years. It felt like an eternity in perdition. I've earned the roots I desperately want to put down.

My wallet skid across the bathroom counter with a heavy thunk. The fluorescent lights doing nothing for my already world-weary features. The four-day scruff on my cheeks itched like hell and reminded me once again, I neglected to pick up a shaving kit from the local pharmacy. Every time I tried to leave, someone else wanted me in another bullshit meeting. I barely unpacked before the Chief wanted my ass front and center to brief me on my duties while in Kansas City.

The sulfur-scented water I splashed across my face did little to startle me into wakefulness. I couldn't even remember what state I was in. Was it Missouri or Kansas? Who the fuck names two cities in two different states with the same name?

Cracking open my wallet I searched through the various papers within its confines looking for my dossier sheet, because now until I knew where the fuck I was, I wouldn't be able to settle my brain. Considering it was already two in the morning, screaming down the hall would not solve my conundrum.

Hodgkins. Not the piece of paper I wanted to see. I didn't have the luxury to reflect on that at the moment. My hotel was across the street. Eventually, they'd figure out the plan of action. Then I could finally settle in whatever housing they put me in. Until then, I needed to land the plane on what state I was presently in.

Camille

"Puke."

That one word was too much for me to handle. Bile burned in my throat. The putrid scent invaded my nostrils threatened to upend whatever contents occupied my stomach.

"Camille? Can you hear me? I need you to open your eyes."

As more stimuli assaulted me, the room began to spin, despite only seeing the back of my eyelids.

"Can't."

I needed my eyes to cooperate with me, so I could find the bathroom. However, lying still until the world stopped tilting seemed to be the better solution at the moment.

"Ms. Saint, you have a pretty nasty head injury. I need you to open your eyes for me."

The no-nonsense tone of the woman, I assumed was the same one who patted my chest. She began again, imploring me to do the very thing I simply couldn't oblige.

"Ugh." I felt as if I'd done a round of cross fit followed by ninety minutes in a Bikram class. I couldn't get my tongue to detach from the roof of my mouth. The desert had decided to take up residence between my teeth and tongue.

Fully coherent sentences seemed to be out of the realm of possibility a well.

Ms. Saint, they need you to open your eyes so they can monitor your concussion."

That voice sounded familiar. Sort of twangy. Local. For the life of me though, I couldn't associate the voice with anyone off the top of my head.

"Thirsty."

One-word phrases seemed to be the best way to keep the bile at bay.

"Ms. Saint. Cammie. You've taken a pretty hard blow to the head. We need you to open your eyes. Just for a minute."

Jesus if it took opening my fucking eyes to get a damn glass of water, then fine. I'll open them. Of course, the task of getting a single eyelid to cooperate had been monumental. The moment I did, the most violent torrent of pain assaulted my brain from the onslaught of brightness the overhead lights expelled. Immediately, with a whimpered groan and a handful of four-letter words my eyelid shut of its own volition, against the intrusion.

"Cut the overheads. Give her a second to adjust."

The twangy man snapped directives at the woman.

"How about now? Can you try again Cammie?"

I lifted my eye to half-mast, waiting for another assault to my retina which never came. After a few moments, the second eyelid also opened. The bald-headed officer from earlier stood over me.

"Spiderman."

"Good to see you rejoining the land of the living. You've been out for quite a while."

"Where?"

Common sense and the unmistakable stench of disinfectant answered that question. Hospital. What I had wanted to say was, *what the hell is going on?* The throbbing pain in my head made full sentences an impossibility.

"U of K Hospital. You suffered an attack near your car. The security guard phoned it in."

I closed my eyes, grimacing as my head made contact with the pillow. A logical timeline proved too difficult to process. I needed water and then sleep.

"Ms. Saint. Cammie? Please try and stay awake for a few minutes more. The doctor needs to see you." The nurse came in to focus. Her mouth set in an impatient frown.

So much noise. The lamp hummed. Monitors beeped. Shoes squeaked on the floor as people rushed past the door. Does saline dripping into an I.V. have a sound? I'm certain I heard it.

"What is the last thing you remember from today?" Spiderman asked.

Why did I call him Spiderman? It hurt my head to think about it. I tried to take a mental inventory of all the things I had done that day, not sure they were true memories.

"Do you remember talking to me today?" The man asked. "You must because you called me Spiderman when you opened your eyes."

"Sir, perhaps it would be best to sit in the lounge for a few minutes until the doctor examines her. Perhaps once she's had some food in her system, she'll be able to answer some of your questions."

The doctor had cold hands and an even chillier demeanor. He gave me his name. But I had already forgotten it. He had a mustache. It curled into his lip as he talked. It distracted me from nearly everything he said. Each time he spoke, those shit-brown hairs would tuck under his lip and get pulled into his mouth. I wondered if it bothered him. If it tickled his lip or made his nose itch. He didn't seem to notice. Watching it made me want to sneeze.

He asked me to lift each arm, but my limbs refused to cooperate. He asked me to count like a pre-schooler--but when I tried to recall the progression of numbers, my brain checked out. He asked other banal questions like what color was the house Mrs. Smith had in the story he told and what was the eleventh letter of the alphabet--honestly, I think he tried to be an obnoxious asshole on purpose. The light he shone was too bright to tolerate. Everything he did set me on edge and had me wishing for anything familiar. He eventually backed out of the room, mumbling some directives to the nurse about follow up tests and scans.

"Do you have any family that should be notified?" The nurse asked while she helped me readjust in bed, before sliding a tray over my lap.

"Just eat what you can." She said in response to the tray of food she placed on said wheeled tray.

In the twenty-nine years on earth, I consumed an infinite number of meals. However, the pudding cup, soup, roll and sad looking canned fruit salad confounded me.

The nurse took the plastic lid from the pudding and put the spoon in. I didn't like her watching me. She made me nervous. Her eyes laser-focused on my attempts to get that stupid plastic spoon to line up with my mouth. I gave up. Nauseous and exhausted, the last thing I needed was someone watching me eat.

"Is there someone I should call?" She asked again, spooning a dollop of pudding on to the spoon and holding it in front of my mouth. Did she expect me to eat off her spoon like a child? She would be sitting there for an awfully long time if she waited for that.

"Boss."

I had a stack of work needing my attention the next day. The timing couldn't be worse for me to be laid up. The moment I opened my mouth the pudding went in. She chuckled at me.

"What about your parents? Do they live around here? Or maybe a husband or a boyfriend? You didn't come in with a cell phone, but surely someone is wondering where you are?"

"Her boyfriend is on the way. I expect he'll be here any minute. He was on the phone with her when it disconnected. He has a good head on his shoulders."

The last comment he directed towards me. I wish I could remember his name.

"Apparently you were arguing when the line went dead. He originally thought you hung up on him. But then when you wouldn't return any of his phone calls or texts he got worried and called the police to double check no reports had come in from Arrowhead Stadium. Dispatch told him they brought a mid-twenties female with light brown hair to the U of K."

Danny was on his way. The police officer talked too fast and too loud. Most of what he said didn't make sense. But I understood that. My boyfriend would be here soon.

"Here, I can do it."

The officer sat to my right, taking feeding duties from the nurse who stood in response to the overhead page.

"Do you remember talking to me earlier?" He asked again, offering me another bite. "I'm Officer Parker. Peter Parker. We met at your work this afternoon."

His face and neck pinkened. That's why I called him Spider-man. I remembered that at least.

"The doctors are really worried. You have been unresponsive for almost two hours."

I could only nod. Minutes passed in silence as I tried to choke down a couple sips of apple juice or a mouthful of pudding. Swallowing the pudding had become quite the task and took all of my focus. I felt off-kilter. Like I'd taken an entire box of Benadryl and then boarded the Tilt-O-Whirl. All I wanted to do was close my eyes and sleep.

Peter Parker had kind eyes and a warm smile. He was older. Not grandpa old, but probably late thirties or early forties. He had the fair skin and light eyes which usually accompanied blonde hair--if he had any. His fingers were well kept, and he didn't have any scars or bruises on his hands I assumed most cops would have if they were scrabbling with law-breakers on the daily. I bet if you saw him in church on a Sunday, in a button down and a pair of khakis laid out for him by his wife, you wouldn't know he was a cop.

"Is there anyone else I can call for you?"

He switched from the pudding to the soup, trying to contain the broth on the shitty plastic spoon which drooped under the weight of its contents.

"What about a parent, or a sibling? Do they live in another state? I'm sure they still want to hear about what happened."

This was the worst part of being the only child of a deceased parent, single parent. The second people found out that you were alone; they got this look in their eyes which was almost harder to deal with than the reality of a dead parent. I desperately wanted to shake my head and be done with it. My head felt too heavy or funny to shake though.

"Cammie. My God, babe! You scared the hell out of me!"

Good old Danny. For once in our relationship, he possessed perfect timing.

He burst through the door, collapsing on my bed, and yanked me into a hug.

"Mr. Olsen, she's had a traumatic brain injury. Pulling her isn't wise. She is having issues with spatial relations and motor function."

Danny let me go, and I bounced, painfully against my pillow.

"Office Parker, KCPD." Parker stood and extended his hand to Danny. "We spoke earlier by phone. If I can get a statement from you real quick, I can be on my way. I'm sure after what a trying evening it's been you want to be alone with Cammie."

He smiled at me when he said it. I had to admit that just the slightest tinge of disappointment pinged through me at the realization he was leaving. For some inexplicable reason, his presence calmed me. For the first time tonight, I felt satiated and calm.

Danny and Officer Park stepped out of the room and stood on the opposite side of the door. I could hear the hushed murmur of their voices through the crack in the door. Unable to fight against my drooping eyelids, I closed my eyes and allowed myself to be entranced by their voices.

"Didn't hear anything..." I recognized Danny's scratchy voice, "like I told the receptionist at the station, we were talking and then nothing. I thought she'd hung up on me."

"Attempted abduction...scared away..." the twangy voice broke through my haze. "...keep her a few days...impaired speech...delayed motor function...need an MRI and a CT Scan."

Abduction? Why would anyone want to abduct me? I wasn't anyone important. I worked for a football team, sure. But why would anyone care about me? I wasn't a player, or a cheerleader even. I had nothing of value to offer.

Mulling over those thoughts and trying to come up with a reason proved too exhausting for me to process. Shortly after, I succumbed to sleep. I vaguely remember Danny shaking me awake to say hello and see if I needed anything, but within seconds I sank back into the murky depths of my own subconscious.

The following days went by in a haze of dreamless sleep interrupted by doctors waking me up, asking me to perform mundane tests, grunting at my progress, ordering nurses to send me down for more testing, more sleep and then more tests.

A week into my hospital stay I started to feel like I had a personality again, and not an uncommunicative zombie. My words returned at a much slower pace than my ability to raise my hand or to point to the picture of the greenhouse.

Danny missed his classes to be with me. Like that didn't weigh heavily on my conscience. He never complained or talked about it to me, but based on the questions he asked of the doctors, I knew he needed to get back.

The other more recent development were the vivid dreams I kept having. I would wake up screaming and shaking, but the second I opened my eyes, the memory of them totally disappeared.

From what Officer Parker had been able to piece together, two men had been dragging me towards their van when our night security detail spotted them. They fled when the security guard approached. Parker told me if it hadn't been for him finding me when he did, I'd be dead. They had hit me in the back of the skull where the brain meets the brain stem. They called it a 'killing blow' because it caused the brain stem to detach. Lucky for me the blow wasn't hard enough to cause too much damage--just knock me out cold for a longer period of time than the doctors felt comfortable with. Because of it, the doctors projected recovery time to be at least a few months, and much longer before I felt 100%.

I had health insurance as well as both short and long-term disability through the company thank goodness. According to Danny and Officer Parker, the company had coordinated a fundraiser so I wouldn't be burdened with hospital bills while trying to recover. If I had all of my faculties, I'd be thrilled with that piece of information because I always worried about how much money I had in my savings account.

"Morning Babe."

Danny arrived, handing me a cup of smuggled coffee from the Starbucks across the street. Hospital food couldn't be described as appetizing, having to drink the mud they called coffee? Torturous.

"How are you feeling today?"

"Better."

I don't think there is anything more heavenly than the first sip of coffee in the morning, regardless where you get it. Because trust me, I was by no means a $5 a cup status coffee drinker.

"Thank you."

Danny hadn't been in my more than three minutes and he had he refused to settle. He bounced from the chair next to my bed, to the windowsill, to standing and leaning against the doorjamb.

"Babe, you can't deny I have been super supportive this entire week, right?"

I nodded, waiting for him to continue.

"I'm so behind in my classes Cammie. I'm getting emails non-stop from my professors. They don't understand my absence Cam, because you're my *girlfriend* and not a blood relative. I took an entire week off from school already, and it's the most important time of my program."

"I understand." I did. I couldn't be upset about it. Danny had been there all week, engaged and without complaint. At the same time, a tiny piece of my heart broke, because once he left, I didn't have anyone to help me.

"Great. I'm going to go and grab my stuff and check out of the hotel. I'll bring your bag back with the final receipt before I leave for Columbia."

"The hotel?"

I never thought about where Danny had stayed all week. Obviously, he didn't live in Kansas City, but I guess I assumed his friend Isaac let him crash at his place.

"You were staying at the Marriott when the accident happened. They found the keycard in your wallet. Since you already had the room, I went there. It was the middle of the night when I got here. You paid for the room through today, so it made sense not to waste what you had already paid for."

He smiled, bent down and kissed my forehead.

"I'll be back in thirty minutes. Do you want me to grab anything while I'm out?"

I shook my head again, afraid if I tried to say anything my emotions would surface. That would be unfair to Danny. Once he left, I allowed a couple minutes of self-pity. I couldn't place where the intense reaction to him leaving came from. He wasn't leaving for good. Logically, I knew he would check on me. If I really needed him, he only lived ninety minutes away. His departure, however, hit home on the disservice I had done to myself by never making any deep or lasting connections.

I needed a game plan on how to handle this on my own. There were taxis or ubers for things like the grocery store and doctors appointments. I needed to work on standing without assistance at the moment, so I could get around my house. Taking a shower would be challenging. I could practice using the bathroom by myself while I still had nurse supervision. Fear had no place in my planning, and yet it hung over me like a pregnant storm cloud.

"Hey, why all the tears?"

Officer Parker popped in and out frequently. He made it part of his rounds--these check-ins. He would inquire into any new developments in my memory. Which, there weren't. Even if there was, trying to access the words to discuss them was also a roadblock to my recovery.

"I'm okay."

I turned my head to hide the evidence of my indulgence.

"I was in the area," his voice told me he didn't buy what I told him, "and thought you might be sick of hospital food."

Even if their logo weren't on the front of the bag, the smell alone was a dead giveaway to the contents within.

"Fluffy Fresh!"

The best donut shop in Missouri or Kansas, hands down. I mean, Kansas City possessed more than a few donut shops, but in these matters, either you were a *jet* or a *shark*. For me, I was a Fluffy Fresh girl, without question.

"I'm a bit of a donut purist." Officer Parker pulled the tray table from the corner and placed it over my lap, "so I only got glazed."

If he handed me a donut hole covered in dirt I would have still been thrilled. Anything would be better than another Jell-O cup and meat of questionable origin. I am certain Officer Park absolutely knows what my O face looks like as I devoured the two donuts he gave me. It was as if Moses and I had just chilled in the desert together for forty days where not a morsel of food or drop of water could be found. He spared me total embarrassment by politely ignoring my caveman grunts and orgasmic groans, choosing instead to focus on the police file he laid on the tray table.

"Are they discharging you?"

I wished they would. As much as the prospect of navigating everything alone terrified me, I also didn't know how many more days I could tolerate being cooped up and bedridden. My TV options were sparse, at best. One of my two visitors presently was at the hotel packing. My mind refused to focus so novels, crossword puzzles, trashy entertainment magazines all impossible options.

"Have they said anything about your therapies?"

"Speech started yesterday."

It helped. Kind of. The problem wasn't so much forming words. I was able to have entire conversations in my head. Hell, I could probably wax poetic on the symbolism of water in Murakami's *Kafka on the Shore*. In my head anyway. Just trying to get the word Murakami to my mouth. That's where the problem lay. I could usually keep my brain and mouth aligned for about five words. Seven if they were short words.

"Alright, babe. The car is all packed up and I'm ready to head out. I'll call you when I'm back at school okay?"

Danny breezed in, my weekender bag in hand. He set it on the windowsill before turning to me. If nothing else, I would have clean clothes. Danny had been good about getting a handful of items when the accident happened, but I was wearing the same pajama bottoms and t-shirt I wore a week ago.

"You're *leaving*?"

Officer Parker's mortified judgment had a satisfied fist bump playing inside my head. Though technically unfair to Danny, me being upset.

"He has classes."

"My professors are all over my ass" Danny interjected over my defense of him, "This is my last trimester, and I can't take any more time off without having to take a leave and push my graduation back."

"Who's gonna take care of you?" Parker's attention turned to me, his entire demeanor shifted from friendly to downright concerned. "Did either of you call the insurance company?"

Obviously, the 'either' in his question really meant had Danny.

" What about the new door? She needs a door before she can

go home. Speaking of home," he continued his concern gaining momentum, "How will you get there? How will you manage once you're there? If something happens to you, how do you plan to communicate with 9-1-1?"

"Dude she isn't even getting released yet. She's here until next weekend at least. I'll try to make it back up here on Saturday or Sunday, and *if* you're released by then I'll take you home and get you settled."

"You'll *try* to get home this weekend? Are you kidding me, Mr. Olsen? She's practically an invalid. You can't make soft plans with someone who can just barely take care of herself. How on earth do you have no concern over this?"

Danny crossed his forearms in front of his chest, the veins in his arms bulging as he did.

"I don't know who you think you are Officer Parker, but I don't need to defend myself to you. As much as I wish things were different, you don't get a whole lot of compassion or under-standing from teachers when your *girlfriend* is in the hospital. She's not my mom or my sister, or grandma or any other blood relative laid out in the student absence policy. Unfortunately, as much as I care for Cam, I can't risk my academics. Getting an Incomplete for this trimester doesn't mean I get the eighteen thou-sand dollars refunded to me. I have to shell out another eighteen grand next trimester when I repeat it."

I didn't understand why Parker fought him so hard on this. I didn't like that Danny had to go home either, but it couldn't be helped. It was a shitty situation with no solution amenable to all parties.

"Can you at least make sure her house is safe to return to? Like follow up with the insurance company and verify the work is complete?"

"Cam, you have friends here who can help you with that stuff, don't you?" Danny turned to me, practically begging both in voice and those ridiculously expressive eyebrows I usually found so endearing. "How am I supposed to take care of any of this all the way in Columbia?"

Parker appeared to be at the end of his tolerance with Danny." With a frustrated huff, he grabbed his file from the tray and stormed off to the nurses' station.

"I can figure it out."

I could. Someone would be able to help me. I mean, the people at work had said 'if there is anything at all you need, don't hesitate to ask.' So I could always ask them. Since no one had suggested discharge though, fretting over it was unnecessary.

"I'll call you later, okay?" Danny pressed his lips against mine one last time before turning and walking out the door.

5

Camille

"Can you manage the stairs?"

They were tiny stairs. I knew Parker wanted to help. He was my newest accessory--at my elbow constantly--since Danny went back to school. He was the one who coordinated with my HOA to get the window and door fixed; liaised with the Chiefs to get my house cleaned and put to rights. I tried to keep an accurate tally of everyone I needed to pay back. The people I work with went to great lengths to replace almost all of the damaged goods in my house, either with the exact replica or close to it. No one should have to pay for me to have a new couch or new throw pillows, or new whatever else they replaced for me. It seemed selfish to consider keeping those things.

"I'm fine Parker. I barely need to lift my leg to get up them."

"Your nurse's name is Janet." His arms spread out behind me like he anticipated me suddenly blacking out and tumbling back down. "She should be here any minute. I told her to meet us here at one."

Parker pulled his focus away from me to stop and look at his watch.

30

"Huh. I guess when you go across town with lights and sirens, you get here ahead of your anticipated schedule."

He wouldn't let me unlock my own door, but rather juggled the various items that the hospital sent me home with, along with my overnight bag, and the 'few things' he picked up for me at the grocery store. It went beyond the call of duty. I still had no clue why he did all of this for me.

In the past week, he visited me almost every day. He kept me company, read articles out of the trashy magazines Danny left for me and worked with me on my vocabulary and memory recall as per the doctor's instructions. My words aren't a hundred percent but improving. I could manage about two sentences before my thought train took a detour or derailed altogether.

"You know, you can call me Peter. You don't need to keep calling me Parker or Officer Parker."

I watched as he set all of my stuff inside my door, before guiding me by the elbow to my new--but almost like my old--gray couch.

"I appreciate your help." I tried to find a way to say thank you for the whole trip home from the hospital, but every time I went to say it something else came up in conversation.

"Thanks aren't needed."

I liked his smile. It was so genuine.

I watched him flit around my living room, setting my prescriptions on my dining room table, and placing my new walking cane to my right hanging from the sofa arm.

The teal pillows that my arm rested against distracted me from my observations of Peter. The ones in the room previously had been gutted, their stuffing creating a snowy landscape in the old living room. These looked nearly identical. Why would people go to all this trouble? I could only continue to gape at my surroundings. The peacock curtains weren't exactly the same, but similar enough, my crappy old hand-me-down TV had been replaced with a slick SmartTv over my fireplace. I would never be able to pay for that. It was easily a four thousand dollar TV based on what I'd seen in the sale papers.

"Most of this was donated by the football team or the organization."

Peter explained as he collected the rest of the items by the door.

"Are you in any pain? Do you need a pill? The discharge nurse..."

"Parker--I'm good. I got it."

I didn't mean to sound snippy, but the way he flittered about set me on edge. There was too much for me to process and I was quickly becoming overwhelmed.

"I'm sorry. I just. It's so much. You've done so much."

How do you repay a favor to a cop? The list of people to repay made my head spin, but Peter sat at the top of the list. How do you monetize the kindness he showed me in the past days?

I tried to stand in an attempt to walk to my bedroom and lie down, but my feet weren't having anything to do with that command. No sooner had I stood, then I fell back down -hard-- thankfully into the plush cushion of the sofa.

"Janet should be here any minute. If it's all right with you, I can grab you a blanket and pillow from your bedroom. You look beat. I'll set the sofa up all comfy. Trust me, being a cop, I'm used to couch time."

I think Peter was joking. Though I didn't understand why being a cop and sleeping on a couch would go hand in hand. Maybe because they worked such odd shifts? Winnowing out that reasoning wasn't at the top of my priority list, however. I nodded my permission, and that was all Peter needed to skitter down the hall only to return seconds later weighed down with pillows and a blanket.

"Oh! That must be Janet!"

Jesus, did the buzzer always sound that loud? My God if that torture were to continue every time someone came by to pay me a visit, I'd be thrust into an aneurysm by tomorrow. Of course, people weren't beating my door down to visit.

The pair excused themselves into my kitchen once introductions had been made to Janet, and she instructed me to make myself comfortable on the sofa. I didn't argue. I felt like these days I couldn't get enough sleep. Personally, I didn't think I needed a nurse. Sure I was a bit unsteady, but once I readjusted, I could most things. It seemed like such a waste to pay for someone to babysit me every day. Parker insisted though. Especially since Danny couldn't dig out from underneath his workload.

I tried to pay attention to the light murmurs of conversation in the kitchen. The subtle arcs of the pitch of their voices were hard to make out and required too much effort. It was soothing though. What felt like seconds later, Peter startled me awake with a vigorous shake of my shoulder.

Trying to surface from my sleep proved impossible. It took ages for my conscious to cooperate and allow me to wake up.

"You were screaming."

Was Parker still here--or here again? While I slept it had gone dark outside. Why did I have a nurse if he planned om hovering all day long?

"What are you doing here?"

"I called to check in with Janet and she told me you were still sleeping. It's been six hours."

I couldn't stop trembling. In a hoodie and flannel pants, covered with a down comforter I couldn't imagine I wasn't warm enough. Why couldn't I stop shaking?

"She's a nurse, is she not?"

"Technically she is a CNA. So, no she isn't a nurse in the way you think she is. She can give you medicine, check your vitals, and make sure you're breathing and the like, but anything severe would require an emergency room visit."

The trembling got worse. I swung my legs over the couch and tried to put myself into a seated position, but immediately succumbed to a bout of vertigo.

"Hey. You're looking pretty peaked. Should we go back to the hospital?"

He ran the back of his hand across my forehead. I may have been soothed if I knew this guy for more than two and a half weeks.

"I'm okay. Just a bit woozy." I tried to politely shift my body away from his touch without hurting his feelings. He pushed to his feet and stomped off, I assumed in response to my brush off. Instead, he returned moments later with a bowl of chicken noodle soup and a fresh roll.

"You haven't eaten all day." He crouched in front of me and placed the tray on my lap. "You're due for another pain pill as well, but food first. Janet's shift ends in about a half hour. Starting tomorrow she'll be back every day at eight."

He took a seat on the ottoman, so he could look directly at me.

"She'll stay through the day. Any doctor's appointments you have, or errands that need to be run, she'll take you to. She said she doesn't mind making meals for you if it's too much to handle. Every day she'll leave around six unless you need her for more time. You'll be responsible for evenings and getting yourself to bed."

"Peter, I'm not an invalid. I just got knocked on the head."

He regarded me with the strangest look. When he tilted his head, he was kind of handsome. Not that I crushed on him in any way. But his concern, how much time he spent making sure I was okay--I liked it. And, I could see how someone would find him attractive.

"Should I be worried?" I asked. It was a joke, but inflection hadn't returned when I found my words.

"About what?" Peter cocked his eyebrow in a confused pout.

"Well, you're with me every day since the attack in some way, shape or form. I'm sure someone is missing your presence."

Janet busied herself in the kitchen. I could hear here washing pots and pans, and putting dishes away in my cabinets. The thought made me cringe. Sure I was unsteady, but she shouldn't be forced to also take on my domestic duties. Surely that didn't fit under the normal purview of a CAN, did it? I made a mental note to research that once everyone left for the day.

"...so she understands the crazy hours. Plus, she knows that once I'm involved in a case, I get a little protective until the bad guy is put away. Hazards of the job I guess."

I hadn't been paying attention. Obviously, someone waited for him, so at least I knew there was no misguided hope of getting in my pants.

Janet brought in a glass of juice with two pills.

"I'm sorry I wasn't better company on your first day, Janet."

I accepted the pills and tossed them back without the juice.

"Weren't you bored all day without anyone to talk to?"

She looked older than she did earlier. Of course, I was in a bit of a haze. For some reason, though I assumed she was close in age to me. Now that I saw her up close, she looked like she could be my mom. Her dishwater blonde hair was pulled back into a messy bun, and she wore those little half glasses older people wear when reading the small print. Hers were bedazzled at the corners.

"No worries Camille. Or is there a nickname you prefer? The file didn't say."

She stuffed a book into the purse cradled in the crook of her elbow, before gathering her sweater and car keys from the dining room table.

"Cammie. Cam. Either one. The only person to ever call me Camille was my Mom, and only when I was in trouble."

I tried to laugh at the joke, but the mention of my mom shot a lance right through my heart. She died a few months after taking my job with the Chiefs after I graduated and moved to Kansas City. She had been living in Chicago, and apparently fell down the stairs to her apartment and broke her neck. An older lady, Mrs. Marengo lived on the bottom floor of their two flat, but she didn't hear her fall. By the time anyone noticed her in the snow at the bottom of the stairwell, it was too late.

At times like this, when I wasn't a hundred percent and I wanted to curl into a ball and hide from the world, I missed her the most. I missed hearing her bustle about through the house. Hearing her hum songs while she dusted and straightened nick knacks and paper piles. I missed hearing her gasp and yell at the TV when *The Young and the Restless* was on.

Our neighborhood--*Back of the Yards*--was not friendly to outsiders. It was one of those neighborhoods where crime rates are reported more than anything good that happens in there. She had worked in a candy factory. Like full on *I Love Lucy* shit. I could smell her before she ever walked into the house.

That was what I missed more than anything. The smell. She always smelled like chocolate or caramel, or whatever candy she worked on that day.

Of all the cities we lived in, Chicago was our longest stint in a single area. A year of high school and all of undergrad and graduate school, it was almost *home* to me.

"I'm pretty resourceful when I need to keep busy."

Janet pulled me out of my musings.

"There's always a good book to read, or some tidying up I can do. And of course, with modern day cable, there's always something on the idiot box to winnow away the entire day. I have two daughters at home, high schoolers, and they've introduced me to Netflix. I take binge-watching to a whole new level."

"Janet you and I are going to get along great," I told her. "Tomorrow, you, me, the couch and any series of your choice."

I liked her laugh. She had a Mom laugh. The kind that lit you up from the inside because you knew you were the one responsible for it.

"It's a date! I'll see you at eight!" She snorted as she opened the door.

"I'm a poet and I didn't even know it!"

Despite the cheesy line, a silly grin seated itself on my face.

"I think that's a first."

I forgot Peter was still there. He hadn't moved. He was still poised almost in front of me on my ottoman, though he must have turned to face Janet when she joined us in the living room.

"What's a first?"

"Your smile. I think that's the first time I've seen you smile."

Self-consciousness swept through me faster than the laughter that bubbled up. The smile which caused my cheeks to ache a moment earlier, released.

"You have a nice smile." Peter continued, the flush creeping up his ears, "I didn't mean to embarrass you. I mean it was nice to see you like your old self again. Not that I know what you are like when you are 'yourself.' Just...it's good to see you moving from paid-addled zombie to having a personality again."

His face went garnet and his eyes went wide. I should have put him out of his misery considering how much he rambled, digging himself further into that black hole of embarrassment. It was so entertaining though.

"Pete. It's fine." I rescued him from his own rambling. "Thanks for coming to check on me."

He reached behind him for his briefcase, pulling out a new iPhone.

"I almost forgot. Your old phone was destroyed. It must have hit the ground pretty hard. I don't think they're going to be able to repair it. It's at the precinct. They checked it for prints but didn't find any. It has to be stored for evidence."

I couldn't stop staring at it. My old phone was a barely surviving iPhone 5. I didn't want to spend money upgrading it when the six when it came out, and then in a blink, they released the seven and I was like *why bother*. So I planned to use the phone until it died.

This one was pink. And so big. It was like having a Kindle for a phone.

"They were able to transfer over all of your old data from the other phone. I programmed my cell phone in there too," he kept talking, but the shiny new object in front of me already distracted me. "You can call whenever you want. Or text or whatever. I don't want you to feel like you're all alone because you aren't."

The muscles in my shoulders tensed, and I could feel my entire body riding on a chilly wave.

"Why would you think I'm alone? Just because Danny is back at school? Do you think that I'm some kind of friendless loser?"

My emotional about-face was irrational. Intellectually I knew this. But at that moment, an angry bull of rage poked my rib cage begging to be let out. Parker hadn't expected it. His hands flew up in defense, and the smiling demeanor melted from his face into wide-eyed befuddlement.

"Cammie, no! Not at all. Without Danny here, you ... well I didn't want you to be afraid. You know, in case you were worried about being in this apartment alone after what happened. I'm less than a mile down the street. I'd make it here before the police would if you called 911."

"I'm sorry Peter. I don't know what's come over me. I think I'm tired."

It was a cop out... no pun intended. I knew his answer before he explained himself. He'd shown me nothing but kindness the last two weeks, and I launched on him like he was my worst enemy. Mortified didn't even scratch the surface of the emotions I felt.

"Can we pick up this conversation tomorrow?"

"Of course." He unfolded himself off my ottoman. "Is there anything else I can help you with before I leave? Are you planning on sleeping on the sofa, or would you like help to get down the hall to your bed? Or do you need help getting to the restroom?"

Just hearing him say restroom in relation to helping me or implying we'd be anywhere near my bed together, gave me the creeps. Not in a self-protective way, but in *my little brother saw me naked in a towel*, kind of way. Not that I had a little brother. Or ever had the experience of anyone seeing me naked whom I hadn't intended to show my goodies too. But with him, it was just--weird.

"Would you mind if I stopped over again in the morning? I have a few questions I need to ask. It would be great if I had the answers when I went into work tomorrow."

Anything to get him to leave. I wanted to be alone. I needed to process so many things that were coming at me too fast.

"I'll see you in the morning, Cam. I'll be back around eight-ish. Right around the same time that Janet gets here."

I shuffled behind him to my door, realizing when my legs started to wobble that I'd left my cane on the sofa. I needed to set an alarm on my phone or something to get up every hour or so and walk around. Maybe if I did that, vertigo would go away quicker.

I concurrently realized it had been hours since I used the bathroom, and since the bathroom was closer to my bedroom than the living room, I ended up in bed. Without my down comforter, and short one pillow.

6

VAUGHN

Every office looked the same: standardized cubicles in some kind of nondescript gray, fluorescent lights over-head that sucked the life out of you, institutional beige cinderblock walls. The men and women busying about their day, annoyed you dare breathe their air, or be in the same space as them, as they rushed back and forth from office to office completing their important governmental tasks.

No matter the city, it all remained the same. Hell, the govies even dressed the same. Black, gray, or navy pant, crisp white button-down shirts, black nondescript tie shoes. Some of the women, if they were feeling bold, wore a skirt. If they were feeling extra adventurous, a black heel.

Every city had the same procedure. Sit down with the locals, grease the egos, and whisper sweet promises that fed their egos about how I wasn't there to make them look bad. Except for Kansas City. Fucking Kansas City. I was in Missouri, by the way. In case anyone had a burning desire to know whether or not that cluster fuck of confusion had cleared itself up. It had.

Anyhow, Kansas City not only housed branches of the DEA and the FBI, but also the CIA. This shit-tastic town in the middle of Anywhere, USA was knee deep in bureaucratic bullshit. Why was I here?

"Vaughn, we need to go have lunch."

Carter, the HGIC of the Kansas City branch of the DEA sat across from me in his standard, government-issued pleather chair-- trust me, they all had the same, ugly, not quite brown, but not exactly black leather-like chair and a particle board desk painted to look like real wood. It wasn't.

The candidates in both political parties like to talk about bloated governmental spending and $500 toilet seats, but I had no clued where that shit was. I have been through at *least* seven of these buildings now, and they all looked like the inside of a prison.

"Now why would I want to go and do a thing like that?"

I kicked my heels up on the edge of the desk and rocked my chair backward.

"When I'm dropping my good, hard-earned dollars on a meal out, I want to actually enjoy it. Not suffer through the meal, making niceties and trying not to get indigestion."

Carter tossed a file across the desk, leaning back and tucking his arms behind his head.

"Quit busting my balls, Vaughn. You being here is about to unleash a tsunami of bruised egos and pissing contents down on this department."

"It's the same bullshit everywhere I go, Carter. This is no different."

It was, and I knew it. It would be a day wasted to sit down with these blowhards and listen to them postulate upon how this was technically their case, and they appreciated my help. Essentially, I needed to know it was their show, I was simply an extra.

Fuck. That.

If I was being sent anywhere it was for one of two reasons. Either the people in the city didn't know their asshole from a hole in the ground and they needed me to play Mary Poppins, or the case was about to become a powder keg and I was the only one with enough experience in that kind of shit show to know what to do in those situations. I'm pretty sure this was the latter and not the former.

"Carter, I've been here for five days and I haven't even gotten my housing assignment yet. Your cheapskate department put me up in some roach motel that used to be owned by Norman Bates, and I've been wearing the same three shirts because my stuff has been mysteriously diverted from whatever low budget Help-U-Move you used to bring it here. If you really want me sitting down and breaking bread with all of these guys with next to no sleep and a list of grievances a mile long, by all means, make the reservation."

Carter's rugged mug would never win any beauty pageants, especially not at that moment as it morphed from sallow to bruised raspberry. With a gaseous huff, Carter leaned forward and pushed his desk intercom.

"Lacey--can you come in here please?"

The tallest drink of water I had ever had the pleasure of laying eyes on poked her head into the room, sauntering closer when Carter waved her in. How does a middle-aged slob like him, who more than likely hasn't seen his toes for at least ten years, manage to score a looker like Lacey as his assistant? Some guys have all the luck.

"Can you help Agent Vaughn out with a few issues? He still hasn't received his housing assignment. I'm pretty sure he is being put up in Ashwood Villages, but can you double check that? Also, liaise with the offices in Centennial? Agent Vaughn's personal effects have gone missing. I'd like to get him in and settled by the time we return from lunch. If the moving truck is more than a day away, please text me and let me know. We'll need to take care of obtaining some items for Agent Vaughn's stay in Kansas City."

As she nodded along to Carter's requests, signaling she was listening, a curlicue of her strawberry blonde hair would fall on her face. She'd brush it away, and tuck it back behind her ear, only to have to repeat the process a minute later. Too bad I'd sworn off redheads. She and I could have a hell of a time together. As if reading my impure thoughts Carter cut me an annoyed look before asking Lacey, "How are the wedding plans coming along? When do you get married again? Next Month?"

"October, sir." She smiled at him crossing her arms beneath her bust--which did nothing for my wayward thoughts.

Even if Carter hadn't inquired, the impossible to miss iceberg on her hand pretty much shouted that she was promised to another.

"Maggie couldn't stop gushing over the invitations." Carter continued, "Ours arrived just yesterday."

"Seriously?"

The woman went from serious and businesslike to panicked and hairsbreadth from suicidal in a nanosecond.

"I sent those two and a half weeks ago! You only live down the street, and you're just getting it *now?* I wonder if there are other people who haven't received theirs either. Maybe that's why I've barely received any responses back.

Sensing her mounting panic, and trying to avoid having to do CPR on the poor girl, I decided to step in.

"Look darlin', I'm sure the Captain here noticed that my eyes took the detour up to your face when you stepped in here and was trying to subtly let me know, without embarrassing you, that you were off-limits."

Lacey's face tinged the same color as her hair--well, close anyhow. I turned on the charm, smiled the toothpaste smile I was accused of possessing and winked at her, which was met with a dramatic throat clearing from Carter.

"Laying it on a bit thick, aren't we Vaughn?"

"Lacey, your soon-to-be husband is a very lucky man. Thank you for helping me get settled in Missouri."

I stood, signaling to Carter that we could go. The sooner I could remove myself from this charade disguised as a lunch, the faster I could be loading myself into my new abode and throwing back a fifth of Jack.

7

Camille

"What the hell is that?"

Janet bolted from her feet and ran to the windows looking out my front stoop.

"I didn't realize the circus is in town."

Orphan Black had been the marathon of choice. The afore-mentioned circus disrupted what had been a pretty quiet day. We were almost to the end of Season 3, and despite suckling from charity's teet, I didn't think I could wait for Season 4 to become free on Amazon. We needed answers.

"Maybe I'm getting a new neighbor. 2B has been empty for as long as I've lived here. I didn't even know it was for sale."

"Well, all I see is a moving van and a couple of burly looking guys trying to navigate a couch up the staircase. You might want to let building management know because I'm certain they left scuff up the wall."

There was a good chance she would open the door and start telling them how to do their job. Or chastise them for being too loud. It wouldn't be the first time.

Earlier in the week, it had been the UPS guy who had dared to ring the doorbell to deliver some flowers from Mina while I napped. Then, the landscapers dared to cut the grass while we watched a dramatic turning point in *Orphan Black*. And now she wanted to yell at movers? She was too much.

"Man Janet, you would hate Chicago."

She let go of the curtain and looked over her shoulder at me.

"I didn't know you lived in Chicago."

"Yup, in *Back of the Yards*. If there wasn't a train passing through on the way to the rail yard, or horns blaring from the Stevenson, you'd hear the Ortegas screaming at one of their kids down the street, or music from the Discoteca on Damen."

"Did you grow up in Chicago?"

Janet reclaimed her space on the other end of my new sofa. It is a million times more comfortable than my old one. It's so deep it near swallows you every time you sit down in it.

"No."

Too late, I remembered why I didn't share personal tidbits. Questions. Everything became a question. One question became two which morphed into a long trail of crap I didn't want to get in to with anyone. She didn't push.

It made me feel guilty though. Allowing the conversation to hang. I could be *Riley* and *Addison's* best friends I knew so much about them. They attended Saint Pius high school; Riley would be a senior when classes began after the Labor Day holiday. She captained the debate team and hoped to gain early acceptance to Yale. Addison, a sophomore, played volleyball in fall and softball in the spring. She wanted to be a Mizzou Tiger, just like her parents. She had gotten her driver's license and was absolutely furious she had to share a car with her sister.

If you asked me, she should feel lucky she even got a car. My two feet transported me through most of my life. If I couldn't get there on foot, I had to figure out a bus or a train, or some other way to get me from point a to point b.

"I only lived in Chicago for about a year. My last year of high school. My mom still lived there when I was in college and grad-uate school."

Janet nodded. A look at her watch apparently signaled it time for something of mine, be it a pill or a meal. I didn't know which.

"Keep talking. I'm still listening. I just realized it's two o'clock and I never made you anything for lunch."

"You know, I do have use of my limbs. It's my head that took a hit. I'm capable of making my own lunch."

Every time she brought me something, a glass of water, a blanket--lunch--I imagined my mother standing in the corner of the room, arms folded, glaring at me before whispering *Who do you think you are? The Queen of Sheba? Get up off that duff of yours.*

We didn't depend on others to take care of us. We took care of ourselves.

"Cammie you are the easiest case I've ever worked. Let me at least do the few things that I am, otherwise, I'll feel guilty for getting a paycheck. I've done nothing but sit and watch Netflix."

I could hear her busying herself in the kitchen, opening various drawers, the fridge, cabinets--she returned in a blink with a couple of sandwiches and drinks.

"So you were in Chicago for high school and college..."

"No, I was in Chicago for a year of high school. My mom wanted to make sure I could get into a good college. She read in the newspaper that the best way to get noticed by scholarship boards and selection committees was to have attended a magnet or charter school. She packed up our Geo, and decided Chicago was my best chance at both a decent Charter school and an opportunity to get a scholarship."

"Where did you live before Chicago?"

"Where haven't I lived?"

I tried not to sound bitter. Honestly, my Mom did the best she could. Being a single mom couldn't have been easy. Being a nomad, however, isn't the easiest way to grow up.

"I was born in Los Angeles from what my Mom told me. I don't remember much about it, other than memories my Mom has told me. I only have one really vivid memory. We were in a house with palm trees and a pool. I had a green two-piece bathing suit with silver stars on it, and a ruffle on the butt and across the bust. I remember almost nothing about Los Angeles. I remember moving away from L.A. We were in the car for a long time. It was incredibly hot, and it seemed like forever until we arrived in Miami. From Miami we moved to I think Oklahoma City. Then it was Dallas, New Orleans, Indianapolis and eventually Chicago."

"My goodness! Your pen pal list must be a mile long! All of those cities."

Janet shook her head, taking a long gulp of tea from her mug. I told her enough. I didn't want to get into any more of my life. We sat in silence, both looking out at the park outside my condo.

"You know. We've been cooped up inside all day long. It's too beautiful of a day to be hiding in here. Let's stretch those legs a bit. The fresh air will do us good too."

8

VAUGHN

Lunch was a complete waste of time. Not that I expected anything less. Everyone wanted to puff their chest spread their peacock feathers and mark their territory around the Jefe case. Yeah. Fuck. That.

I've worked the Jefe case for seven years. I focused on nothing but him for the last three. I didn't give a fuck if Kansas City purported to be his main inline into the United States. He has been mine since my days in Miami. A dead *secuaces* from the Mercado cartel washed ashore on 35th Street Beach. An oddity because we assumed that Mercado only worked California and the Baja coast.

A dead henchman in Jefe's territory though made us wonder if there was a connection. During the autopsy they discovered his eyes were burned out, his tongue severed and force-fed to him, along with some other gruesome details, before tossed into the Gulf. There was so much water in his lungs that autopsy listed his cause of death as drowning, which meant that poor SOB felt every toe-curling, cringe-inducing second.

Eventually, we connected the dots that lead him to my man Jefe, and the deeper I got into his case, and the closer I came to tracking him down--the harder my boner got for taking him down. Of then, of course, there was Baxter.

Noah Baxter of West Linn, Oregon. Son of Marie and Hank Baxter. Brother to Alice and Gabe, uncle to Penny, Sally, Ethan, and Shane. In our line of work, your identity is sacrosanct. Not many even get the privilege of knowing your full know let alone your entire lineage. Those are things you keep close to the chest, not just to protect the ones you love, but also to protect yourself.

He was more than a partner though. Even more than my best friend. We went to college together. Graduated the Academy in the same class, worked together as partners. Regardless of how tight we were professionally, he, first and foremost, was my brother.

The wound festered and burned the longer Jefe slipped from our hands. Because of Jefe, I flew solo these days. He took away the best friend I ever had. Jefe would go down, or I'd die trying.

I made that promise to Bax every day I opened my eyes and still pursued these bastards. I made a similar blood oath to Bax's family when I handed them the flag from his coffin. I made promises to Bax too, but that was neither here nor there. Not until I dethroned Jefe.

"I realize I'm just a local beat cop but if there's anything I can help you with... other than being your taxi...I know my way around these parts pretty well. So, just let me know if there's anything you need."

Barney Fife sitting next to me pulled me from my daydreams. Not that he was a bad guy, just unremarkable in the cattle call of people I'd exchanged pleasantries with. I couldn't remember Bob from Tom from Sam. I didn't of Missouri as a southern state, yet Barney had a southern twang. What the hell did I know, though? As we established earlier, I didn't even know the difference between Kansas and Missouri.

"I appreciate the lift. I'm sorry...I don't remember what your name is."

He glanced at me for a brief second before focusing back on the road.

"Parker. Peter Parker. And other than Chief Carter and my own boss, there isn't anyone else I knew prior to lunch. There's no way in heck I would be able to remember any of their names if I needed to get their names right standing in front of a firing squad."

No way in heck. I tried to suppress my laughter. The keyword was tried. Instead, it came out sounding more like a huff that sounded more arrogant than entertained.

"So, are your folks Spiderman fans?"

"My dad is. They featured him on the news a while back because he has the biggest comic book collection in Missouri. Including an original Adventures in Spiderman signed by Sigel and Schuster."

Based on the way he said it, I gleaned I should be impressed by the feat and gave the appropriate reaction. Honest though, I'm not a comic book guy. I mean I watched the movies and cartoons as a kid, my Spiderman knowledge was as shallow as a puddle.

"It's no big deal. The lift. I'm headed in your direction anyway to check on a friend. I'm not going out of my way. Do they have a car coming for you in the morning, or will you need a ride to HQ tomorrow?"

I had no idea. Long legs Lacey never told me the plan. I'm not under cover...yet. I needed to figure out who the players were in this city and get to know the routes in and out.

"For the moment I'm pretty much doing casework. I have files from the Bureau and Agency I need to read through, to get an idea of who's who. What kind of beat do you usually face?"

When I worked in Centennial, drugs made up eighty percent of their calls. If they weren't busting meth labs they were arresting dealers or breaking up Drunk and Disorderlies. In Idaho, it had been more of the same except XTC/MOLI instead of meth. Same with Cali and Nola except those were coke and heroin respectively.

"I can't believe KC has any kind of drug inline. It's so rare we get more than the usual's around here. You know, DUIs, gangs, accidents, a drunken husband knocking his wife around. Three weeks ago was the first time we even had to face any kind of unarmed assault. Poor girl. She just got out of the hospital last week. Terrible head injury. That's where I'm headed. To check in on her."

I didn't think that cops made house calls, but what did I know? Maybe Kansas City is the new Mayberry.

The neighborhood seemed decent. It looked like it a nice part of town, mostly middle-class type cars. You know, the late model Hondas and Toyotas, with a sprinkling of status symbols like Beemers and the like.

"I'm headed to Nine Carrington Ct, Unit A, where do they have you staying?"

I looked at the slip of paper that Lacey had given to me. Wouldn't you know it; I was in Nine Carrington Ct, Unit B. I showed him the slip of paper and expected no less than the Barney Fife *well I'll be* response I received.

"Hiya Spiderman."

I looked in the direction of the throaty whisper and found two women walking towards us from the park.

"Cammie! I can't believe you're up and walking about! Where's your cane?"

The woman whose arm had previously been linked through her companion's pushed both hands into the pockets of her zip sweatshirt wore. You know the kind. The ones from the lingerie store that said, *"Pink"* on them.

"Janet decided we needed fresh air. She said marathon watching Orphan Black isn't helping me heal any faster."

She had a throaty laugh. The kind that would put Janis Joplin to shame.

"Just around the park. It's not even two blocks. I helped her to keep balance so her muscles begin relying on themselves to stay upright. It may be slow going, but it's better this way."

The no-nonsense woman with graying hair and bedazzled

glasses wouldn't get an argument from me, even though she looked like she expected one. What did I care if the chick walked with a cane or not?

"See. I knew they scratched the wood."

She continued to tsk as we followed them up the stairs. Her finger traced the entirety of the gash from the lower stairwell to the upper stairwell

"Did you see that sofa? It was obscene in its size."

We made it up the last five stairs, ending up awkwardly standing between the two condos. Cammie looked at Parker then to me and back to Parker with a question in her eyes.

"I just stopped by to see how you were doing. I guess just by being up and around, you answered that question for me! Oh, and I gave this guy a lift. And wouldn't you know it, he's your new neighbor."

"Vaughn." I extended my hand in greeting, "The guy with the obscenely large sofa."

Cammie regarded me for a long moment before extending her dead fish hand and pretending to shake in greeting.

"You should tell your moving company they need to be more careful. That gash is hideous. I'm sure you'll be hearing from the management company about that."

The one with the bedazzled glasses interjected her unwelcome opinion. Despite getting verbally dressed down by bedazzled glasses, Cammie's eyes hadn't left mine.

The August sun remained warm, despite it currently setting. Except of course right on the porch where we stood. I don't think it could have been any colder if Mr. Freeze himself blew a snowstorm onto said porch.

I turned on the panty dropping charm, smiling that same megawatt smile I'd used on Lacey earlier. I never claimed exclusivity of use or limited the number of women on the receiving end.

"I'll be sure to let my company know. I'm certain their make sure to handle any repairs."

Bedazzled still didn't seem satisfied, but Cammie at least smirked in my direction.

"Well Parker, I'll be seeing you around."

I extended my hand and nodded my thanks for the ride.

"You have my number if you need a ride to HQ tomorrow."

I cringed when he said it. Granted HQ could have meant the Police Station to anyone who overheard. I liked to keep my profession on the down low to civilians.

So many years associating with drug dealers had shown me how many people hid something or someone. Not in the physical sense, but everyone knows a person or is related to a person that wouldn't want to have a run-in with the law.

"Does he work with you, Peter?"

I heard her throaty voice again as I turned into my home-away-from-home. The condo possessed a wholesome charm. It came mostly furnished. Regardless I had my own possessions I liked to bring with me.

My own bed, because who sleeps on a used mattress? I know DEA guys. And, just, no. I bring my own armchair and sofa because again, I know DEA guys. Plus, rental sofas are always lumpy, they're kept well past their prime and are always made of some substandard, cheap fabric that makes them smell like they've been rotting in a dumpster. And finally, my rowing machine, because when I need to focus in on a case, workouts clear my head the fastest. Everything else I let the hosting agency worry about.

As I inspected the one bedroom with a den condo, learning the layout of my new digs, I wondered if Lacey had been there earlier directing. Maybe the movers figured it out on their own, but I never specified where I wanted things and they figured it out. They set my furniture the same places I would have. My armchair and rowing machine in the den, my sofa directly underneath the windows, and the bedroom positioned in its most functional arrangement. The fridge, pantry, and medicine cabinets were also well stocked.

I shot an email off to Carter asking him to thank Lacey for the setup. This kind of hospitality had not been expected. At all. Most of the time when moving to a new location, I got to serve my time in some dingy apartment on the side of town no one wanted to live in. Either this was typical M.O. in Kansas city, or they expected me to be here a while.

9

Camille

Fresh air and a couple laps around a kid's park do amazing things for your well being. Granted, I had to stop and catch my breath on a park bench--twice--but getting my body moving had cleared my head and got the life back into my limbs. I didn't have a miraculous recovery. Benny Hinn hadn't slapped my forehead and declared me healed. My recovery is still slow moving. For the first time since the hospital though, I felt more like me.

"You and Janet hit it off."

Peter accepted the bottle of water I gave to him, before dropping ungracefully into the sofa cushions.

"Surprisingly, we are fairly similar. Our tastes on a lot of things--movies, tv shows, celebrity crushes...are the same. Plus, she talks but doesn't push. She doesn't mind silence if my brain takes a break. Never laughs when I can't access my words fast enough. And, she even reads to me out of that hot and horny romance novel she brings with her."

"I heard that!" she called from the kitchen, "it was one sex scene, and now she's weirded out!"

"It was way more than an innocent little scene," I tell Peter, trying not to drown in the blood rushing to my face.

"...And it used words that would make a sailor blush."

"I promise you, cock does not come close to the words that could be described as embarrassing a sailor."

Janet called once again from the kitchen.

"You know you are more than welcome to join the conversation from *this* room, seeing as how screaming hurts the head of the patient in this room. You know, the one with the brain trauma."

I turned to wink at Peter, realizing that he too became as red as I had been a moment ago. Apparently, *cock* is enough to make a cop blush.

"I'm about to leave."

Janet gathered her knitting and book from the dining table.

"The crockpot is on simmer, whenever you're hungry. It's chicken and dumplings. It's my go-to when the girls are under the weather. Sure it's going to be ninety tomorrow, but sometimes a little comfort food is the best thing for us."

"We need to get to the bottom of this case, Cam."

Peter followed me to the kitchen to help gather plates and such. When I grabbed two bowls, he didn't protest, so I assumed he wanted to stay for dinner.

"Peter, I told you, I was on the phone with Danny and then woke up in the hospital. That's the extent of my memory."

"Just one. Any more than that Nancy will have my hide."

That is a first. Peter hasn't ever mentioned his wife by name. Following his directive, I ladled a single dumpling into his bowl we sat down at the table.

"What about the break in? Anything unusual? You've had a few days to take inventory. Anything of note missing?"

"Well... No, nevermind, it's dumb"

"Anything helps Cam, even if you think it's dumb. It might end up breaking the case."

"It wasn't missing. It's just odd. I had a statue on my mantle.

56

I've had it since childhood. My mom must have bought it for me because I don't ever remember *not* having it."

Peter nodded his encouragement to continue, inhaling Janet's stew while I talked.

"That night, someone smashed it to smithereens. There was nothing left but plaster dust. It's so silly, yet so obnoxious, you know? Who would bother to take the time to pulverize a piece of junk that more than likely came from Walgreens for chump change? If it had been knocked over and the head broke, or it cracked or chipped that would make more sense. But completely obliterated? It felt like whoever broke it... you're probably going to say I watch too many crime shows..."

I sounded crazy in my own head, despite Peter's rapt attention I felt embarrassed to suggest it.

"...It felt personal. Like someone knew it was important to me and wanted to make sure I had no chance to repair it."

Peter nodded noting what I relayed in his notebook.

"Are you sure that you haven't had any fights recently? Co-workers, maybe an old roommate? Heck, perhaps an old college friend who knows about your fancy job? "

The sun just started to set outside. I can hear the kids in the complex screaming and carrying on, gleaning the last few moments of summer before they went back to school after the Labor Day holiday.

"Peter, I went to school in Illinois. My college roommate moved to the east coast for graduate school and is now a PhD Candidate at Boston University. I talked to her last Christmas. In college and grad school, I kept a low profile. I didn't know many people but you can have whatever information you need."

"What about online? Any social media? Chat rooms you belong to or message boards?"

"Those still exist?"

I stood at the windows, drawn to them by the sounds of the kids. They were getting ready to play Ghosts in the Graveyard. I couldn't look away. Hypnotized by the flashlights darting from patch of grass to patch of grass as the "ghost" tried to collect its souls for his graveyard. In these moments, watching the purity of joy from those kids that I realized how much I missed as a kid. Despite all that my mom did for me, working crap jobs to make sure we had food to eat and I had shoes to wear, I didn't get to have days like the one those kids were having. Where I could run and play in the security of my home and my friends, blissfully unaware of the dangers that lurked in every corner.

You must be careful Camille. You don't understand how much I worry. It's just me, little prima, and I would never forgive myself if something happened to you. Promise me you'll stay close okay? Play with the kids in the building.

The memory filled my mind and stole me away from whatever Peter asked me.

But Mom, I don't want to play with the Garcia boys. Their house smells gross, and their abuelita won't ever let us watch what we want to watch.
Mrs. Garcia is an old lady who earned the right to rest her feet and watch what makes her happy Camille. You're a six-year-old girl. You shouldn't be inside rotting your brain away anyway. If you don't want to play in the alley, go to the library. There are plenty of places you can travel to, all within the pages of a good book.
The librarian always shushes us. She makes more noise going 'SHHHHH' than we ever do talking about the books we're reading.

"Cammie? Earth to Cammie."
"Sorry Peter, I got distracted by the little kids in the park, and then all of the sudden I had a memory of my Mom."
"Musta been a good one."
"I was laughing at my younger self."
I couldn't sit still. My hands braided and unbraided my hair in a never-ending cycle.

"My mom didn't let me watch television as a kid. When we moved to Miami we lived in a two flat with the Garcia family. Diego and Juan were my age, and we played together a lot. Their abuelita refused to share the television when she watched us. We spent a lot of time at the library. I was such a precocious kid."

A chuckle bubbled up, surprising me with its appearance. With a chagrined roll of my eyes, I returned my focus to the yard where a man in a t-shirt had replaced the laughing kids and jog shorts.

"So you made a new friend at work, huh?"

I asked Peter, tossing my head in the direction of Vaughn.

"I don't know about a friend."

He rubbed the back of his neck. I learned that motion indicated '*I'm really uncomfortable*'.

"There was this big pow-wow at work between the suits and the street guys. Vaughn's new to the area so I gave him a lift. Little did I know he'd be moving in right next to you."

My new neighbor danced on the balls of his feet, bouncing back and forth like Rhonda Roussey before she goes in for the kill shot. He bounced in the parking lot, his earbud strands swinging back and forth like a thin jump rope.

"Now I know you'll be safe, with him next door."

Peter's observances probably didn't stop there, but being so intrigued by my shadowboxing neighbor, I stopped listening. In the time it took me to look at Peter to turning my focus out the window, Vaughn became swallowed by the shadows.

10

VAUGHN

They needed to get me a car. Trying to coordinate between pick up and drop off had me flashing back to pimples and puberty. I spent the previous evening combing through the files I was sent. I'm 90% up to speed with the players in Kansas City in relation to the Jefe' cartel.

Chasing down Jefe these past few years, I could see how Kansas City could be an inline. And, I'm pissed it took me this long to figure it out. Kansas City appeared a larger piece of this puzzle than we anticipated. Something kept nagging at me. Like Kansas City might be the key that took Jefe down. I don't know how. I needed to sort out why. But something said this city would be his demise. It was ballsy, granted. When every organization the government tasked with tracking and extricating bad guys were housed along one main strip in the middle of the heartland? Ballsy as fuck. My gut told me though, if I waited it out in Missouri, Jefe would come to me.

I wanted to go to my condo. My rowing machine called to me like a siren. I thought clearest when I beat the hell out of my body. All of that blood pumping through my veins helped clear my head of all the unnecessary crap. Twenty years working drug cartels guarantees you'll never sleep peacefully again.

Barney Fife had given me his business card for whenever I needed a lift. I craved the clarity of movement, choosing instead to walk. Hoofing it to HQ gave me enough time to clear my head. Earlier an intern carted me to the library. I remembered enough about the route to return me to HQ without incident.

"Vaughn."

Carter had some kind of sixth sense, being aware of the exact moment I arrived anywhere in his vicinity. His bellow carried all the way to the front door. The guy probably had a camera trained on the parking lot so he'd be notified the very moment I came back.

"Good afternoon Lacey," absorbed in her task as she was, she startled the moment I said hello.

"Well, hello, Special Agent Vaughn."

Her mouth turned up into an entertained smile.

She pushed back from her desk and crossed her arms, "You know you don't need to walk. We have any number of agents available to drive you."

My shirt was near translucent by the time I got back to HQ. It was nearly a two-mile walk from the library, and the afternoon temp steadily climbed into the mid-nineties.

"I appreciate that I do, but do you know when I'll be able to get a car? I'm grateful for all the generosity thus far. I'm truly touched by everything you did to get me settled, but I'm here to put this case to bed. I can't do that if I'm constantly trying to juggle rides, hon."

I was so close to winning her sympathy when *hon* fell from my mouth. It isn't intentional or meant to be condescending, but her pouty frown told me I stepped into a steaming pile of shit.

"Vaughn! Stop flirting with my assistant. I told you, she's spoken for. Now get your ass in here, I need to talk to you."

Fuckin' Carter. Way to throw gasoline on an already delicate situation. She probably thought everything I said was laced with

61

innuendo or charm. It wasn't. I had received the message loud and clear. Even without the obvious gestures to show off the *glacier that sunk the titan*ic iceberg her fiance turned into a ring.

"I was simply inquiring about a car. Other than saying thank you for getting me set up in my new house, and begging for the aforementioned mode of transportation I did no such thing."

The tattered plaid chair should have my name weaved into the back of it at this point. I was pretty sure that my ass indentation was still in that chair from earlier that morning. Since arriving in Kansas City. I spent more time listening to Carter yammer than I had actually getting anything done.

"I just got off the phone with Hendricks over at CIA."

Carter leaned back in his chair, the bottom of his white pressed shirt pulling out from his pants. The hairy roll of skin that hung over his belt buckle exposed itself to my line of sight, making it impossible to focus on anything else.

"He said there has been a lot of chatter from Jefe's men the last few days. Hendrick's team is certain that they're gearing up for some major transaction to go down. I need you to go meet with their team and see what the hell all of this is about."

He slid an email across my desk from his counterpart, David Hendrick's, CIA. While I scanned the email, he unwrapped his lunch. An amalgamation of processed meats from the sub shop down the street. If you could get past the overwhelming stench of onion, the sandwich actually looked decent and reminded me I had yet to eat or drink anything, and considering I expelled my weight in sweat, I needed to tend to that post haste.

From what I could surmise based on a cursory read of the email, there seemed to be discussions regarding a payday. They kept referring to a transfer--so said Hendricks. I guess if I wanted the full story I needed to hear it from the horse's mouth.

"I need a car."

"You're a pain in my ass, Vaughn." Carter said around the sub he bit into, "We don't have any. CIA is two blocks up fourth. You can't miss it."

He wiped his mouth, trying to finish gnawing down the massive slab of meat sandwiched between those pieces of bread. Bits of his sandwich projectile from those lips, as he laughed at his joke before he even said it.

"It says Central Intelligence Agency in big letters across the front of the building."

It was times like right now--when you expected the government to have its shit together--that I fully understand the world's frustration with bureaucracy.

I don't understand what is so difficult about obtaining a car. Four blocks passed fairly quickly, especially since I had my own annoyances at the government to fuel my journey, and the CIA had every drink one could imagine at their disposal.

I clearly picked the wrong agency to work for if this was how every agent at the CIA lived their daily grind. A kitchen full of gratis food and beverage, no institutional gray walls or fiberboard desks. In fact, I noted as I followed whatever junior level staffer they'd sent to collect me, the carpet beneath my feet was plush beyond belief. I could probably take my shoes off and squish my toes in it. It was boudoir level opulence. Must be nice.

"Special Agent Vaughn, these are Agents Lisner, Butler and Dukard. They're the special detectives assigned to this case. Since our meeting yesterday, I've brief them on the information gleaned from the meeting. Based on that data and our own intelligence my men wanted a sit down with you. It seems the wire has intercepted a hell of a lot of chatter recently. I'll let Butler fill you in on the rest. He's the one that's been listening."

Agent Butler and I exchanged pleasantries before sitting around their conference table and getting to why I was here.

"I need to say before we get started, your work on the Mercado cartel was impressive. A wanted fugitive for three years, and you get the file, take a look at all of the evidence we examined till our eyes bled, and discover the transport was occurring through high-end crystal? Who would believe that wealthy southern socialites for years have been serving Aunt Bessie's' Red

Velvet Cake on a platter made entirely of cocaine? Just brilliant...."

I tuned out halfway through the adulations. Not that I didn't appreciate the praise. I did. Who doesn't like to be respected for their work? The thing was, it's never as simple as they make it out to be. And, in all actuality, a piece of crystal made entirely of cocaine never made it to the purchasing market. The pieces that were made of coke would dissolve when soaked in water. That would make it a bit hard for those ladies to use more than once.

My team spent months on that case. We took it apart piece by piece. The tipoff had been a specific type of crystal from Mexico arriving on cruise ships docked in Galveston. The company claimed hundreds of thousands of dollars in damaged freight every year.

It was more than a little odd that Mexico was importing crystal. They were not well known for their crystal and stemware. We wrote it off though because there's plenty of sand in Mexico, and what is glass but heated sand?

We wondered why they continued to utilize the same cruise line month after month if they kept damaging their freight. One nugget of information led to another, which eventually became a trail for us follow. I don't think any of us had a decent night sleep for the eight or so month's leading to Mercado's arrest. There were a lot of dead ends and roadblocks, but we got him. He would live out the rest of his life behind bars.

"So what's this chatter that Hendrick's is talking about?"

Agent Butler ran a tired hand own his face, pulling his glasses off and rubbing against his eyes. It looked like the trio had pulled a few all-nighters, but I was more enthralled with the hunks of beef he called biceps. They were bigger than my thighs. How he fit into the CIA standard oxford with those things was beyond my comprehension. Also, why does a guy--who works for the Agency notorious for thick-waisted desk jockeys who spend more time at the local Starbucks--have to look that cut? He's CIA for Christ's sake.

"A few weeks ago the lines opened up between Jefe's Cabo Primero, Segundo, and Tercero."

The agent named Dukard began pulling pictures of the men from a folder.

"Francisco, Omar, and Guermo Ocatillo are his Cabo's here in Missouri. Omar the oldest, is his primero, Francisco his Segundo, and Guermo--whom they call Chuchi because of his, um, proclivities, is the youngest."

Chuchi roughly translated meant little girl. But it was a slang term meant to offend. Given Guermo preferred men to women, the insult made sense.

"Around August the second, the chatter got real loud."

Butler cut in, laying transcripts of conversation across the table.

"I'm telling you, their communication was occurring almost on the hour. Around roughly twenty-one hundred the chatter intensified to nearly every fifteen minutes then at twenty-one forty-five, silence. They must have missed whatever pickup was supposed to occur, because the next day, same thing. Intense chatter near sixteen hundred that ended at twenty-one hundred. Whatever they were supposed to pick up, they missed again. The chatter is still going on. It's on a different channel, totally encoded. There's something they are doing real soon."

The transcripts held the same information that Butler just finished summarizing. Something didn't sit right though. Obviously, translations aren't the best. It's like playing a game of telephone. You need to attempt to understand a garbled transmission, sometimes from a building or two away, and then also translate from Spanish to English.

"Can you email me the original file?"

"Sir..."

Dukard looked at Butler and Lisner, panicked.

"This is Agency property."

Internally I said a prayer. Okay, prayer may be a generous definition of muttering Jesus Christ under my breath. At least I was thinking about the guy upstairs though, right? This is exactly the reason why I found all those fucking lunches to be a pointless waste of time. A complete exercise in futility.

"Correct me if I'm wrong, but what exactly was the purpose of me sitting down and breaking bread with Hendrick's and the rest of the fellas for that big pow wow? You remember it right, Butler? My intelligence is your intelligence? Anything you need is at our disposal?"

I tried really hard to keep the attitude in check. Well, tried is a subjective term.

"What I need? Your evidence. At my disposal."

Butler smirked at me and passed the folder on the table.

"We made you copies."

I took a deep breath and counted to ten. Fuck it, I gave up at six.

"These are paper copies."

"Yes. Paper copies of everything we just talked about."

"I need the digital file."

"Everything is written out, right there."

Lisner pointed at the folder with the pen he nervously clicked as Butler and I exchanged niceties.

Apparently, intelligence was not necessary at the CIA despite it being part of their name.

"Again." I made sure to slow my speech and enunciate. "I need the digital file. There may be something that you guys missed. I want to hear the conversation myself."

"It's all in Spanish."

Butler crossed those pythons across his chest, staring me down as he rocked his chair back on two legs.

"Hablo espanol con fluidez."

"I dunno guys," Dukard chimed in, looking across to Butler. "Do you think we should call Hendricks?"

11

Camille

I don't know how long I'm going to be able to tolerate staying at home doing absolutely nothing other than watch TV and walk around the park. I was already climbing walls in the eight days since getting discharged. Thanks to the extended leave of absence, they'd disabled my email and work login. I couldn't work from home if I wanted to. Granted my concentration level ranked right up around that of a gnat. Being totally unproductive isn't in my DNA.

Janet's attempts at trying to teach me how to knit were futile. I poked myself at least six times with the needles and my yarn skein never seemed to want to stay tangle free. The Christmas afghan I had pictured presenting Danny with on Christmas Morning, more than likely would be ready sometime in the next millennia.

The only breaks in our monotonous days were when we found a new show to watch, or the UPS driver came with a delivery. My condo looked like a funeral home, and if one more person sent me a cookie basket, my ass would be as big as my sofa cushion.

"Oh goody, more food."

The doorbell chimed and Janet jumped to answer it. I stopped trying to beat her to the door. She always had a good ten seconds on me. Between pushing off the sofa, directing my limbs to straighten, and my core to keep me balanced, my damaged synapses weren't able to sort through it all at once. I ignored the imperious stares coming from my imagined mother tapping her foot at me from her permanent position in the corner of the room, every time I allowed Janet to take care of me.

"Not food!"

Janet sang from the front door.

"Something way better!"

Mina came tearing into my apartment and launched herself at me.

"Girl, you had me scared shitless. Don't go up and almost dying on me like that again."

Above the initial shock that Mina stood in my apartment, the fierce hug that practically choked the breath out of me added a new layer of surprise. I smelled the artificial strawberry of her hairspray and the subtle floral of her perfume--that's how closely cradled to her personhood I was.

"Head injury Mina."

Her grip finally loosened, allowing me to move back to neutral territory and away from her death grip.

"How scary! I swear we've all been looking over our shoulders ever since it happened. The players walk us to our cars if practice ends at the same time. Donovan and Hunt blame themselves. Like it's their fault some whacko was skeezing around the parking lot looking for a girl to kidnap."

She launched into full warp speed, summing up everything that had happened since my attack.

"I think there are at least three more fundraisers planned for you!"

The groan that leaked from my mouth didn't indicate any pain I was in but rather in reaction to the thought of more charity arriving. My balance book filled up faster than I could cross it off. I was fine now. Mending slowly, but mending. I didn't need fundraisers and certainly not any televised appeals.

"Everyone has done way too much, already."

Just the tally of new items from my living room/dining room and kitchen took up seven pages in my little journal.

"There's no way I'm going to be able to pay this all back."

I made the comment to myself, not to Mina, but she interjected anyway.

"You don't honestly think everyone expects to be repaid? They want to help because they can't believe a member of their Chiefs family is going through this."

"Mina, there are people in this world suffering. Truly suffering. People right here in Missouri that can't afford to put food on the table or a roof over their head. I'm safe. I have a roof over my head. Janet helps me. My occupational therapy is progressing--slowly--but steadily. Hopefully, I'll be back to work real soon. The only thing I'm truly suffering from is boredom."

Janet being ever the hostess produced a pitcher of tea which she wordlessly set in front of us before turning to disappear back to the kitchen. She missed my imploring look, hoping she'd stay and help keep the chatter flowing. I'm glad for the company, don't get me wrong, but other than work things and topical water cooler talk, Mina and I didn't have much to talk about.

"Is it weird that I'm here?"

Mina kicked off her heels, padding around my living room in her stocking feet.

"I realized on the drive over here that despite knowing you for almost three years, that I've never been to your house."

Her fingers skimmed my mantle as she inspected the various knick-knacks that had been brought in to make the place feel "homey." Since most of my original things had been decimated, these stand-in decorations were as generic as picture frames with pretend families in them.

"Did they tell you about the break-in?"

Mina nodded, further inspecting the items on my bookshelf. Thankfully, most of my books had been salvaged. Some torn jackets, a few broken bindings, but for the most part, they were damaged but not destroyed.

"I didn't know you liked books."

She tipped a copy of A Tale of Two Cities from the shelf, her eyebrows raised in question.

"We moved a lot growing up." My voice changed pitch, high to my own ears. "Books were the only constant."

I cleared my throat trying to cover the sudden tightness in my throat with a cough.

"I hear you." Mina slumped into the sofa next to me. So close to me, in fact, that our legs would touch if I shifted mere inches to my left.

"It was my me, my ma, and my two brothers. She worked as a maid during the day, and at a *lavadaria* at night a couple days a week to bring home some extra cash."

I didn't know Mina was Hispanic with her caramel colored hair and hazel eyes, her pronunciation gave it away.

"Did you grow up in Kansas City?"

A true friend would know this. We'd been work friends for so long. The bulk of our conversations revolved around who drove us crazy at work, tasks that needed to be completed, why Kim Kardashian decided to dye her hair blonde, and other banal water cooler chat. I would assume at some point she had mentioned her family, or at the very least talked about going home for the holidays, but for the life of me, I couldn't remember it.

"Patterson, New Jersey. I got a full scholarship to the University of Kentucky, worked at UK for a bit and then took a job with the athletic department at Mizzou. From there, this job practically fell into my lap."

As much as I appreciated Mina coming over to visit me, we hadn't been more than work friends. The long pauses in conversation left so much silence I could count the number of items Janet loaded into my dishwasher.

"It's so damn hot outside."

That was the conversation kiss of death. The second a conversation moves into weather territory, there's just no coming back from it.

"I haven't been out today. Janet and I went for a walk yesterday after the sun went down."

"Mina? Why don't you ladies get some fresh air?"

Janet called from the kitchen.

"The exercise will do Cammie some good. She needed to get those brain synapses used to firing commands again."

"We could head to the pool if you want?"

I offered, grateful it remained open a few more days.

"You can borrow a suit. We can swim, or just lay out."

"The pool is a fabulous idea!" Janet chimed, once again, from the kitchen, "Once I set dinner in the crock pot I'll join you guys. Dipping my feet in the water sounds like the perfect way to cool off!"

If going to the pool ended the uncomfortable, stilted conversation, then that's what we would do. Even if I wasn't bikini ready.

12

VAUGHN

Meeting with the Agency had taken the better part of two days. Carter is worse than that clingy girlfriend who needed constant reassurance. I didn't know much, but I knew I was on to something. We had disbursed with a plan to meet up with KCPD in the morning. We needed a time-line to match up against the chatter from the Agency. *Spiderman* could give me an assist in that regard.

The slog around the city for a second day had drained me of any desire to do anything more than mix a drink and float in the pool while it still remained open. With a Yeti full of John Daly, I made my way down to the center of my complex.

The hoards of screaming children running and cannonballing into the water couldn't detract me from my goal. The days had been long and too fucking hot to care about sharing my little slice of heaven with a handful of annoying little ankle biters. I stuck to the corner of the deepest part of the pool, content to hang from the edge and move with the pitch and yaw of the waves created by said children.

Halfway through my twenty-four ounces of booze, two gorgeous women arrived, taking a few chairs right near my towel and flip-flops. Totally oblivious to everyone else in the pool, they chatted about football players. It was odd, in and of itself. I didn't know any women who gave a rat's ass about football, but to find two of them in the same place? Talk about a hard-on waiting to happen. I'm sure if the pool had been a few degrees warmer my lower half may have cooperated.

Both blonde-*ish,* of the bottled variety I assumed. The one more honey than caramel though? Sweet sin, she had an ass for days. I could easily see myself spending time worshipping every inch of those globes.

Honey and Caramel took a lap around the pool, chatting with each other, blind to the more than obvious ogling from the horndog tweens. Honestly, if the kids didn't pick up their chins and close their pie holes, a mass drowning was imminent.

Honey's bikini wasn't quite pink but not red either--whatever the correct description of the color is, I called it sunset in the sand. Laying against her bronze skin combined they were a work of art.

"Travis somehow wrangled Eric and Rich into this stupid scheme, and all three of them carried my car into the tunnel and left it there. I literally spent like an hour walking around like a moron looking for my fucking car. That made Dorsey mad because we're all supposed to be coming in and leaving work in pairs or groups and making sure we stay safe and whatnot. You know, because of what happened to you."

Caramel cleared her throat and looked nervously at her friend before continuing.

"Anyway, he just wanted to lighten the mood. We're all on edge since it happened. Everyone is worried about you--and now for their own safety since they never caught the guy."

Caramel stepped into the pool to my right, not paying me any attention whatsoever as she hung on to the ladder rungs and lowered herself in.

"I miss everyone so much!" Honey squat into a sit, draping her legs over the lip of the pool. The pair had no idea she had given me the view of a lifetime. That swimsuit of hers hugged her skin and left nothing to the imagination. Southern Vaughn made quick work of showing his appreciation for the peep show.

"Kelce sent me the biggest basket of flowers I had ever seen. I'm pretty sure they are as big as I am."

"Travis Kelce?"

The words came out of my mouth before I could come up with a smoother way to insert myself into their conversation. "The football player?"

In unison, their heads turned in my direction. Honey lowered her sunglasses and shot me the most imperious of looks. Wouldn't you fucking know it. Honey is my new neighbor.

"Excuse us? Eavesdrop much? Private conversation."

I saw the second she recognized me. It was in her eyes. They shifted slightly from narrowed with complete disgust to a bit wide briefly, before sliding back into that saucy glare. She could best some of the nation's top poker players with a mask like that. If I hadn't been schooled in reading people for years, I would have never caught her indifference slip.

"Hard not to hear when you're an arm's length away from me."

I swung my hand off the lip of the pool towards where they congregated, which judging by their looks of disgust, was the wrong place to put my hand.

"Jesus first you eavesdrop then try to cop a feel? Real nice. C'mon Cam, it's less crowded over here."

Caramel cocked her head towards the other end of the pool. Seconds away from losing out not only on what sounded like an exceedingly interesting conversation but also the opportunity to appreciate those female forms close up.

"Please stay Cam." I implored, trying to sound like the nice guy I actually am and not the creeper who accidentally copped a feel.

Cam's eyebrows shot up before slamming into a deep set V.

"You're friend just used your name. But, we're neighbors, remember? We met last night? The guy with the couch that gashed the wall? Your friend Janet read me the riot act. She may or may not have called the HOA on me? There's a slim chance I'll be evicted two days after I moved in... so why not stay and chat for a few more minutes?"

Word's came tumbling out of my mouth like a Niagaran waterfall of desperation. My mouth, I could feel superglued into a John Wayne Gacy kind of clown smile. She would forever label me a creeper, regardless of how I tried to recover. The near brush in against her ample chest--not that I looked--okay... you know I did and now the "hey I'm a friendly neighbor bit." Every guy-next-door-turned-murder tale started that way.

Deep breath. Maybe if air forced its way in, no more stupid words could fall out. An additional swig from the Yeti insured it.

"I'm Vaughn."

I extended my hand, much lower this time. I aimed for her midsection and forced my eyes to stay laser-focused on her own. I know she recognized me. But she could be shit with names.

"I moved here from Denver. We seem to have a friend in common? My friend Spiderman."

I nearly lept from the pool and clicked my heels when that garnered me a chuckle. I felt like a boxer getting the TKO of the night.

"That's so funny, I call him Spiderman too!"

"Well, with a name like Peter Parker--you're kind of asking for it."

Cam smiled and nodded, pushing her sunglasses back over her eyes before leaning against her hands and stretching towards the sunlight. My eyes remained under strict orders not to follow the elegant slope of her neck down to those delicious pillows nestled so sumptuously in her bikini top.

"So," I had to lick my lips and clear my throat--twice--to get my voice to work again.

"How is it that you know Travis Kelce?"

Caramel pushed off the wall, floating in the middle of the pool. Her bathing suit left nothing to the imagination. I would not be enticed into looking, however, after gaining an inch of ground I had won engaging with Cam.

"We work with him."

Caramel muttered waving her arms in the water to keep her afloat.

They worked with him. Stated so casually. As if I had asked what state we resided in, or what color the water was.

"I'm surprised Peter didn't tell you." Cam added, "He about drooled all over my conference room the first time

he came to visit me."

"Nope, he forgot to mention that little tidbit. Must have thought I was a Cowboys fan."

"You're from Dallas?"

I could only nod. Cam lowered herself into the water bit by bit, the temperature of the pool having a pleasant--to me anyway-- reaction to the chilly water. I couldn't stop my eyes from drifting south to where her body protested the temperate changed with two turgid peaks. I realized all too late that my infatuation with Ms. Cam threw me off my game! I had come from Denver. As in Colorado. Dallas had been three cities ago. Dallas was on my mind because the conversation I had with the guys at the Agency earlier.

The assumption, of course, tended to be that if you lived in Dallas, you had to be a Cowboys fan. I bet you'd be excommuni- cated from the city if you weren't. I despised them though. Hated them as much as I hated the Michigan Wolverines. My hatred for all things maize and blue, however, wasn't something I typically shared with anyone while assigned.

"Nope. Lived there for a while."

I flipped my sunglasses down, taking a long pull from my cup as I surveyed the water. If my game got knocked off kilter from a couple of hard nipples pushing against a bathing suit, I wouldn't allow anyone to make eye contact with me.

"Me too! Well, as a kid anyway."

"I sure do miss the 'cue there. Colorado couldn't hold a candle to the 'que in Texas."

Her head tilted and I was graced with another of those looks. The girl should be a preschool teacher. She would make the most ill-behaved child toe the line.

"Colorado? I thought you came from Texas?"

I pushed off the wall, half diving under the water. I needed a few seconds to gather my scattered thoughts. This is the reason I stayed away from people while on assignment. I should know this by know. My dick, unfortunately, did not want to listen to me. It liked talking to this girl fine. Even if my mouth ended up divulging every state secret I owned in the process.

"I'm a nomad."

A group of cannonballing kids slammed into the water simultaneously, causing a wave that shoved me directly into Cam. My reflexes thankfully fast enough that my body didn't end up pushing her up against the lip of the wall. Her soft body, the silk slickness of her leg sliding between the pair of mine, her nails running down my chest in reaction to the sudden movement of our bodies against each other. Those actions overwhelmed my nervous system. An explosion of riotous sensation pulsed through my body settling in my tailbone, tingling with enough strength that my enjoyment of our predicament became prominent in my short.

She gasped, fingers flexing against my chest. I know she felt it. Even with her eyes shuttered behind sunglasses, the pout of her mouth, the crease of her eyebrows, screamed to me that she had. With little effort she pushed my body away from hers, an embarrassed smile floating across her lips.

"I'm sorry."

I wasn't.

"Those damn kids."

I'd probably give them twenty dollars to recreate the scenario again.

"Cam! How ya doin'?"

Her friend Janet, the one who wanted to sling my balls up earlier in the week, called from the entrance of the pool. In her oversized sparkly sunglasses, sunblock tinged nose, and an armful of pool accouterments, the woman screamed soccer mom.

"Are you feeling alright?"

Cam pushed off the wall, sliding past me towards the opposite end of the pool with Caramel hot on her tail. So much for getting to know my neighbor better.

~

THE REST of the week's passage of time didn't get marked by how many pieces of the puzzle I could put together, or how many brick walls I came up against trying to figure out the ins and outs of the Jefe Cartel. Rather, time passed according to the coming and going of my new neighbor.

Cammie and Janet existed like Siamese twins joined at the hip. They barely left the house. The lone exception occurred every morning at eight-thirty on the nose. I made sure to leave for the office at the same time. I gave up waiting for the agency to get me a car, and rented my own. Sure I drove a piece of shit Chevy Aveo, but it was my dime, and I'd be damned if I spent more than twenty-five dollars a day on it. Even if I looked like a clown with a toy car.

Cammie and I had progressed from the polite smile/nod combo to an actual good morning and have a nice day. Sure, we moved slowly, but I counted it as a win. I couldn't remember the last time I had to work this hard to get a general pleasantry from a woman. Maybe junior high.

The pair also took a walk around the neighborhood, every evening. Every other day the resident Officer Friendly paid a visit, after which came by so we could talk shop. Not that local PD could help much, but I needed him to feel as if he mattered to my case--in the off chance anything went down I needed to be the first to know about it.

Honestly, though he did little more than listen to my thoughts and theories, nodding where appropriate--I liked not being so damn lonely for once. He and I went down the street to watch pre-season football once. The Chiefs--of course.

I had given Parker plenty of opportunities to mention that my neighbor worked for the football team, but he never said a peep. It clearly wasn't a state secret. Cammie's friend--whose name was Mina, I learned--had been pretty open with the fact that they worked there.

By the Friday night of Labor Day weekend, *I* had enough of staring at file folders and listening to phone taps. Since it was Labor Day weekend, I intended to enjoy my earned holiday as a worker for the good old US of A, and planned to start my long weekend with a twelve pack of beer, a pizza, and a UFC fight on Pay Per View.

Parked planned to come over and watch with me, as his wife had a 'girls night' planned with her college friends.

"What do you mean we can't watch the fight?"

I had learned in a couple of weeks that I lived here that the walls were nothing more than decoration--soundproofing in the units was non-existent. In my line of work, not the most convenient wrench to get thrown. My options were to drive to HQ every time I needed to have a confidential conversation or be that asshole that blares his stereo or TV to scramble any eavesdropping technology someone might be using.

Parker nodded at me as he scooted past me into my apartment, case of beer and something that smelled fucking awesome stacked on top of it. I could hear the argument brewing next door from where I stood.

"Danny, I told you. I need to watch my money.
I'm not working."
"Babe--it's Johnson vs Dodson.
Do you know how important this fight is?
I would have never come home this weekend

if I knew you weren't gonna order the fight."
"Why not call Isaac and see if he bought it?"

I shouldn't be eavesdropping. Pete had already finished laying out the casserole I assume his wife sent him with, and had put all of his beer into the fridge and now regarded me with impatience.

"The boyfriend sounds like a dick." I tossed my head in the direction of her apartment.

"YOU wanted me to come and visit you this weekend Cam, so why would I spend my time with Isaac?"

You didn't need supersonic hearing for the last sentence. Even Parker heard it, seated in the middle of my living room.

"Do you think I should go and check on things?"

What did I know? Did people normally insert themselves into other people's arguments? I doubted it, even if it did appear to be escalating.

"Well, the kids hurt. She may be home from the hospital, but there's a long road before she's healed."

More mumbled conversation that neither of us could hear. I assumed the argument ended. I slowly shut the door just prior to the yelling erupting again.

"DAMMIT CAMMIE! WHY AM I HERE THEN? I'M UP TO MY EYEBALLS IN WORK!"

Not my business. It wasn't Parker's business either, but as soon as the screaming started he was out the door faster than the damsel could scream out her distress.

"Cammie?"

He used the rabbit tap. That stereotypical two knuckled rap on the door that you see used in every cop movie. I didn't think anyone actually used it. Then again, I never hung out with a beat cop. By the time they called me in, social niceties had been surpassed. My guys broke down doors with battering rams and shot laser beams into houses.

"It's Officer Parker, is everything okay?"

Officer Parker. My eyes rolled of their own accord. She called him Peter every time they interacted.

The door flew open with the boyfriend at the door.

"Officer Parker? Everything is fine."

He smiled that all American, boy-next-door smile.

"Just a little disagreement."

"Cammie?" Parker inserted his shoulder between the door and the boyfriend's body, "how ya doin?"

"You know what babe, maybe you're right. I'm going to hand out with Isaac after all. I'll see you later."

Before any of us could further that conversation along, the guy had his wallet, his keys, and bound down the stairs, and out into the parking lot. A blue F-150 with bass shaking the windows peeled out of the parking lot seconds later. Of course, the guy drove a douche-mobile.

"I'll be over in a couple of minutes."

Parker turned to me before quietly shutting Cammie's door.

A couple of minutes turned into almost a half an hour, but once I opened the door and saw not one but two people standing there I didn't complain.

"I invited Cammie along. There's plenty of food, and since Danny decided to visit his friend, I thought she might want to come and hang out with us."

In a tank top and a pair of those soft pants that spelled love against her ass, Cammie stood in my doorway nervously twisting her fingers. Almost like she expected me to turn her away and send her back to her condo. Like hell, I would. Her hair hung in a loose braid, with these tiny wisps of hair floated around her face barely skimming her eyebrows. I couldn't do more than wave them into my apartment, as I had totally lost the ability to speak.

The girl had no makeup on. Her eyes shone, but not in the excited I want to fuck your brains out kind of way. She looked like she'd spent the evening crying. Complete gut punch. Tears were my weakness. Growing up with a Mom and a sister, heart-broken women were my kryptonite.

"Hi, neighbor."

I couldn't talk around the sand in my throat. I don't know I went from being one episode of skin to skin contact away from a hard-on, to wanting to put a blanket around her, pull her into my lap, and run my hands through her hair.

"Are we going to watch the fight or what?"

Count on Parker to interrupt my moment. Wait. Damn, I stood there like a damn moron blocking the entrance to my apartment.

"O.T. is good then?" Parker asked her around a mouthful of whatever casserole his wife had put together.

The woman could cook. I didn't remember the last home cooked meal I ate. The chicken concoction she sent with Peter was heaven in a pan. Cammie nodded pushing her food around her plate. I inhaled three helpings without shame, and honestly, I considered asking her for the remnants she couldn't finish.

"I think so. My words aren't fully back yet but they're getting there."

"Any recollections from the attack?"

Peter asked because apparently, we can't have a night of normalcy where three people ate dinner and watched TV together. Everything always came back to the job. Don't get me wrong in any other situation it would be impressive]as hell. Tonight though, I wanted to enjoy the company they provided.

"No, sorry. Like I said, Danny was talking then I woke up in the hospital."

"What about the dreams? Any more strange dreams?"

"Nope, all the medicine sends me into a pit of blackness for ten straight hours."

"Ten hours?" I whistled, "I can't remember the last time I got ten hours of sleep."

"My body is going to hate me when I have to start getting up at five again and going to bed at midnight."

I got her to laugh. Sure, she laughed at her own joke, or at her impending dilemma, but she laughed. I wanted to make her do it again. Laughter was much better than the subdued and pensive woman who sat with us all night. Not that I knew much about her, but I assumed she didn't normally act this way. I wanted to cheer her up and take away that glassy-eyed blank stare.

"After Georgetown, I joined the force," I told her trying to keep as vague as possible.

"The first six weeks is what they call hell week. They only refer to it as a week because you literally lose track of time. They keep you up for days. They make you stand outside in the rain--or in my case snow--they put you in dark rooms so you have no idea if its day or night. Then when you're ears are buzzing and your brain refuses to focus because you're so out of sorts, they make you take test after test until you mentally have nothing left.

It's six weeks of pure torture. Anyhow, during one of these marathon sessions where we'd been up for almost two days, I needed to use the bathroom real bad. I snuck in during a time when the CO took his leave, hoping I could go really fast and come back and no one would be the wiser. So there I am trying like hell to stay away while sitting in the bathroom, and wouldn't you know I fell asleep right there, in the john, with my pants around my ankles."

"He came back didn't he?"

Internally I gave myself a fist bump. Cammie leaned a bit closer. Her eyes, not totally alert, but not nearly as empty looking as they had been.

"Not only did he come back," I continued, "but when he did, I was the person he wanted to speak with. Of course, I was completely down for the count. They had to turn the lights on and everything to search for me. Which meant that they had to reset the exercise for everyone in the class."

"Oh God." Her hands pressed against her cheeks to cover an empathetic groan.

"Once the exercise finished, I received bucketful of snow down my pants in the middle of the night because the guys were so pissed at me."

"That's awful!"

"That isn't the worst of it, though I'm pretty sure I had frost-bite on my ass for the rest of the program. Oh, hey the fights about to start!"

I used to never be a fan of UFC. I never saw the point of it. How can a bunch of idiots essentially having street fights in a ring, be entertaining for anyone? But when you're trying to track down drug dealers, drug pushers, and drug lord--they all tended to hang out in the same types of places. UFC fighting is a great cover for them. Over the years while on stings or busts, I picked up the sport and now I'll admit I'm a total convert.

The Johnson/Dodson fight was a pretty big deal for hard-core fans. They didn't get enough clicks for the fight to be national news. Both still middle-tier fighters, it still remained a big deal for those who had witnessed their rise that they finally faced off.

Cammie's temper tantrum throwing boyfriend didn't win any points with me, I could empathize with him. The excitement over tonight's fight was palpable.

"It's a big deal huh?"

She asked as if reading my mind. It amazes me how women can fold their bodies into the strangest positions, like living origami. Cammie presently perched at the opposite end of my sofa, her legs tucked underneath her, her body folded over the pillow with her hand resting on her chin.

"Yeah. Fans have been begging for this matchup for at least two years."

She caught me staring at her but didn't look away. Her mouth twitched as she held my gaze, a curious smirk lifting one side of her lips up before trying to refocus on the television.

I couldn't focus on the fight. The biggest fight of the year, and instead I found myself wondering what her lips tasted like. What they felt like when pressed together in a half smirk like she had on her face a minute ago. I wondered how those close trimmed finger-nails felt when arched and piercing into the skin.

Did her legs feel as smooth dry as they had when slicked with water? There was an intoxicating smell surrounding her. It smelled as if she had danced in the rain, before dashing through a euca-lyptus field. I couldn't tell if it was perfume, or shampoo, or fabric softener.

I wanted to cradle her against my chest, bury my nose in her hair, and against her neck. To run my lips along the soft cotton of her tank top and feel the ribbed texture against them. I was hard for her, and nothing more than a few sentences had ever been exchanged between us.

"Gawd! Out in five rounds! You've gotta be kidding me!"

Parker's hands flapped wildly in my periphery, from where he sat in my recliner.

Shit. I missed the whole fight. Five and half minutes and it was over. Glad I wasted ninety-nine dollars to watch that. Correction. The Agency wasted ninety-nine dollars on that fight.

"Were you even watching?"

Nailed me on that one. Count on Parker to call me out.

"Of course."

He looked at me again, confused, before standing and collecting the beer bottles from the coffee table.

"I'm gonna head back home."

Cammie stood and stretched before walking towards the kitchen.

"Thanks for helping out Peter."

He got a hug from her. Like a full-blown, breasts smashed against his body, arms wrapped around his back, hug.

"It was great talking to you, Vaughn."

A wave. That was the gist of our goodbye. A simple wave over her shoulder before only the silent hush of the door closing could be heard. No '*thank you.*' No 'I *hope we can talk again soon.*' Nothing. I bet she saw me ogling her. I probably made her uncomfortable. Great. Just great.

13

Camille

My escape couldn't have been fast enough. There is something wrong with me. I don't know what. Perhaps the hit to my head, or maybe the medicine. Vaughn could turn me on with a well placed smile and look.

Vaughn, I'm sure, could smell how turned on he made me. Despite being all the way across the couch. Every time he smiled. my lady bits would contract. When he laughed? I Gushed.

I know he looked at me. I could feel it on my skin. Like when you're laying poolside, and a cloud passes over the sun. That second of shade makes you notice the difference between sun and shade. When the sun returns, it's hot kiss tempts every millimeter of skin. That was what his interest felt like. My skin puckered in awareness every time. I still trembled from the most delicious sensations floating through my blood stream.

Speaking of pools, our encounter? I couldn't stop thinking about it. The way his legs felt against mine. Being caged, but not trapped. To see his **d**ark stubble of his five o'clock shadow and the entertained glint of those stormy blue eyes?

Janet came at the perfect time. Her rescue saved me from

embarrassment. I practically begged him to kiss me. My mind refused to think of anything else.

His mouth formed a perfect heart. The top lip full and rounded, his bottom lip pouted enough to form a bow. I wanted to suck on it. Or bite it. Or run my tongue down its crease.

Sweet Jesus. I had a boyfriend. A great boyfriend. He made a lot of sacrifices for me. Girls with boyfriends did not covet their hot neighbors. Even if their boyfriend acted like an asshole.

Danny was still at Isaac's. I wasn't a fan of Isaac. Not that he was bad news per se but he seemed shady. He worked whatever angle he could find. He sold supplements or something -I guess having to hustle all day long, carried into your personal life.

We never got off on the right foot. Isaac and Danny were inseparable through undergrad according to Danny. Then Danny went to grad school. Isaac wanted nothing to do with more college. When Danny took the internship with the Chiefs, Isaac could't wait to spend three with his college best friend.

But, Danny met me--and Isaac inadvertently became the third wheel. That is my assumption anyway. It's not like Isaac and I routinely share our feelings.

I fixed Mina up with Isaac once in hopes of socializing as a foursome, but no such luck. Mina preferred men with deeper pockets and a solid five year plan. Drifter man-children were not her scene.

These days I barely get a hello from Isaac Typically it's an arctic stare and a grimace he tried to pass off as a smile.

"Baby..." Danny stumbled into the condo as I was about to step into my bathtub.

Silently I cursed his inconvenient arrival. The bathtub and I had a date. After the Vaughn workup-- a book, a bath, some self pleasure were the plan for the evening.

"Don't *baby* me Danny. You acted like a huge dick."

I wrapped my robe tighter around my body shooting him a wasted look of disgust. Danny's glassy eyes told me his buzz left him incapable of interpreting any emotional subtext. My actions were completely lost on him.

"Aww c'mon Cam. Don't be like that."

He swayed a bit as he walked. Hopefully, he got a ride home from Isaac. He certainly didn't have enough faculties to drive.

"I'm sorry for the way I acted. I miss you so much when I'm gone."

Regardless of how he annoyed me, it felt nice to be cradled against his chest.

"This is the first time you seem like *you*. I wanted to spend the night showing you how badly I missed you, and how relieved I am that you're okay."

Danny rubbed his erection against my thighs, trying and failing to hit any place that would tingle.

14

VAUGHN

"**C**ome on baby." I heard through the wall.

CLEARLY. I might add. Like I could have been laying in bed with them.

"I haven't seen you in weeks."

"Seriously Danny?" I heard Cammie huff, "I'm not supposed to be doing anything that causes my head to move or bounce unnecessarily."

"I'll do all the work baby."

I could picture him laying next to her, running his hands between her legs. Caressing her well-defined thighs. *Fuck.* Thinking about it made me hard.

"Danny," she sounded annoyed, but I could tell by the lilt in her voice he had gained her acquiescence.

What a dick. Who pressures their sick girlfriend for sex?

"Mmm baby. You smell so good."

This guy couldn't be for real?

"I want you so bad. Feel me. Feel what you do to me, baby."

I wanted to puke, and not because of the three helpings of Parker's casserole or the six-pack of beer I washed it down with.

These certainly were shoddy builds if the walls were this thin. There should be building codes or firewalls, or *anything* to protect a neighbor from having to hear these kinds of things?

"Yeah Cammie, oh god. That's it. Right there. Yesssss."

Great. The meathead was a talker. My eyes were going to permanently be stuck in the back of head listening to his drivel.

"Baby. Mmm, Baby. So good."

How could she find this attractive? Honestly. What kind of guy calls a grown woman, baby?

Then, the thumping began.

Thump. Grunt. Thump. Grunt. Thump, thump *oooh yeah.* Thump. Thump.

That's it. There is no way in hell I would be party to the entire theater of their fuck. I whipped off my covers, stumbled out of bed in a half beer induced, half hormone addled haze and beelined for the shower. If anything could drown out their ...*sounds*...I hoped it would be the sound of the bathroom fan and water hitting the glass enclosure.

The hot water served as the perfect salve. I lost myself in the quiet solitude of the enclosure, oblivious to the passage of time. The subtlest of sounds teased from my haze. I tried not to take a breath. The foreign sound refused my attempts to place it. It came again, louder and more distinct. It was a female moan.

Was nowhere safe? First the bedroom and now the bathroom? I heard a groan again. Then a soft thunk against the shower wall. Afraid to take a breath, I waited for the foghorn boyfriend to join in. Only silence.

You know who did come? My gorgeous neighbor. And not quietly either. Where in the hell was the boyfriend? Did he leave his girlfriend and high and dry? Did she need to take care of herself in the privacy of her shower? What kind of douche is insistent upon sex only to fuck her until his satisfaction ? Who does that? Isn't it like common courtesy to make sure your girlfriend is still hanging in and enjoying the ride?

My brain flooded with images of her simply laying there, bored. Her body moving up the bed with each of his dramatic thrusts. Dead eyes instead of ones that danced with passion. Her mouth set in a pouty frown instead of agape and ready to cry out in apogee. Instead of her own sweat setting her whole body into a maelstrom of hot and cold sensations, she instead lifelessly received bullets of sweat from her partner's exertions as he sought his own pleasure.

Who wouldn't want to experience a woman as beautiful as his girlfriend is? Especially at the height of her pleasure? In a relationship, those moments are my favorite--sexual pleasure aside. The beauty that is only witnessed by a select few. Where vulnerability and pleasure intersect.

My hand found a path down to where my own need announced itself. Already rock hard, I swayed into the hole my fingers provided, rather than pumping. Just a few thoughts and I nearly came. I wanted to draw it out at least a little bit especially since I wasn't even mentally present for the initial build up. Imagining Cammie's back arched, mouth wide open on a silent scream, I arrived at the point of no return.

Imagining her legs spread as wide as they could go, rolled up on the top of her toes so she could push up to meet my downward thrust, catapulted me into that abyss of pleasure on a less than quiet exclamation.

What the hell is happening to me? I couldn't seem to get Cammie out of my mind. Now she was part of my jerk-reel? This is not good

"So TELL me again what we are looking for?"

I convinced Carter I needed help from KCPD to lay down a timeline of crimes committed in the last month. I wanted to compare it to the chatter I had *finally* gotten from the CIA. Sharing evidence should not be such rigmarole. Since peter and I formed a friendship, this was the most natural progression to bring him into my confidences.

"I need you to go through the list you got from your Sergeant. Highlight every crime committed between these times on August the third and August the fifth. Let me know if anything stands out or seems odd"

We were seated at my dining room table. I'm not used to working with someone in such proximity. Of course, Baxter and I worked together for years, but never practically on top of each other. And Parker is a mouth breather. Worse still, when he finds something interesting enough to warrant a highlight, he makes this obnoxious 'ohh" kind of half hum/half exclamation before dragging the highlighter across the paper in a way that ensured it made the most noise possible.

This is probably why I worked alone.

"Anything?"

There wasn't much chatter on the audio Butler and his crew hadn't already briefed me on. I figured it would probably be a dead end, but I hoped they missed something.

"Not yet."

Parker continued to peruse his files, loudly breathing from his mouth. Still making those noises I could hear through my earbuds over the sounds of the Cabo's discussing their grab. The audio was so grainy it was near impossible to clearly make out what they were saying. Even after cleaning it up, there is still too much background noise to get a lock on what they were saying definitively.

"Huh."

Parker is a many of many words.

"What?"

"What, what?"

Good Lord. He really is Barney Fife. Parker is a good guy, don't get me wrong. Knew his football. Is fun to shoot the shit with. But in all honesty, I'm not sure how long I would be able to use him as my sidekick. Parker was in my apartment less than an hour, and already I reconsidered my offer.

"You made a noise."

"Oh."

He capped the highlighter, and set it down perfectly parallel to the other writing instruments he lined up.

"Cammie's house got broken in to on the third, and then she got attacked in the parking lot on the fourth."

Peter yanked his backpack onto my table, taking out various files from within. He unbound a thin file and spread it out between us.

"Here's the preliminaries from her break in. They couldn't find any prints. Not even a quarter of a print. The detectives thought it is odd someone committing a petty robbery would take the time to wear gloves."

I half listened. It would take me a quarter of the time to read through the file than wait for him to explain it to me.

"It says here nothing was taken."

"Yep. Weird, huh? They break in--shatter the door jamb, destroy the lock, make all this effort to get *into* her house, but then take nothing. The entire apartment is tossed--they must be looking for something."

"God these pictures."

You couldn't tell someone occupied the space there. The entire room had been a tornado of destruction. The couch--totally gutted. The curtains looked as if a feral lion tried to climb them and failed. The carpet, shredded. The television, bookshelf, glass coffee table, and TV stand all shattered. Same path of destruction in the kitchen and dining room.

"It's weird isn't it? That they would go through all that effort but not find anything worth taking?"

"It makes it feel pretty personal."

"That's what we said too. But when I talked to Cammie, she could not name a single person who might have it out for her. I talked to her college roommates--their names are listed there in the file--and they said Cammie kept to herself and doesn't possess a huge circle of friends. Neither of them could imagine anyone wanting to hurt her."

Reading over the statements from the roommates they didn't pull any punches. While they weren't unkind, they certainly didn't hold back. One of her roommates--a Rowen Eisenberg--currently studying at Boston University insinuated Cammie is a socially inept loner. The statement said after living with her for a semester Rowen realized she preferred solitude to socialization.

"...and then the very next day she's attacked in a parking lot?"

What could be missing? It circled around my brain like those old cartoon characters when they got bopped on the head from a nemesis.

"Took a hit to the back of the head. The hospital called it a kill shot. She's lucky the security guard found her in time. We don't know what the perp wanted with her. To rape her, abduct her, rob her...there's some shady areas around the football stadium.

The security guard making his rounds said the perp looped her by the armpits and dragged her towards his vehicle. Six two, two twenty, mustache, collar length hair, dark blue or black jacket and jeans. We searched for days. The locals gave us wall to wall cover-age. Hell, the Chiefs put up sketches during the games and offered a reward in hopes someone would come forward. No luck."

According to the file, the accuracy of the sketch isn't at fifty percent. Distance, lack of lighting, the security guards own less than stellar eyesight--a good twenty percent of the population probably looked like the guy they sketched out.

I should talk to Cammie. The thought teased at my psyche while I flipped through the file. Damn if it isn't the best idea I had all day. Plus then I had an excuse to see her. This case didn't pertain to mine, from what I gathered. She is just a girl, living in a semi-decent neighborhood. Being a pretty girl like she is, having a high profile position like she did, it is more than likely her perp is someone with whom she interacted and didn't realize. It is most likely something simple like a gas station attendant at the local BP.

15

Camille

"It's the cop from next door!" Janet called to me from the front door.

Janet asked if she could leave early. School just started and she tried to juggle the two girls schedules. Addison had some kind of after school event. Softball maybe? My memory isn't the most reliable.

"Are you up for seeing visitors?"

Janet peeked around the corner from the foyer into my living room where I notified the post office of my change of permanent residence.

"Do you know what he wants?" I whispered so Vaughn wouldn't know I tried to give him the slip.

"He asked if he could talk to you for a few minutes. I need to head out though, so if you don't feel comfortable with him being here with you alone I can tell hi to come back at another time."

"He's a cop Janet.." She is so protective of me, it's sweet. No one has ever been this concerned about me before.

"Just because he's a cop doesn't negate the fact he's a man with a weapon."

"Is that what they're calling it in your dirty books these days?"

95

"Camille. I'm not talking about his cock. I mean his actual gun. The one holstered at his hip."

"I think you watch too many cop shows Janet. I don't think I've ever seen him with a gun holster."

"Yes or no Camille? Addison is going to have my head if I show up late."

I wore no makeup. I don't think I took a shower. My hair is tied up in a half-hearted bun, and I wasn't wearing a bra.

"Send him in. Hopefully, he'll be quick."

No clue why I said that.

"Camille."

The guy made me feel hot even when I looked and felt like shit. I didn't remember him being so tall. His form filled my entire doorway. I needed to strain my neck to see his face.

"Hey."

Why was I blushing? This is my house. He came over to see me. It isn't like he doesn't know I am a recovering invalid. Surely he knew to expect I would be in lounge around the house clothes.

"Do you want something to drink?"

I asked, realizing after the fact that meant he needed to bare witness to the arduous process I required in order to do so. Expecting him to accept the offer, if nothing else than to ease the discomfort, I tried to worm my way off the sofa in the best possible position for me to not get dizzy and lose my balance.

"I'm still here!" Janet called dashing in behind Agent Vaughn. "I'll get you two settled and then I'll be off. Agent Vaughn, is that a yes to the drink?"

"Sure. Whatever you have is fine."

Janet brought yet another pitcher of iced tea out. It seemed her go to whenever anyone came over. I drank more iced tea in the last three weeks than in my entire life.

"So what brings you over, Agent Vaughn."

I smiled my thanks as Janet silently waved goodbye and saw herself out. Vaughn accepted the proffered glass which I nearly dropped when his fingers innocently brushed against mine. It is a simple touch. I probably accidentally brush body parts with people a million times in a regular day. A bump of shoulders passing through a door, a slide of knee against knee sitting on the subway, these simplistic actions never do anything more than pull me from whatever thought I'm focused on long enough to register them. Yet I feel two of Vaughn's fingers on my own, and my entire circulatory system shocks awake.

"How are things with you and ...I'm sorry I forgot the boyfriend's name."

He took a lap around my living room taking stock of the knickknacks on my fireplace mantle and the books on my shelves. Did no one just sit and have a conversation anymore? Briefly I considered if I made people uncomfortable by not standing in greeting.

"His name is Danny, Agent Vaughn. And if you came to have a conversation, I prefer to have it to your face and not your back."

His raised eyebrows spoke volumes over the glass he shoved in his mouth. I guess that came out bitchier than I intended.

"So the two of you kissed and made up then?"

He continued, taking a seat in the armchair perpendicular to the couch.

"We aren't fighting."

"Sounded like an argument to me. Or do you normally allow your boyfriends to steamroll right over you and guilt you for not being able to afford to purchase a ninety-nine dollar pay-per-view?"

Who is this guy? My dad? I don't remember asking my fairy godmother for a stand-in sibling or father figure. And, who is he to comment--or listen in for that matter--to a fight I did or didn't have with my boyfriend?

"Um, invasive much? Is there a point to your visit Agent Vaugh? Is this simple neighborly curiosity?"

"Look--"

He crossed his leg one over the other, giving me a nice look at his well-defined calves. He wore athletic shorts and the movement of his leg revealed a huge red embroidered O on the bottom corner.

"A Buckeye, seriously?"

He was about to explain something, but I couldn't continue a conversation with him any further until I knew whether or not he actually attended the most hated school in the Midwest.

"You got something against the Big O?"

The big O. What a putz. If my eyes rolled any further into the back of my head I might give myself a seizure.

"No, not at all. If you're a fan of completely overrated colleges, then by all means, sport your *Big O.* "

"Overrated? Over*rated?* Look I'm sorry your hair is all up because I think you're way too pretty to be allowing your boyfriend to treat you like shit, but talking smack about my team? That's worse than below the belt. It's a hit to the hanging fruit."

"Hanging fruit?"

That drew an actual laugh right out of me.

With a sheepish shrug he explained, "I grew up in a house full of women. I wasn't allowed to say the word balls or nuts for that matter."

Wait. Did he say I am pretty? I think he did.

"Danny is back at school."

He cocked his head, looking completely baffled.

"You asked where my boyfriend was. He went back to school. He actually left Saturday morning."

If you can call three in the morning 'Saturday morning.' He woke me up in the middle of the night to tell me he was leaving. All the work that waited for him stressed him out. Apparently, he couldn't sleep knowing he had so much to take care of back at school. I couldn't put up an argument since I had been barely coherent.

Whatever. I am still pretty pissed. I didn't respond to any of his text messages all weekend long. It is childish and petty, I know. I should at least respond to one so he knew I am safe. I didn't feel very charitable right now.

"I spoke with Officer Parker earlier today, and I'm hoping you will be able to go over one more time, exactly what happened to you lately."

Why did they all keep obsessing over this? Nothing changed.

"Agent Vaughn, I'm sorry but there isn't anything I remember that Officer Parker doesn't already know."

He has a really nice smile. A little crooked. The left lip pointed just the tiniest bit south when the right side headed north.

"Humor me? Just for five minutes. I heard from a little birdie you love these."

From the laptop bag, I didn't realize he brought with him, he produced a familiar looking white bag with a very familiar logo.

"Fluffy Fresh! Those are my favorite."

His laugh was so nice. Like a sprinkler in the summer. Inviting with just a little bit of something that caused your heart to start.

"I'll need to remember to thank Officer Parker for the tip."

"So you must be higher up on the chain than he is since he calls you *Agent* Vaughn."

I think I made him nervous. He did this thing with his lip when I asked questions. He traced the outline of his lip with his thumb.

"Let's just say he and I do not operate at the same level, no. So--can you help me out?"

He broke out that smile again, and I'm ashamed to admit he charmed one right out of me in return.

"Can you recount for me what has happened to you from the minute you walked in and your apartment is trashed?"

"I don't know how much I remember." I hedged; worried something important would be left out. "I was in the hospital--I'm sure Parker told you. I got hit on the head. Since then," I rubbed at the base of my skull--a remembered pain flaring up. "my mind isn't what it used to be."

Vaughn's thumb took a journey around his pouty lips while digesting what I said.

"Okay, let's try this. Can you trust me for a couple of minutes? I promise I'm not going to leave this seat."

Even my new oversized leather chair isn't big enough to swallow Agent Vaughn. Everyone else who sat in it became dwarfed by its size. I personally could snuggle into its width with room left over on both sides. Not him though, his broad shoulders nearly spanned the entire back of the chair.

"Look," he continued. "I want to try something. If you're uncomfortable with it, we can stop at any time."

Trust him? I barely knew the guy. Aside from spending one night in his apartment watching the fight, and a half hour chatting it up at the pool.

"I want you to lay down and close your eyes."

Is he crazy? Like I would do that with him sitting there watching me. It had been hard napping around Janet, and that sleep I couldn't fight since it was medically induced.

"I'm not sleeping with you, Vaughn."

I meant not sleeping while he sat in the room. I'm choosing to blame the mistake on the head injury, and not the fact there is something about him that set me on edge, in a good way.

"Well, I can assure you that you won't be sleeping."

Vaughn got flustered.

Smooth, self-assured, Agent Vaughn could put a wrinkle in that well-tailored demeanor. And he blushed! Not a slight shade of pink either. A full on blush that traveled all the way to his ears. He caught his innuendo before the sentence finished clearing his mouth. His flustered look is adorably boyish.

"What I meant is that I'm trying to do a relaxation exercise. Sometimes in that floaty feeling you get when your eyes are closed and your mind wanders, your brain puts its guard down for a second and reveals things you might not otherwise."

Resigned I swung my legs back up the couch, curling into a modified fetal position, facing him.

"It works best if you're on your back, but if that is more comfortable we can try it."

I couldn't lay on my back with him perpendicular to me. I wore Yoga pants. With no panties on. Getting dressed is a chore in the morning, and I couldn't be bothered to find any. I am certain I have camel toe, and my shirt isn't long enough to cover. So, curled in a fetal position it would be.

He placed his cell phone on the table in front of me. Face up. His screen made little dancing patterns of colored light--bouncing off each corner and multiplying.

Watching it made my eyes get heavy like I wanted to go to sleep.

"Are you hypnotizing me?"

I regretted this decision immediately. What kind of idiot am I letting some strange gut into my apartment? A girl alone and not in possession of their full faculties? For fuck's sake, I couldn't stand without getting dizzy. Now I had a man in my apartment and no one but Janet knew he is here

"No. It's a relaxation technique. I promise. And I'm not moving. Remember. I'm cemented into this ridiculously comfortable chair of yours."

I glanced over at him. His legs were crossed again. He isn't wearing any socks with his gym shoes.

"How far did you run?"

I tried to stifle a yawn with no success.

"About three miles."

I heard the surprise in his voice.

"I've never seen you in shorts before. And you're not wearing any socks."

"They rub against my toes while I run, and I'm not keen on blisters."

"Do you usually do three miles?"

Is that a far distance? I don't run. I hate running, in fact. Yoga, Pilates, even a cardio box class, but running? Ugh, pass.

"if I need to think, three miles gets the blood pumping."

"You don't look sweaty. You don't even smell. In fact, you smell really nice."

My mouth needed a memo that everything in my head did not need to be voiced.

"I like to run."

He stated simply. Thankfully ignoring my comment about him smelling nice. He did that lip thing again.

"I like this chair."

I could hear his legs moving against the leather.

"You can thank the Chief's organization for it."

I stifled another yawn, if I shouldn't be falling asleep why couldn't I stop yawning?

"Did they buy you a new chair after the break-in?" He asked.

"The chair, this couch, that humongous television, the rug, all that crap on my fireplace mantle, these comfy pillows, the curtains--what didn't they buy."

He has a nice voice. It is so soft. Just the slightest hint of gravel, like he woke up and came over to share a secret with me.

"There was nothing left."

This floaty feeling he talked about is so nice.

"What do you mean there was nothing left?"

"In my house."

"They took it all? Robbed you everything?"

"No," I giggled.

Why is that so funny?

"There was nothing left because they destroyed it. Even my ballerina."

"They broke your ballerina?"

"No, they pulverized it. It is just a pile of dust now."

"Why? Who would do this to you?"

"Dunno."

"Do you like the people you work with?"

"Of course. Look at everything they've done. I'm going to have to eat ramen for a long time because of this."

"Because you're not working? Do you need money?"

"No, I have so much of that now. I don't know how I'm going to pay it all back."

"Who do you need to pay back?"

"Everyone."

"It's nice people care about you."

"It's too much."

"You must touch a lot of people if you receive such an outpouring of charity."

"*no se caso de ceridad.*"

16

VAUGHN

I got the idea during my jog around the park. A total long shot, but I remembered reading somewhere the conscious and the subconscious exist on a separate plane. Sometimes if the conscious mind couldn't or wouldn't cooperate due to a physical injury or emotional trauma the subconscious memory would.

I'm not a psychologist or a licensed hypnotist. This isn't hypnosis though. I simply tried to get her to relax to the point where she could "float." I did some of my best thinking in that floaty state right before I fell asleep. A lot of problems in my cases were solved in that in between. It's why I always slept with notepads and pens next to my bed. If something came to me I could jot it down. Not saying a hundred percent of the time it worked--or my writing is decipherable. But there have been times where it is that 9th inning strikeout I needed.

"No se caso de caridad"

I'm no one's charity case.

Did she speak Spanish? She never mentioned knowing Spanish.

"Did you take Spanish in school?"

"No."

"Then how do you know it?"

"I don't."

I wrote *Spanish*?!? On the notepad that rested in my lap. I didn't push. She is being so responsive thus far. My fear is if I make her aware of an inconsistency, she'd shut down.

"You're no one's charity case?"

"Mom."

It was a whine. Like a little kid annoyed with something, a parent said.

I wrong down *Mom-Spanish-No se caso de caridad*, circled it and put a question mark next to it. Grateful to have the recording to refer to later on. I forgot to mention it to her, but I don't think it would pertain to my case anyway.

"After your break in you went back to work the next day and then what?"

"Spiderman."

"You mean Officer Parker?"

"Yes, he came to my office to ask me questions."

Must have been a helluva interrogation session if her subconscious mind remembered it.

"I worked late. It was dark when I went to my car."

"Tell me what you did. Take me through it. You are working at your desk. You realize how late it is. You shut down your computer and then what?"

"Hmm."

Her sigh is the cutest sound. I shouldn't be noticing things like that. This is a case. Or, at least part of my case. Hell, more than likely part of Peter's case. But she is a witness regardless. *Agent* Vaughn needed to come back and help me exorcise Vaughn the neighbor hanging out with a cute girl.

I should have gone home and changed before coming over. Maybe the fact I sat here in running shorts is what made me feel too relaxed.

"Danny called me."

Her voice broke me out of my haze.

"To say goodnight?"

I doubted it. From the few interactions I had with him, he didn't seem the 'goodnight I love you' type.

"No. He couldn't come for the weekend. It's his last trimester. He's busy and stressed."

"Were you arguing?"

The police file noted this. I already knew it. I tried to convince myself the only reason I asked was to help jog her memory of the case. In no way did I try to further incite her already hurt feelings against Danny for the argument over Pay-Per-View.

"He didn't want me to come and visit him. I wouldn't have been a bother. I could have kept myself entertained while he worked."

There is hurt there. Even in her dreamy state, I could hear her struggling with her own voice to keep it in check. I heard the warble of disappointment though.

"So you hung up on him?"

No. I was talking to him and then the world went back."

Her voice got real quiet, but I could hear her mumble something. I debated asking her to repeat it, but again wanted to keep the subconscious going without alerting the conscious. I hoped the mic picked it up.

"Do you know anyone who is mad at you?"

"No." she giggled.

"Why is that funny?"

"Because I don't know anyone."

"What do you mean? You know lot's of someone's."

"No. Just Danny. He's it."

I didn't need to know about her devotion and undying love for some douchebag. Honestly.

"What about his friends. Do you get along with all of them?"

"I think so?"

Her eyebrows came together in a V and her nose scrunched like she contemplated something.

"Does one of Danny's friends not like you?"

"More like I don't like him."

"You don't like who?"

"Isaac."

I wrote down his name and circled it, making a note to call the asshole boyfriend and ask him about Isaac.

"The guy Danny went to watch the fight with? How come?"

"Dunno. He just ...he's a hustler."

I had no clue what that meant but I wrote it down anyway. Maybe Parker met this friend. Or at least has some intel on him.

Cammie shifted a bit, tucking her hand between her legs and shifting further into the couch. I became so distracted by her straying hand I lost focus on my task. She succumbed to the call of sleep.

It didn't happen fast. I couldn't stop staring at the hand. Is she touching herself? It looked fairly innocent. My dirty mind immediately went to other things. While I sat there and stared, trying to get control of my untoward thoughts and burgeoning interest, she sighed before letting out the tiniest snore.

Despite promising I would remain seated in the chair, I wagered it is creepier to stay and watch her sleep. After scribbling a quick note for her, tenting it so it would be the first thing she saw, I grabbed my phone, covered her with the throw and saw myself out.

I replayed the interview again in my apartment. That mumbled phrase was there but barely discernible. Frustrated, I forwarded it to my guys in surveillance. They had all kinds of specialized software to be able to get that snippet for me. I hoped it wouldn't take more than a few days.

17

Camille

Something beeped. I couldn't place the sound, but somewhere an incessant meep pulled me from my dreamless sleep. My living room was nearly dark, something pulled at the edge of my conscious ...some kind of memory set me on edge.

I shot up and glanced at the leather chair, fighting off the sharp sting of vertigo. *Agent Vaughn.* I could still see his indentation, even if the darkening sky told me I slept for a while. How long did he sit there and watch me? I groped for my cell phone, too lazy to reach up and turn on the light.

> *You fell asleep. Didn't want to wake you.*
> *Let myself out. Thanks for trusting me*
> *Vaughn*

The piece of paper fluttered to the floor as I tried to place my cell phone. I guess he didn't watch me after all. Odd that I fell asleep in the first place. I pushed myself upright, waiting for my body to adjust to the new position before shuffling to the light switch.

The occupational therapist told me it would take a while for vertigo to dissipate. She too emphasized how grateful I should be vertigo is my only issue. If I got paid a nickel for every time someone told me the 'kill shot' to the back of my skull could have done much worse, I could probably pay back everyone who donated to my cause.

Of course, I was grateful. But at the same time, I grew impatient with my body. I wanted to feel normal in my skin again. I wanted to be able to get up and go to the bathroom without having to wait for the room to right itself. I wanted to work. I never spent this long away from work, ever.

The beep sounded again from somewhere in the kitchen. I found my phone, next to the stove, with a reminder to call Janet and check in with her. Gosh, she is a helicopter. She leaves early once, and the worry sets in. Danny sent me a few texts too, but I ignore those briefly in favor of setting my babysitter's mind at ease.

"Hi, Janet!" I singsong as soon as she picks up.

"Oh, good! So nice to hear your voice and know you're okay."

"Yes, you're lovely little notification woke me up from my nap. What kind of nurse are you, preventing your charge from her much needed rest?"

I loved making her laugh. She reminded me of my own Mom. I wondered how Mom's possessed talent for making you shine from the inside out. Like there is a gold medal for joke telling, and you'd just won it.

"I am terribly sorry to inconvenience you with my worry. Go back to sleep then. I will see you bright and early. Are you all locked up?"

I was about to give her the usual, 'you know I am' when I remembered I wasn't. Agent Vaughn let himself out so the deadbolt wasn't engaged.

"I will be as soon as I get off the phone with you."

"Everything go okay with Agent Vaughn?"

"He asked me some questions. I don't think I was much help."

"Well, it's the cops job to determine that. You did your best."

Even her responses screamed Mom.

"I mean I fell asleep in the middle of him questioning me."

"I'm sure it isn't the first time it has happened. Oh dear, I'm sorry I have to let you go! Addison is calling me. I'll see you in the morning okay hon?"

She could put a smile on my face from miles away. It was strange how quickly she had become such a focus in my life. Of course--I saw her every day and didn't have much choice in the matter. But paid nurse or not, having her to call and knowing she worried about me gave me the warm fuzzies.

I scrolled through my text stream as I made my way to the door to set the bolt. Danny had sent me a novel. Completely atypical. I got a sentence full of actual words, I was lucky.

> *Danny: Babe. We can't keep doing this. I know you're sick but I'm not the guy you need. I can't be that guy. I have goals. I need to finish school. I can't afford to delay graduation. I can't be the person you lean on anymore. I know you're all alone, and it sucks and I'm sorry for it--but that can't be the reason I hang around. It's too much pressure. You need to find someone else willing to be that guy. If need be I'll try to help, but I can't keep coming to Kansas City. I hope you understand.*

Was he breaking up with me over text message? Seriously? I tapped on his name to try calling him. It rang once and then gave me three beeps. I tried a second time and got the same. He blocked me. He fucking blocked me from reaching him. So much for "being around to help if I needed him." What the hell? What was I going to do now?

18

VAUGHN

My day hadn't been nearly as productive as I had hoped it would be. I checked my email every hour to see if I had anything back from the lab. Nothing. Carter was going to throttle me if I called again. I needed to know what she had muttered. It was probably something benign, like 'remind me to pay my water bill,' but I couldn't rest until I knew.

Like a fly which continually buzzed and landed, my mind circled around the things she had said. Why was she no one's charity case? How didn't she realize she spoke Spanish? Why had her laugh sounded so bitter when I mentioned friends? And why on earth did she think Danny was 'the one?'

The guy couldn't be bothered to take care of her in the bedroom, and she was going to chain herself down to that for the rest of her life? I give the guy some credit, he was a graduate student trying to balance schoolwork and a sick girlfriend. That's hard for anyone, let alone a grad student. At the same time, he didn't seem like he was the selfless type. So why did he keep doing it?

Frustrated, I slammed my laptop shut, tossing it to the other side of my bed. My brain wouldn't stop moving. Too many thoughts tornadoing through I couldn't focus on just one. T.V. was out. I was too tired to get out of bed and row--but I needed to do something other than sit in bed and be frustrated by my inability to focus.

That was when I heard it. I thought I imagined it at first. An eternity passed before I heard it again. Spending nearly eighteen years with a house full of women, the sound coming from my shared wall wasn't lost on me. Tears. I distinctly heard tears. Cammie cried in her bedroom. Instead of tapering off, they escalated.

The more intense they became, the higher my anxiety climbed. What was I supposed to do? Knock on her door? Admit our walls were paper-fucking-thin? Find some lame assed excuse to go in and check on her? What if she didn't come to the door because she was too busy crying?

With her head injury though, I couldn't help but worry that hysterics might send her into some kind of fit or something. *Fuck it.* I yanked off my covers, threw on a sweatshirt and charged across the patio, paying little attention to the fact I was barefoot and essentially in pajamas.

"Cammie?" I knocked on the door as loud as possible so she could hear it from her bedroom. Why these condos had no doorbells was beyond me.

"Cammie? It's Agent Vaughn. Are you okay?"

I couldn't hear anything through the front door. It was pin-drop quiet in the neighborhood, just the occasional whiz of traffic going by on the street below, and a dog barking in response to my rapping on her door.

"Cammie? Can you come to the door, please? I need to ask you a question."

I knocked harder, hoping she would hear me. I was about to start pounding when I heard the deadbolt disengage and her head peeked out.

"Agent Vaughn?" Her voice had that distinct warble that exposed her emotions without fully being able to see her face.

"Hey Cammie. May I come in for a second?"

"It's not a good time Agent Vaughn."

The warble got more pronounced. I pushed as gently as I could against her door trying to reveal more of her face so I had a reason to go in.

"Cammie, you sound upset. I just want to make sure that you are okay."

The door opened a bit more and I saw her tear streaked face, swollen eyelids and a pair of eyes t practically glowed from unshed tears. It felt like someone had roundhouse kicked me in my solar plexus. Crying women was the one thing I couldn't handle. It brought me to my knees every.single.time. I blamed my Dad for that.

"Hey, c'mere."

I gained access to her house with little effort. Without needing to cajole her she fell into my arms and sobbed. Her hair smelled good. I shouldn't be thinking about that while she was coming apart in my arms, but she smelled like rain, and I wanted to bask in it.

"Are you hurt? What's wrong? How can I help?"

There was no stemming the tide of words once they started. Intellectually, I knew if she were crying she wouldn't be able to answer. But emotionally, I wanted to know what was wrong so I could *fix* it. So whatever was making her cry could be taken care of.

She looked up at me, tiny dewdrop tears trapped in her eyelashes, and I was ready to pull out my gun and go Tarantino on whatever it was that had made her cry.

I guided her out of the doorframe so I could at least get the door closed. The whole neighborhood didn't need to be party to her upset.

"It's okay. Whatever is wrong, we'll figure it out. Okay?"

That only made her sob harder. Damnit. Her head was tucked into my chest, soaking my sweatshirt with her tears. She wasn't short by any means. Probably five seven, one-fifty if I had to guess, but at that moment, she seemed small. I stooped down, picked her up, and carried her over to the chair I sat in earlier. I was acting purely on instinct at that point. Sure, she was a grown woman, but the only thing I could think to do was to cradle her against my chest and rock her till she calmed down.

"It's okay Cammie." Her hair was petal soft. I didn't know if I was running my hands through it for her own benefit or mine. Eventually, she quieted to the occasional hiccup, and I tried once again to find out what was wrong.

"Want to tell me about what has you this upset?"

She shook her head burying herself further into my chest.

"Should I call someone? Janet maybe? Or your boyfriend?"

That did it. The mention of her boyfriend had her lip quivering, and her eyes filling once again with the tears I had thought she had exorcised.

"Did something happen to him? Is he hurt?"

She looked up at me again, the cell phone I hadn't realized she was holding pointed up so I could read it. I only read the first two sentences but it was all I needed to read.

That shit. Who breaks up with someone over a text message?

"Oh hon, I'm so sorry."

"I don't know what to do."

Big fat tears rolled down her cheeks. How did I become this guy? The one who wiped the tears falling over another guy?

"You'll find someone else."

I told her, trying to sound as genuine as I could despite my eyes fighting to roll back into my head. It was a mistake coming over here for this. I should have minded my own damn business. That piece of shit wasn't worth her fucking tears. I here I was. Committed to this the second I knocked on the damn door.

"You don't understand."

I understood plenty. She'd told me earlier. He was 'the one.' Now she got a cold bucket of reality as to what a douche bag he was.

"He isn't worth all of this upset sweetheart. What kind of asshole doesn't have the guts to call?"

"He blocked my number." She sobbed, starting with the tears all over again.

He wasn't helping his case any.

IT TOOK ten minutes for Cammie to calm. Unfortunately, she had shorted herself out. Right in my arms, she cried until she fell asleep. I wasn't sure what to do. Twice in one day, I had put her to sleep. I tried not to take it personally.

Her cell phone was still angled towards me, so while I debated what to do with Sleeping Beauty, I helped myself to the entirety of the text. I wish I hadn't. I didn't know what he meant by "I know you're all alone," but honestly? Who does that?

Was she all alone? She couldn't be. How did this girl not have a million people rallied around her? I didn't consciously make the decision to, but after reading that I couldn't put her to bed and walk out. On a deeper level, a level may be consciously I wasn't aware of yet if she was alone--I refused to be another person that walked out.

I FELT her shift in my lap before my subconscious pulled me out of my own sleepy haze.

"I guess we both dozed off."

I ran my hand through my hair, trying to get my bearings.

"How are you feeling?"

"Hungry." She mumbled, pushing herself out of my lap only to pivot and slump onto the sofa.

"I can go and grab us some food. What do you feel like?"

"Pizza. And, I can order from GrubHub, no need to go anywhere."

Her face was almost Raphaelite lying there on her face with her hand tucked under her chin. She reminded me of those little cherubs with her sweet smile and tear-stained cheeks.

While I placed an order on my phone, she turned on the TV and selected the next episode of *Orphan Black* from her Prime screen.

"I think you are the only person I know who watches this show."

"Do you watch it too?" I tried getting Janet to watch it with me, but she says the characters confuse her.

"Helena's my favorite." We both said simultaneously, which drew a laugh from her. Laughter was much better than tears.

"So I guess it's safe to say you're okay with watching this with me?"

Even if she asked me to watch Barney the Fucking Dinosaur I would have.

"After watching all of season three," she explained, "as much as I wanted to wait until it was free--I couldn't. I needed answers."

Her face turned bright red, and she chewed her lip for a second apparently while she debated finishing her sentence.

"They left us on such a cliffhanger, you know? I needed answers, so I bit the bullet and shelled over the seventeen dollars and bought the season."

"If you're home all day every day, what is seventeen dollars in the grand scheme of things?"

It was less than twenty bucks. A drop in the bucket if you asked me.

"Well, when you're living off of other people's charity, you have to be smart about where the money is going."

She pointed the remote towards a notebook ledger with a pen tucked into its spine resting an arm's length away from her on her coffee table. She couldn't possibly be keeping track of everything she spent her money on, could she?

"I have savings," she continued, bouncing the remote against

her thigh, "but I don't know long I'm going to be out of work for. The doctors don't have a definitive answer."

She tapped the remote against her thigh, looking out the windows to the park below. I didn't tell her this, but with her curtains open as they were--anyone who walked the park could see her watching them. After she asked me this morning if I'd been out running, I realized she watches me from her window. Like that hadn't beat my chest a bit.

"I guess I'm a bit of a hypocrite. Maybe that's why Danny broke up with me. I sit here indulging in my favorite show with little regard for the almost twenty dollars I spent on it, but couldn't be bothered to order the fight he had been looking forward to watching."

Her reasoning astounded me.

"Maybe if the fight had been so important to him, he could have offered to pay for it himself. You shouldn't beat yourself up, Cam. How long have you guys been dating?"

"Dated, as in past tense."

She rolled her eyes heavenward.

"It was just over a year."

"If he hadn't been such an asshole I would have invited both of you over to watch the fight. That was what Parker was on the way over to do before he skipped out. Honestly, though, it's better than his true colors showed now. Now, you can find a guy who will show up and stand tall when you need someone to lean on."

19

Camille

Before the conversation had a chance to veer into the uncomfortable, the doorbell rang. Vaughn the gentleman, paid for dinner, which I appreciated. Though maybe my griping about the seventeen dollars I spent on my TV show made him feel bad about my situation. I hadn't meant to guilt him into buying.

"I'll be right back."

Vaughn set the two pizzas on my coffee table, along with the plastic plates and such the delivery guy had given him and dashed out the front door. He returned moments later with a couple of John Daly's in his hand.

"I'm not allowed to drink."

I handed him a plate full of pizza, assuming the plain sausage was for him.

"The reason they tell you not to drink isn't that it's dangerous. It's because the effects of alcohol will be intensified due to your medication. Therefore I think the *one* drink I have for you will be fine. You're not going anywhere, and you've had a hell of a day. Cut yourself some slack and have a couple sips. The worst that happens is you fall asleep on me again."

I got one of his smiles, which thrilled me despite the dour mood. It had been a shit day that was for damn sure. I was at home and in all reality, I didn't need to stumble to my bed if I didn't want to. Clearly, the cop was trustworthy. He *had* come to my rescue earlier, and he bought me dinner. I threw caution to the wind and said fuck it, clinking my bottle top to his.

"Did you grow up around here?"

Vaughn asked, while he pulled the throw off the back of the sofa and covered my feet. We had spent the better part of three hours watching *Orphan Black* and chatting. While Vaughn had started the evening in the leather chair and then moved to the floor so he could eat his pizza, he and I currently shared the length of my sofa, resting our feet on the ottoman he switched out for the coffee table.

Despite the temperate weather we had been having, thunderstorms had swept in while we watched TV. The air had chilled significantly. I debated lighting a fire in my fireplace.

"No, I moved to Kansas City when I got my job."

He looked at me like he expected me to continue. The guy wasn't exactly an encyclopedia himself, so he'd need to give to get.

"You aren't making this very easy you know."

His mouth twisted into a lazy smile.

"Making what easy?"

I asked knowing what he meant but playing coy. It was the best way to exit this little exchange gracefully.

He stood, grabbed the two boxes of pizza and headed towards my kitchen. I could hear him bustling about, opening the fridge door and closing it before returning with a garbage bag in his hand. Before I could ask, he was out the door closing it behind him. I assumed he was off to the dumpsters.

Mentally I tracked his movements, picturing him bouncing down the stairs walking across the parking lot to the dumpsters, turning around and jogging back up the stairs. However, Vaughn in my head returned much faster than the actual Vaughn. He hadn't said any kind of goodbye, so I assumed he was coming back. Surely playing coy hadn't made him *that* mad had it? The longer it took for him to return, the more worried I became. It was still raining kind of hard, I'd assumed that would have sped up the process not slowed it down.

He walked through the door, dry as a desert, as I was about to get up and go searching for him.

"Chicago." I blurted, ahead of any questions as to where he'd been.

"What?"

"You wanted to know where I'm from. I'm from Chicago."

He tumbled onto the couch, kicking his feet up and settling against the pillows with graceful efficiency. He offered me a second John Daly, which I declined. I still hadn't finished the first one, and I was starting to feel a bit buoyant.

"Huh." He took a long pull from his bottle, "I guess that explains how you know Spanish."

"I don't. Well, I guess a few words maybe. Abuelita is grandma. Lavadaria is Laundromat. A couple of swears I picked up over the years... you know just things you learn from friends."

20

VAUGHN

How strange. Was it possible someone could speak a language but have absolutely no idea they could? Even her pronunciation had been spot on. Etymology and linguistics weren't my specialty. I had no idea what the rules of comprehension and speaking were in regards to secondary languages. But, it was the strangest thing I ever experienced.

"So where in Chicago did you grow up?"

"I didn't grow up there, I lived there in like high school and college. But when we did live there, it was in Back of the Yards."

Rough neighborhood. I'm not from Chicago either, but given the former President *was* it tended to make the news quite often. Back of the Yards was known for its gangs and drug violence.

"You moved *to* Back of the Yards from somewhere else?"

"It's not as bad as they make it on television."

I had no idea why I was so tickled by her sideways glance. That look she cut me with made me want to laugh every time. Not that it was funny. Shit no, it meant business. But it was such a dichotomy. She could look so angelic and sweet one second until she pulled out that optic blast like she was the female version of Cyclops.

"My mom wanted to make sure I got into a good college. She heard the best way to do it was through Charter Schools. Chicago has some of the best in the country."

She shrugged picking at the paper on her bottle. It was empty but every time I offered another she refused. Not like I was trying to get her drunk. But, at the same time, I needed information from her. If a couple of drinks loosened her lips enough to help me figure out her story, then so be it. The faster I could get information out of her, the faster I could tell Parker this girl had nothing to do with my case and move on.

"Where does your mom live?"

I'm such a dumbass. I should have seen the landmine from a mile away. How else would she be 'alone' as Danny had said she was?

It should have been totally obvious to me from the fact her mom wasn't hovering over her every second of every day. At some point, a mother, regardless of how close or how distant, would come to their daughter's aid if she was hurt and in need of help. Hell, my mother would be on a flight faster than the guys could give her information on what hospital I was in.

"I'm sorry." I cut in before she had a chance to respond.

To make things even more awkward, I pulled her into my side in some kind of weird half hug.

"I should have realized."

I had no idea how the hell to turn this conversation around. I was supposedly trained in interrogation and information strategy. I had a dual Master's degree in Psychology and Public Policy from Georgetown, not to mention the years of training from the Agency itself. A few weeks spent with a beautiful neighbor, and everything I'd learned was out the window.

"I take it you have an out-of-the-picture Dad too?"

She shrugged, pulling another Daly from the box, popping the top and taking a long pull. I never considered how seductive the contraction of throat muscles could be, but watching her work those few sips down had my mouth going dry.

"I don't know who my Dad is. It's possible he's still alive." She shrugged again working the label with her thumbnail. "I asked about him a few times as I was growing up. Each time I brought him up my mother would get annoyed I was curious."

I nodded watching the lightning make patterns across the sky.

"So, you're Dad is out of the picture too, huh?"

Where had she gotten that?

"You said, too, earlier. I had an out of the picture Dad, too. Which would imply you also were raised by a single Mom?"

Damn. There was that brain/mouth thing again. I could probably play it off like I had meant in addition to a mom who wasn't around, but my mouth decided to volunteer information before my brain had a chance to vet the response.

"Not so much out of the picture, as much as never asked for that picture in the first place."

Too late. Had to go full disclosure. Well, at least modified full disclosure.

"Let's just say my Mom and Dad didn't have a traditional relationship, and when he found out my Mom was pregnant, his actual family took offense to him spending time with us."

"Oh no!"

Cammie's legs were curled under her, and she had turned toward me so we could make eye contact as we spoke. She cradled her head in the palm of her hand, resting it on the back of the sofa.

"it's fine." I lied. "It happened a long time ago."

It had. But, it still chapped my ass every time I saw the guy on T.V.

"It seems like everyone I know is part of the single mom's club. Not that I know many people."

It was the first time I'd seen her blush. With her bronzed skin it was hard to tell **if** she was blushing, but her cheeks turned a deep rose. I doubted it was the booze.

"I don't get that."

I pressed my luck, hoping the booze was loosening her closely guarded life.

"You just don't seem the loner type."

She shrugged her shoulders again, clearing the last few drops from her bottle.

"A rolling stone gathers no moss."

Wasn't that the truth?

"That's why I bought this house."

She waved her hand towards the middle of the condo.

"It's mine."

"It's nice to have a place to call home," I agreed, taking in her surroundings,.

I hadn't paid much attention to her little condo. Even in the shiny newness of the furniture, the place felt homey--lived in.

"You have good taste."

"Thanks, but it's easy to have good taste when a multi-million dollar organization is decorating your house for you. I could have never afforded to buy these things. My apartment before the break-in looked nothing like this."

She giggled, flopping her head back on the sofa. The glassy look in her eyes told me she had more than likely met her drink limit for the evening. Her hair had come loose from her ponytail, covering her left eye almost entirely. Despite being blocked from view, the entertained delight that brightened her eyes tugged at my heart. As cheesy as it sounds. It was nice to be around someone who despite having a fairly shitty day could still shine so brightly.

"Tal belleza..." So beautiful. I told her, tucking the errant strands of hair behind her ear. *"esa sonrisa"* that smile.

I continued, tracing her lips.

"¿por qué alguien dejarte ir" Why would anyone let you go?

Her eyes had closed when my fingertips had grazed her face, a subtle smile twisting up her plump lips. There was an extended pause. Her breathing deepened. Her eyes remained closed. If it wasn't for her eyebrows furrowing and her smile eroding into a frown, I would have been sure she was asleep.

"Nadie se queda."

The solemnity in her voice nearly caused me to forget she had once again answered in Spanish. No one ever stays. she told me.

My body acted on instinct. It wasn't lustful. I wasn't trying to take advantage of a vulnerable girl. But, hearing those mournful words, coupled with the pout in her mouth, I wanted to take it away.

I wanted to replace her sadness with something else. A joke would have been smarter - not that I knew any. I held her by the graceful slope in her neck, fusing my mouth against hers. Her lips tasted like the ice tea and lemonade we had been sipping on. They were warm and pliable. They moved against mine with equal interest. Despite massive warning bells going off in my head telling me to pump the brakes on the lip lock, I couldn't back away.

When I opened my eyes and saw hers dazedly looking back at me, I couldn't help but double down. I took my time exploring both the top and bottom lip individually. Sampling my way across one before moving on to the other. She wasn't pushing me away. She wasn't trying to pull away. That made me want to kiss her more, kiss her longer.

Her arms wrapped around my rib cage, those well-manicured fingers nails stretching across the length of my back, shooting riots of sensation up and down my spinal chord. The throaty noises she made were driving me crazy. With every pass of her lips against mine and each groan or sigh that vibrated my lips, we were becoming less vertical and moving into horizontal territory.

"Cammie..."

Someone needed to be the responsible one.

"Agent Vaughn..." the breathy way she said my name had me diving in for round two. I loved the way her face fit so well in my hand. Like her jaw was meant to be cradled in my palm.

"We need to slow this down sweetheart."

I didn't want to. Neither did the southern Vaughn, which was super obvious considering I was wearing a flimsy pair of lounge pants. There was no way she didn't know I was into her in a major way.

"I don't want to slow down," she whispered, running her lips against my jaw, making her way to my neck. "Why do we need to slow down when it feels so good."

Each vowel was a drawn out half groan only emphasized the gravel in her voice. It was an IV of desire mainlining straight to my groin. My sordid thoughts were imagining that voice begging for more and moaning in apogee. I needed to get out of there before I lost the gentlemanly hold I had on my lust.

With one last kiss, I pulled away leaving her panting and dazed. Her kiss swollen lips were shining with the evidence of our passionate exchange. Just seeing it made me want to dive back in for another. I knew if I did I wouldn't be able to stop.

We'd both had some drinks. That good for nothing boyfriend of hers had broken up with her. This was not the right time to start something new. It was a billboard proclaiming me as the rebound.

"I should probably head home."

I wanted to stay. I had been expecting her to agree. To say something like "oh man, look how late it is, yeah you do need to go." But she never said a word.

She traced the outline of her lips like she was committing what we did to memory. She pushed herself off the sofa and placed a steadying hand on my shoulder while she waited to get her bearings. The pile of her hoodie was so soft, and warm from her body heat.

My hands of their own volition ran up and down the length of her arms, hypnotizing me to the sweeping motion. Her cheeks were flushed and her hair pointed every which way. Still, she looked gorgeous.

"I don't even know your name." She whispered before moving in to place a kiss on my cheek.

My lips tracked ever so softly across her own before drawing a path from her jaw up to her ear. "Benjamin."

I whispered, kissing it before backing away towards the door.

"Benjamin."

Her voice was no louder than mine had been, but even at that low volume, the slight timbre in her voice had me fighting hard not to move back into the room and beg her to say it again. In that room, within the palm of her well-manicured hand, she held a power few did. She didn't even realize she had it.

"I'll talk to you tomorrow Camille Saint."

I had a date with a freezing cold shower. Otherwise, hell would freeze before I got any shuteye. I knew I'd forever be haunted by honey colored eyes and an easy smile.

21

Camille

anny who? Okay, that wasn't a hundred percent true. After that kiss though? Damn. It was the kind that had swelling orchestral scores beneath it. Benjamin Vaughn just out kissed every other man ever.

Benjamin. Ben. Benjamin Vaughn. It flowed so well. I said it aloud a few times to test its weight o my tongue. Even saying his name felt like a kiss.

I should probably feel guilty that I just kissed Benjamin Vaughn less than twenty-four hours after Danny broke up with me, but in all honesty--I felt like he had broken up with me months prior. Even before the accident. Before he left to go back to school if I was truly being honest with myself.

Danny wasn't in a place where he is ready to settle down. The whole better and worse thing isn't his thing. He stuck by my side the entire time I was in the hospital. He gets major points for that. If he were truly the asshole that everyone thought he was, he wouldn't have made sure I was taken care of. While my feelings were hurt over the way he did it, and the situation itself, I couldn't hate him for it.

Too wound up to sleep after the kiss to end all kisses, I drew a bath instead. I hoped the warm water would lull me into that super relaxed state where falling asleep was as easy as closing one's eyes. I started to feel just the tiniest bit guilty that all I could think about was Benjamin and his mouth.

It had rebound written all over it. Did rebounds feel like rebounds though? Was a person consciously aware that they were involved in a rebound? Or did it just feel nice to have someone in their life? It wasn't like he'd be in Kansas City forever. Even if he was a rebound for me, it was possible he wasn't looking for the long haul anyway.

It was at a time like this that I wished I had girlfriends. I needed someone to call and pick apart the subtext of relationships.

Actually. A little after eleven. Was that too late to text some-one? I was awake, but then again I could sleep whenever I wanted. I wondered if Mina was still awake.

> *Cammie: Hi, it's Cammie. Are you still awake?*

I patiently waited to see if the ellipses appeared on my phone signaling she was about to respond. I'd never actually texted her to talk about non-work problems before, it felt kind of weird that I wasn't just launching into a tirade about whatever fire I was expe-riencing that required her assistance putting out.

> *Mina: Hey! LT! What's up?*
> *Cammie: So, Danny broke up w/me. Over txt.*

Yeah, I know I just got finished saying that I didn't blame him for breaking up with me, but that didn't mean I wasn't totally salty about the way he did it. Honestly, who can't even be adult enough to make a phone call?

> *Mina: Dafuq? 😖 In a TXT?! 😡 Srsly? When? Why?*

Mina was the only person I knew who provided the appropriate reaction at the exact moment that you needed it. She also apparently thought she was a teenager growing up in Compton.

> Cammie: *This morning. Yes, seriously. bc he couldn't be there for me like I needed him to. He's Danny doing Danny.* 🐿️

She texted me an eye roll emoji followed by the middle finger emoji that I was so glad I now had the new iPhone. That middle finger was going to be getting a lot of mileage.

> Cammie: *But I have another reason for texting you.*
> Mina: *ORLY?*

God, I was blushing. I hadn't even gotten to the reason for the text, and I could warm the bath with my own embarrassment.

> Cammie: *You know my next door neighbor? The guy from the pool?*
> Mina: *Mr. Secret Agent man?* 🕵️ 🔥
> Cammie: *We don't know that he's a "secret" agent man... I just know that he's an agent.*
> Mina: *Yeah yeah whatever let me keep my fantasies that man is a hot slab of sex on a buttered bun.* 💦
> Cammie: *OMG Mina.. you're too much!*
> Mina: *So what did you want to tell me about Mr. Hottie?*
> Cammie: *He came over tonight. He heard me crying this afternoon. When Danny broke up with me. I ugly cried all over his hoodie.*
> Mina: *That was nice of him*
> Cammie: *He ordered us pizza. And I had two drinks, even though the doctor told me not to be drinking.*

Mina: Quick someone call 911. Cammie broke
   the law!
Cammie: LOL
Mina: I bet Mr. Secret Agent Man could handcuff
   you and read you your rights
Mina: If you tell him you've been really naughty
   maybe he'll be forced to perform a strip search.
Cammie: Mina! You're killing me!
Mina: So, why are to texting me your confessions?
Mina: Did something happen?
Mina: Did he ask you to locate the weapon of mass
   destruction... in his pants? 🥒 ✳️🌀
Cammie: OMG hahaha
Cammie: He kissed me. 😍
Cammie: Or maybe I kissed him
Cammie: We kissed--like Notebook kissed. 💋
Mina: Ugh you fucking ruined it.
Cammie: ???
Mina: You ruined my dirty cop fantasy. Damn you.
Mina: You don't Ryan Gossling all over my tie me up
   tie me down slap me in the face with your 'baton'
   fantasy.
Cammie: OMG. I'm seriously going to have to burn
   out my eyeballs.
Cammie: I'm going to be blind. Because of you.
Cammie: Thank you for making me blind on top of
   already being a head case invalid.
Mina: Bwahaha

Texting Mina had been just what I needed. It had been so long since I'd had girl talk of any kind. I mean I had Janet, but she was--Janet. It would be like talking about sex with my mother.

Cammie: Does kissing him like four hours after
   getting the 'it's me not you' speech make me a ho?

Mina: So what if it does?
Mina: It's your life. No one else is living it.
Mina: Did you want the kiss?
Cammie: God yes. I probably would have had sex
with him if he had asked.
Cammie: It's been so long.
Mina: Well, you'll get no judgment from me. And
honestly, who else is left to judge?

I know she hadn't meant that to sound bad, but it smarted a bit. Truly there wasn't really much of anyone to judge my life. What I did was one hundred percent my own business. There were no meddlesome family members to get in the way of me living my life the way I wanted to live it. It was a liberating thought for sure, but simultaneously a bit depressing.

Mina: So what's holding you back then? Trying to be
a "good girl?"
Mina: Seriously, I know you're probably the
quintessential good Catholic girl who like went to
mass and shit and said Novena's and lit candles
but you're almost thirty years old. You have a
Master's Degree, a damn good job; you went to
college on a full scholarship. You've checked all the
good girl boxes. If you're looking for permission-
you have mine.
Mina: Go and jump that hottie's boner.
Mina: AHHHAHAH I had meant jump his BONES
but apparently autocorrect has a dirty mind too!
🙈
Mina: And if you're looking for absolution--you don't
fucking need it querida
Cammie: Thank you ya know for being around to
text me.
Mina: Anytime love!

I had been about to text her goodnight when I heard a groan that did not come from my apartment. At least I didn't think it did. I held my breath trying with all I had to hear the sound again. I nearly dropped my phone in the tub when something--or someone clunked against my wall. I tilted my head against the wall to see if that allowed me to hear anything any better, but whatever I had heard must have been the last of it. As I got out of the tub and pulled the drain, I could have sworn I heard someone call my name. Instinctively I called 'hello,' like an asshole, and nearly jumped out of my skin when a few minutes later a text message came in with a 202 area code--Washington, DC.

> *202: Don't you know that the person who calls out*
> *'hello' is always the first one to get the axe?*
> *Cammie: Who is this?*

I kind of had an inkling as to who my mystery texter was. Especially since he'd already admitted to me he had attended Georgetown, and since he had heard me crying earlier that day probably could hear practically everything that went on in this apartment, and Oh my God, that realization practically drown me in embarrassment.

> *202: I tell you my name less than twenty minutes ago*
> *and already you've forgotten it? I'm heartbroken.*

There was no way I'd be forgetting Benjamin Vaughn anytime soon. And I didn't want to either.

> *Cammie: How'd you even get my number? Actually, I*
> *probably don't want to know. Let me guess, you*
> *have friends like at the FBI or something and it*
> *only took one phone call and the whole bureau is*
> *hunting down how to contact me.*
> *Vaughn: Technically I could have just pulled it out of*

> *the police file that is sitting on my dining*
> *room table.*

He replied back, which made me feel like a complete idiot; of course, he had the case file.

> *Vaughn: But, I sent myself a text from your phone.*

The angel emoji next to the message took the indignation right out of me.

> *Vaughn: Well I heard your giggle so I guess I'm*
> *forgiven?*

Holy shit. Our walls couldn't seriously be that thin? His head must be on the same wall that mine was. Lovely.

> *Cammie: We need to have a discussion about the*
> *things that have been heard between this wall*
> *we share.*

I was already mortified and he hadn't even replied back yet.

> *Vaughn: Oh you mean how badly you snore at night?*
> *I've had to sleep in the den a few times just to get*
> *away from that chainsawing.*

There was no way. I did not snore. Danny would have told me. The guy was nothing if not protective of his beauty sleep.

> *Cammie: I do NOT snore!*
> *Vaughn: Okay... if you say so.*

22

VAUGHN

"**W**hat do you mean that the audio is undetectable?"

"Vaughn you can't pull audio from a cell phone. The audio file is so compressed it's nearly impossible to drill any deeper without the sound going to shit."

We are a government entity. Supposedly equipped with the best surveillance equipment in the known world, thanks to the Patriot Act. Yet my team couldn't get some undetectable audio from a compressed sound file? It didn't seem like a difficult a task to me.

"What about our guys at the other agencies? Do they have better technology than we have?"

"Probably. I'd check with the Agency over the Bureau. My money is on them for having the highest tech equipment."

I forgot to say thank you before I disconnected my phone call and dialed Special Agent Butler. If anyone would be able to get me what I needed it would be him and his team of archivists.

"Butler, I'm going to be sending you an audio file. I need a rush job on it. "

"Look, Vaughn, you and I both know that no one can take a shit without six signatures and a stamp of approval, you'll get your audio whenever the powers that be give the green light to process it."

"I have authority from the highest levels and yet there's still red tape?"

"I'll put this one in personally. Hopefully, that speeds up the process."

"Thanks, man. Remind me to buy you a beer when this thing is put to bed."

I didn't bother with any kind of formalities. I didn't need to know how his kid soccer game went or if his wife experienced regular orgasms. The likelihood of him being CIA and married is slim. The point being, none of us bothered with informal bullshit. No one wanted to get to know anyone else. The less you knew about people the safer you stayed.

My tete a tete with Cammie the evening previous had been a nice surprise. I had to hold my laughter in when she accused me of having high-ranking friends at the FBI. If she only knew.

I kept forgetting how thin our walls were. At one in the morning, the world is kind of quiet anyway--but the fact that she heard me groaning her name in the shower didn't bode well for me and my evening past times. Even that hadn't gotten her out of my system enough to stop my racing thoughts and fall asleep.

The morning had been a cluster fuck. In all honesty, I couldn't expect anything less after the evening I'd had. Not that spending time with Cammie was anything short of amazing. Even if all we did was watch television and eat pizza.

That kiss though. Jesus, Mary, Joseph and whoever else I could thank--that kiss blew me away. I hadn't expected her to be so soft. I didn't want to stop at kissing. But, I also didn't want to be that creepy date-rapey guy who plows an injured girl with booze and then has sex with her.

I came home intent on getting some work done. Reading and re-reading the files I had, rebuilding my case wall. It was one of the few things that they actually got right in all those cop/detective movies.

It was much easier to see how things connected if you actually plotted them out and physically connected the dots. I liked to stare at mine while I rowed. Something about focusing on it while clearing my head has helped me crack cases more times than I can count.

Thanks to the very sizeable den that the good city of Kansas City provided me, the wall space in this room was beyond accommodating. Of course, my text flirting with Camille had pretty much destroyed any actual focus I could have had. The wall was done and my files arranged with some modicum of semblance.

The new information I'd obtained from Parker and Butler I also included even though I wasn't a hundred percent convinced they had anything to do with Jefe.

"Vaughn, you old bastard where the fuck have you surfaced now?"

It had been at least a year since I'd talked to my friend Yuri over at the ILEA. Having worked one case on its own for the past few years, I had little need of special assistance at the International Law Enforcement Agency. He worked for the Academy side of the agency, and hence had access to hundreds upon thousands of brainiacs and educators from around the world. They wrote papers on every goddamn thing you could think of.

"Yuri my man, to say I missed you would be a lie."

The guy was as Russian as they day were long. Word on the street was that he used to work with the secret service over in Russia but had fallen in love with an American girl and now worked stateside for ILEA. Of course, I didn't know for sure because that would mean actually sitting down and getting to know the guy.

"What kind of favor do you call me for today?"

"I need someone in linguistics. Specifically, someone who can explain to me why a person would be able to speak and understand Spanish when under therapeutic suggestion."

"Look at you with your fancy words. "

"Cut the shit Yuri--who can I talk to who specializes in stuff like this?"

"I'm texting--hold your horse. I should have an answer for you in couple of seconds."

"So where do they have you stationed these days?" He asked to fill the odd silence while we waited for his colleagues to get back to him.

"Kansas City."

"What a cluster of fucks that place is."

I sometimes wondered if he truly didn't understand American idioms, or if he used the 'English is my second language' bit to his advantage.

"You've got that right. Not only do I have Carter so far up my ass, he gave my prostate the all-clear yesterday, but I have the FBI and the CIA here too. I could be a Christmas present I have so much red tape surrounding me."

"Carter needs to talk to O'Hanlon if he mentions what you're there for, and why, he should be able to take a scissor to all that tape. I'm transferring you to Doctor Helen Gavros, she is a visiting scholar from Cambridge and the foremost expert on declarative memory."

He didn't even give me the chance to thank him for his help before transferring, instead, I got to be entertained by the cheesy hold music telling me to keep on the sunny side of life.

"Dr. Gavros."

Funny, she didn't sound like a Brit. I couldn't actually put my finger on where she was from based on her accent.

"Dr. Gavros, this is Special Agent Benjamin Vaughn of the DEA. My colleague Yuri Devlov put me in touch with you, as he said you specialize in..." I glanced down at the notepad in front of me, trying to read the scribble I had noted in regards to her expertise.

"Declarative Memory," she offered for me, "yes, Devlov informed me what your call was regarding. He said that you were working a case where your mark spoke Spanish while hypnotized?"She wasn't fully under. It was a therapeutic suggestion, more like a relaxed state if you will. But yes, while she was in this state--she spoke quite a few different phrases. Also in a follow-up session, she responded to me in Spanish when I asked her a question in the same language."

"And I'm assuming she speaks English normally."

"Yes."

"Is this person Hispanic?"

"No- French perhaps? I'm not entirely sure but her name is Camille Saint. Nothing Hispanic in her surname or in her given name."

"Very interesting. Did she mention knowing Spanish?"

"That's the strange part. Every time I ask her about it, she insists she doesn't know Spanish, at all."

"Very strange indeed." Dr. Gavros was silent on the other end, but I could hear her typing away on her keyboard.

"There is a complex condition known as dissociative memory disorder where something that is being said while under suggestion triggers a memory..."

"...Yes, I'm up to date on the various forms of psychology professor, it was the focus of my master's degree. My question was whether or not someone could simply forget that they know a language."

"Well, if she had a primary language that wasn't English, and English was a learned language later in life, it could be that she is reverting back to what had been her primary language. But you said that she wasn't Hispanic."

"I didn't think she was. But I guess I can always double check."

"Primary language and secondary languages are processed in different parts of the brain. Without knowing her history I can't say for sure. But sometimes outside influences also can have an effect on language. If she suffered some kind of trauma--a language that she had learned could return. I have read case studies of amnesiacs, Alzheimer patients, the recovering comatose, all speaking languages they weren't aware that they knew--or weren't their native languages, and sometimes they reverted back to their native tongues."

"Yes but that is on a full-time basis, correct? Like they suffer the injury and suddenly they are fluent in a language. This situation is piecemeal. Just a few sentences at a time."

"Its definitely something interesting indeed. I would love to hear more about this case if you want to send the file over to me. I could certainly dig around a do a little bit more research for you."

"I would greatly appreciate that professor, I will be in touch very soon."

Camille

"**S**o were you aware these walls are practically nonexistent?"

I barely allow Janet to get in the door the next morning before revealing the source of my embarrassment.

"How do you know this?"

"Benjamin told me."

"Who?"

"Oh, sorry, Agent Vaughn."

Her arms are practically overflowing with crap. Once again Janet 'needed a few things' at the store so of course she 'just grabbed some things' for me.Again.Despite telling her I am totally capable of ordering things online.

We had a doctor's appointment later. I had said about a hundred novenas the night before hoping they lifted my driving restriction. The faster I could eliminate the hermit thing, the quicker I could go back to work.

"You and Agent Vaughn are on a first name basis now?"

I could feel the blush pour itself all the way down my body. I felt as if I had fallen asleep and received a sunburn.

Janet flopped into the armchair. The ghost of Vaughn over-layed Janet's smaller frame. Which made me think of kissing him, all over again. She ripped her sunglasses off, freezing me with an appraising look.

"Based on that blush--there's a story to tell so spill it!"

I buried my face in my hands, trying to find the words to explain the insanity of yesterday. How did I tell it without being judged?

"So Danny and I broke up."

Starting with the break up had to get me some sympathy points.

"Oh honey, I'm sorry. Your choice, or his?"

"His. He texted me yesterday afternoon. I guess all of this--"

I signaled down my body before circling the air in front of me, "is too much for him. He's trying to finish up school and, I get it. I mean it hurts but I understand."

"Well, I don't! I don't get this generation. Why couldn't he come here to tell you in person? Or at least called you. I mean over a text? How heartless can a person be?"

I appreciated her indignation. I didn't want to dwell on the shitty part of my day when I still floated on a cloud of the end of day awesomeness.

"So anyway. I got the message and I started crying. Like kind of hard."

Janet scooted off the chair and onto the couch pulling me into a fierce hug.

"You should have called! I would have come back! The girls would love to meet you. Oh, Cam, I'm sorry I wasn't here for you."

"It's fine Janet."

It still smarted a bit. I'm not going to cry over it anymore, though. Sure my family was gone, but I had a few people. Janet, Mina, hopefully, Agent Vaughn. I'd say anything to save my face from the depths of her bosom. Janet is a fabulous lady, and the closest thing I had to a friend these days--but the hugs. Oy with hugs. Seriously.

"Anyhow. Agent Vaughn heard me crying, and came and knocked on the door to see if I was okay. Do you know how embarrassing it is? Like, what else has he heard from over here? I'm super paranoid now. Every time I sneeze, I feel like I need to say 'excuse me,' in case he can hear it."

I didn't even want to think about the other types of activities he bore witness to. Like of the um--self-care variety.

"I'm sure the walls aren't that thin. There are fire codes. But if a room is quiet, you would be surprised at the things you can hear through walls. It's the same in my house. You know Addy once told me she regularly heard her Dad and me through the wall! I tell you I about expired right there at the breakfast table when I heard that one."

Vaughn: Do you like Mexican food?

Janet continued to ramble, but I tuned out. The very person of whom we spoke shocked me with a text.

Cammie: Are your ears ringing?
Vaughn: What does that have to do with my question?
Cammie: Janet and I were literally just talking about you
Vaughn: Were you telling her what a fantastic kisser I am? 😏
Vaughn: Because it would be the first thing I would tell her about you
Vaughn: I can't stop thinking about last night.

That blush? The one I had earlier? It had raged into a full-blown forest fire.

"Who on earth are you talking to?"

Janet's voice pulled me away from my conversation with Vaughn.

"You are bright red. And don't get me started on your ridiculous smile."

Her reflexes were lightning fast. I swear her new nickname would be cheetah or panther--or whichever of the cat family was faster. My cell phone was in her hands faster than I could say 'hey what the hell!'

"Agent Vaughn? Are you kissing Agent Vaughn? What the heck did I miss yesterday Camille Saint?!"

"I kissed Agent Vaughn." I parroted, my whole body tingling with the remembered encounter.

"Yes, I gathered from the 'I can't stop thinking about last night' text he sent. Did y'all stop at kissing?"

She handed me my phone back with a smarmy smile on her face and an exaggerated wink that made me want to throw a pillow at her face.

"Need I remind you I'm not one of your daughters."

I tried to look mad. The Agent Vaughn effect refused to make my face cooperate. My comment sobered her real fast though. She went from playful to serious in a nanosecond.

"My gosh Camille, I'm so sorry! You're right! You're a client not one of my kids. It was uncalled for. But after spending so much time with you, I can't help but feel like you're one of mine to shelter and look after."

If I hadn't already been high on Vaughn as I mentioned earlier, the fact she wanted me as part of her nest of birdies to look over just about melted me.

> Vaughn: So I guess that's a no on the Mexican food.
> Vaughn: I hope it's the Mexican food that you're
> opposed to and not that your silence means that
> you, in fact, don't think that I'm a good kisser
> Vaughn: And if that is the case I would like the

opportunity to change your mind in that
department.

"There you go getting all mooney eyed again."

Janet was such a busybody. I huffed in her direction, trying to split my focus between the two of them.

> *Cammie: It depends on who is cooking it.*
> *Vaughn: Um ... okay, good to know you're a Mexican*
>   *Food aficionado*
> *Cammie: In Miami, I was spoiled by the Garcia's*
>   *abuelita*
> *Vaughn: Are you be opposed to leaving your apartment*
>   *for an evening and spending it with me at Zocalo?*

"Sorry, Janet. Agent Vaughn asked me to dinner."

"Are you planning on explaining to me how we ended up not only being on a first name basis with Agent Vaughn but also how you ended up with dinner plans?"

> *Cammie: Dinner sounds great.*
> *Vaughn: It's a date. And I mean that in the literal*
>   *sense. Can you be ready by seven?*
> *Cammie: Well, my social calendar is so long these*
>   *days, I mean between running a world empire of*
>   *minions and scheduling my mani/pedis Hopefully,*
>   *I can squeeze you in.*
> *Vaughn: I'll see you at seven*

"I have a date. With Vaughn. Tonight, at seven."

To say squealing and general obnoxiousness ensued would be an understatement. Technically I couldn't exactly jump up and down but we celebrated. Once we settled down, I regaled her with the previous day's activities. Janet would have a coronary if she knew I drank, so I left that part out. I also went light on how much making out we did. Telling Janet was akin to describing a kiss to my mother. My mother would be crossing herself and lighting a candle over every detail I shared. Especially considering I dated one guy in the morning picked up another the same night.

"A doctor's appointment and a date all in one day. My goodness, how are you going to handle all of the excitement?"

24

VAUGHN

I felt sixteen. I'm sure I developed carpal tunnel twisting my wrist to check my watch. Carter needed to shut his pie hole. Already ten minutes to five, and I still needed to get across town, shower, shave, and get ready for my date with Cammie. My date. With Cammie.

My body thrilled at the thought. I didn't remember when I felt like this last. From a kiss. A single kiss. Granted it was a hot as hell, but we never went further. Not even a copped feel.

Strange one kiss could feel transformative. Like kissing her gave the all-clear to move us towards that next level. I wanted it so bad with Cammie. Feeling this kind of attraction had become a long forgotten emotion.

My dry spell would make Moses weep. For too long I focused solely on the prize. Everything else took aback seat. I don't remember the last time I saw my Mom. The last holiday I spent not getting drunk in a bar? Years ago. Last year I rang in the New Year in Lima, thanks to unreliable intel. Previous to that, I spent Christmas in Cartegena.

Tired didn't scratch the surface. This shit didn't give me the rush it once did. The thrill of discovery had dissipated long ago.

Each piece of the puzzle brought relief. Each step made one less I needed in order to be finished. The faster I could find El Jefe the better.

"Vaughn! Snap out of it. I've asked you the same question six times and you know how much I hate repeating myself!"

"Sorry, sir... "

"What does O'Hanlon have to do with any of this shit?"

"No clue. Yuri said you should try placing a call in to him and explaining the pickle we're in out here."

"You don't just pick up the phone and call the fucking Attorney General of the United States Vaughn. You overestimate my influence, Vaughn."

"I'm assuming he meant you go through the proper channels to get to the Attorney General, Carter. Like, shoot off an email or however you communicate with Larsen and let Larsen deal with contacting the Attorney General."

Larsen is the Administrator for the entire Drug Enforcement Agency. He'd already put all of his weight on both the Bureau and the CIA before I even got here. Clearly, all these blowhards still insisted on a dick-measuring contest instead of doing what we had all sworn an oath to do. Serve and protect.

"Look--can we continue this tomorrow Carter? I'm on a tight schedule today."

My dumb fucking mouth. I regretted it as soon as I said it. IThe good old taxpayers of the U S of A did not pay me to be out chasing tail. I should be here, burning the midnight oil until the case is solved. It's what they want anyway. We aren't supposed to have lives. The Agency is our life. Getting drugs off the street is our life.

Finding a woman, falling in love, getting married, having children--not the life of an Agent.

"Is there something more pressing than doing your job, Vaughn?"

"Tonight there is. Every other night for the last fifteen plus years there hasn't been. But tonight, just tonight I have somewhere to be."

I left Carter there with his mouth agape staring at the space I had just occupied. My ass is going to be in a sling tomorrow. Carter will have my balls and my head, but I just want to feel normal for a few hours.

AT SEVEN ON THE NOSE, I crossed the six or so feet of concrete separating our condos and knocked on her door. I could hear her dancing about inside, moving from one room to another.

"One second!"

Her raspy voice called from somewhere back in her apartment. Probably her bathroom or her bedroom. I tried not to imagine her standing in front of her bathroom mirror in a bra and panties. Putting the finishing touches on her makeup--so she wouldn't stain her dress--before slipping into it. I said I *tried* not to imagine it. I also failed. Miserably.

I saw her shadowed figure approach the door moments later, and I couldn't find a breath to tell her how beautiful she looked. She wore her hair down. Prior to that moment, I'd never seen it. It was a halo of pin straight honey-colored hair, and so much longer than I thought it would be. I could see pieces of it peeking through the triangle made by her bent elbow, caressing her rib cage.

I never had an opinion on the color green before, but based on the dress Cammie was in, it might rank as my new favorite color. Her dress is fairly modest by today's standards. Figure-hugging without being tight. A modest cut not revealing more than a barely perceptible swell of breast. I wanted to kneel at her feet and run my lips all the way up her calves with the way they looked in those heels.

"I'm not a hundred percent sure how I'll fare in the shoes."

She pushed her hair out of her face, and followed my gaze

down her legs to the shoes and pivoted her toe--revealing more of her well-defined calf.

"I haven't been in anything higher than a flip-flop these days, but I don't own any flats fancy enough to wear with a dress."

I would probably get in trouble for messing up her carefully applied lipstick. The earnest way she looked at me, though? Smiling because she felt pretty but still looking vulnerable as hell-- as if I would at her and tell her to go change. The vulnerability did me in. I wanted to nothing but stand there and kiss her until she knew how gorgeous she was in any shoe. Even flats.

Her hands came up and wrapped around my ribs, underneath my suit jacket, their warmth causing goose bumps to rise up and down my body.

"You look beautiful tonight."

I finally found my voice, but my breath was a slippery beast. The kiss had been a breath stealer.

"Hey y'all."

I heard over my shoulder. Parker. What the hell is he doing here?

"Whatcha doin?"

As if he couldn't tell what we were doing considering I had my tongue in her mouth less than five seconds prior.

"Ben and I are about to go out for a bite to eat. What are you doing here?"

I know it is totally innocent. Something which if I had been anybody else in the world it would be commonplace. But Peter is a smart guy. He knew about me. He knew why I was in Kansas City. He knew where I came from who I came for. Therefore he also knew diverting from the formalities of "Agent Vaughn" is a big fucking deal. I'm pretty sure Parker himself didn't know my name.

"Agent Vaughn."

Parker cleared his throat, his gaze swinging back and forth between us. An embarrassed flush crept up Cammie's neck and swallowed her entire demeanor, pushing away from my chest and curling herself into the doorjamb.

"How ya feelin Cammie? What did the doc say today?"

"Oh, she said I'm doing really well. Only the dizzy spells are left. She said maybe by next week, they'll lift my driving restrictions. Then hopefully I can go back to work!"

"Wow, fabulous news! We'll get together and celebrate. I'll bring Nancy along- maybe we can double."

He practically sneered the word out. I knew he had absolutely no intention of doubling with us.

"Agent Vaughn, There's something I need to give to you. Hence the reason for my calling on y'all tonight."

I hated when he used the word y'all. It drove me crazy. Especially since that whole bullshit southern hospitality cop thing is so damn transparent. He only used the Barney Fife routine when uncomfortable.

"Sure."

I pinned him with the dirtiest look I could, before turning to Cammie and apologizing.

"Give me five minutes okay? I'm really sorry about this."

I placed a kiss on her cheek for good measure, before turning towards my apartment and unlocking the door. As soon as we crossed the threshold and the door closed, Parker launched on me.

"What the hell is goin' on Vaughn? Or should I say 'Ben?'"

I expected it, had prepped me for the interrogation, and yet it still set my teeth to grinding.

"What does it look like Parker, we're going out for dinner."

"That looked a whole lot more than dinner. Are you fucking her?"

This guy had some serious balls. Who does that? Who walks up to someone just this side of a stranger, and asks that? I guarantee when I do get the chance to sleep with Cammie--it won't be just a fuck.

"Since when is it your business whom I choose to fuck."

"Vaughn, I'm telling you, back off."

He tried to cage me in my own foyer, refusing to allow me to move into my own apartment. That kind of bullshit intimidation didn't fly with me. Whether he is a cop or not. Deploying those tactics while dealing with the vermin of this area made little difference to me. You didn't act like that towards polite company.

I saw his beat cop intimidation and rose it, planting my feet and crossing my arms. Where local PD is taught to use intimidation as a way to get the information they sought, those working above his pay grade are taught to utilize other means to cull and collect.

"Officer Parker, my neighbor and I are off to enjoy a nice summer evening together. Drop the officer friendly act because I don't buy it. This case isn't the jurisdiction of local PD anymore."

Sensing he had met his equal in the realm of intimidation, he backed off. Choosing instead to cool his heels on the arm of my sofa.

"Look, Vaughn, there is an entire city of women you can slate your hunger with. I get it, honest. Being out in the field. No roots, free spirit, and the whole nine. You can fuck your way from Los Angeles to Mount Pillier down to Key West, and up to Anchorage. But not this one. Not her, Vaughn."

"And why not? Who are you to say who I can and can't pursue?"

I stood sentry at the front door. I didn't want to be having this conversation in the first place, and the less welcoming I seemed, I hoped would wrap this up and allow me to move on to the person I wanted to spend the evening with.

His faced drained from the red heat of aggression to the sallow cast of the distressed.

"That girl is totally alone in this world. She's been subjected to a break-in and a personal attack, which she's still trying to bounce back from. She isn't a piece of ass Vaughn, and in case you forgot she has a boyfriend even if the guy is a fuckwit."

I tried to hide my smugness, reveling in the knowledge I knew something he didn't. Cammie and Parker must not be that close if he never received a breaking news update yesterday.

"They aren't together. She received a Dear Jane over text."

Peter launched from his seat, the aforementioned heat of rage dialing up to full tilt.

"He did what?" He paced the small space surrounding my sofa for all of three heartbeats before another realization hit him. "How do you know?"

"I live next door to her," I shrugged, casually feigning disinterest, "She tells me things."

Never mind the fact I wouldn't know either if I hadn't heard her crying. Watching him get all territorial over the girl gave me the slightest hint of superiority.

"So what? You saw the vacancy sign go up and you move in? What kind of sleaze are you?"

The intellectual cat and mouse game reached my tolerance limit. Him taking shots at my integrity is not the way to continue whatever friendship had begun to build. I had kissed the girl on the eve of her breakup and offered to take her to dinner. He made me sound like a heartless villain.

"Parker, this is your last warning. Say what you want to say and be done with it."

Parker moved from the couch arm to the actual sofa, cradling his head in hands

"She trusts me, okay? She's pretty self-reliant. I mean I guess you kind of need to be in her situation. But you can tell she isn't one to ask for help. Hell, she slept in a hotel room instead of inconveniencing a friend after the break-in.

But that first night in the hospital she let her guard down for me and accepted help. It was just so she could eat her dinner, but she trusted *me* with the task. She trusted me to protect her in that vulnerability, and I'll be damned if I don't honor that trust to protect her, every single day."

Parker looked up at me and every instinct in me rose to its haunches. The glassy eyes, the flushed cheeks, if I wasn't mistaken, Parker loved her.

"You son of a bitch! Give me a reason not to lay you out right here!?"

Despite the training I extolled earlier, sometimes the coolest of cucumbers turn caveman. Seeing intense feelings for a woman whom I had taken a vested interest in yanked the caveman right out of me, Incredible Hulk style.

I fisted Parker's shirt and had his feet tip toeing on my carpet before my brain caught up with my actions.

"Simmer down Vaughn you're acting like an ass!"

Parker pushed against my chest, snapping me out of my fog.

"How would your wife feel knowing about your crush on a little filly fifteen years your junior?"

I sneered. Like nose wrinkled, forehead tight, eyelids at half-mast, sneered. What in the hell is wrong with me? Parker is the only guy in the whole town who had shown any type of kindness towards me. Cammie and I had spent all of the forty-eight hours, in total together over the past month.

I'm overworked. That had to be it. A nice session on my rowing machine, pushing my body to the exhaustion point and a power sleep and I would be completely recovered.

"Crush?"

The dude looked flabbergasted. As if I had just told him he is an heir to a billion-dollar fortune and he shit rainbows.

"Yeah, when you want to protect the girl from being sullied so you can keep up your choir-boy fantasies."

"I'm married."

"Yeah- kind of sad you'd be crushing on a young, vulnerable girl when your one and only is at home."

He laughed at me. Not a giggle or a chortle, but full on laughed.

"I don't have a crush on Cammie. I'm concerned about her. Do I care about her? Of course. But like a little sister, not a lover. Which is exactly why I'm asking what your intentions are, Vaughn.

"I know your type. You guys blow in here thinking you're big shit because you're way above us local peons in pay grade, experience, and training. You think the world should bend to you because of who you are.

"But don't bend a lonely girl who is need of a friend. If all you want is an anonymous piece of ass to warm your bed while you are here--I'm begging you to look somewhere else."

I wanted to laugh. And not because he is comical in any way. I wanted to laugh because I knew so many guys who are exactly like Peter described. The ones who still live off the high of who they are, and ride the adrenaline rush day after day. Ten years ago, it was probably me.

"Look Parker--it's dinner. Just two lonely people enjoying each other's company. That's it."

The book had reached its final chapter. I would not speak on the topic any further. What did he want? Promise rings and chastity clauses?

I pushed off the wall, turning to grab the door handle. I had seven thirty reservations across town. I should have shaken his hand, or given him some kind of assurance his newly adopted 'sister' is safe with me, but fuck it all.

He had no right insinuating himself into my life--especially if he is going to make grandiose generalizations and pin them on me as if I am the sacrificial lamb for all DEA's with a wandering eye.

"I'm sorry Cammie, sometimes case business needs immediate action."

It did sometimes, but not then, and I hated lying when I didn't need to.

25

Camille

I had heard them arguing. We've already established neither of us has any privacy, especially when people are yelling. I never went back inside. I was in heels. Granted they are only two-inch heels, but heels nonetheless. I sat down I wasn't confident I would be able to get back up fast enough to answer the door.

I couldn't make out the words. Our walls weren't *that* thin. I distinctly heard both of their raised voices volleying back and forth though. I won four rounds in QuizUp before Vaughn opened his door and saw me. He looked pretty pissed, but once we made eye contact the storm blew out of his eyes.

"I'm sorry Cammie, sometimes case business needs immediate action."

Without another word, he smiled, reaching for my hand and guided me down the stairs. I heard Peter shut Vaughn's door following behind us by a few steps.

He didn't look any better than Vaughn did. Whatever they'd argued about didn't seem to be settled. Neither of them acknowledged the existence of the other.

"You look stunning Cammie."

Peter's hand curled around my shoulder, slowing me down

enough to hear the whispered compliment. No sooner had I slowed to accept it, his hand left my shoulder and he departed in the opposite direction.

"Have fun tonight."

He called he continued down the sidewalk to his cruiser.

"Is everything okay?"

I ventured towards Agent Vaughn...Benjamin... as he helped me into a black SUV so tall I practically had to vault myself into its seat.

"Fine."

Vaughn muttered making sure my dress was tucked in before closing my door.

"When did you ditch your clown car?"

The SUV was nice. Very Men in Black. Tinted windows so dark no one could see in. Black leather seats, and a dashboard that looked like Mission Control on a spaceship. His hand paused on the ignition, his stormy eyes sparkling even in the darkened interior of his car.

"So you've been watching me?"

He teased, turning to grace me with a smile that had my insides clenching.

"It's kind of hard not to miss a six foot something man fold himself into a car built for a midget."

His laugh was like a mountain spring just after the snow melted. Fast moving and so refreshing, something you wanted to dip your toes in and feel the rush.

"My bosses' assistant is a gem. I swear when I leave KC I'm going to have to buy her the biggest thank you present."

"She probably saw you try to origami yourself into that car and found you a new one post haste."

I tried to keep the conversation light and congenial, but he had reminded me once again his stay here was only temporary.

"How long are you here for?"

I asked, trying to make my question sound conversational. The smile slid right off his face. I swear I blinked and the atmosphere in the car went from light to stormy in a nanosecond.

"Look, Cammie," He turned to look at me while we waited at a stoplight.

"There are some things about my job I can't discuss with anyone other than those involved, like

Officer Parker. I honestly don't know how long I'll be in Kansas City."

He had really nice hands. Not like this was something to notice in the middle of a discussion, but they looked as soft as they felt on my skin, and his nails are well trimmed. Odd, I never noticed any man's hands before Vaughn.

"...It could be a year, it could be six months. I could be out of here two weeks from now. It all depends on how things go down. I want to be upfront with you though," he continued turning in to a parking lot and pulling alongside the valet. "I like spending time with you. So whatever amount of time I'm here, I would like to spend it with you."

I watched him unlatch his seatbelt and slide out of the car, handing it off to the valet before opening my door and helping me out. We stepped inside the upscale restaurant where the familiar scents of cumin and coriander brought me back to my days in Miami.

"Earth to Cammie."

Ben's hand caressed my cheek, those blue eyes honing in on mine with such intent I was certain he could see all the way into my soul.

"Sorry- I spaced out for a minute."

I followed him to the table the hostess guided us to, where he helped me into my seat before taking his own.

"If my kissing you last night was too much, I really am sorry."

He traced the shape of his lip with the nail of his thumb, contemplating what he was going to say next.

"You don't have to apologize for kissing me."

I didn't usually talk about kisses after they occurred. Was this a normal conversation to be having? We kissed. It was fabulous. I wanted more of them. So why are we discussing the subtext of a kiss?

"No, I kind of do."

He placed his napkin on his lap, before perusing the drink list. After a moment, he gave up on that distraction as well.

"Look, Parker seems to think you and I dating is a bad idea. I can understand where he's coming from, knowing I'm not a permanent fixture in Kansas City. But I like you."

His mouth twisted into an embarrassed kind of half smile, before refocusing on the drink menu he had set aside a moment ago. So they had been arguing about me.

"I didn't realize Officer Parker had appointed himself my keeper."

I startled another laugh out of Vaughn. Every time I did it, it felt like I scored the game winning touch down with two seconds on left on the clock. It isn't that Vaughn didn't seem the genial sort--he isn't a grouch running around with a frown on his face all of the time, but being able to make him laugh felt so good.

"This is going to sound strange for a first date," Vaughn laced his fingers together, resting his elbows in front of him.

Even the shadows the flickering table candles made across his face made him look handsome. What was my problem? I couldn't stop observing things about him I never remember thinking about Danny ever. I wracked my brain trying to think of any time in the entirety of our relationship I found subtle shadows made by a candle and highlighting the scruff along his jaw sexy-as-hell.

"How can I be boring you already?" Vaughn chuckled again. "We just sat down."

"I am so sorry Vaughn!"

Busted.

"Would you let me off the hook if I played the pitiful brain-injured girl card? You really aren't boring, I'm just--easily distract-ed." *By your good looks.*

The waitress saved me from further embarrassment producing a pair of drinks I didn't order.

"I took the liberty of ordering for us. Last week some of the guys at work invited me out for drinks here, and the mojitos are probably the most authentic and I've been pretty much all over Central and South America."

His eyes got real wide, and I swear he blushed. Of course in the low candlelight, I couldn't tell for sure. He looked flustered but I had no idea why. I took a sip from the famed mojito and it was more than decent. Not that I was a mojito aficionado by any stretch.

"So what were you going to say was strange for a first date?"

"I was going to tell you someday you are going to be that Mom who puts their kids in place with just a look."

It was my turn to laugh at him.

"It's probably years of being on the receiving end of a look like that," I surprised myself by admitting.

It was a very rare occasion I discussed my mom. Not because she was a bad person. I loved her. She was my mom. Was it hard being transient? Sure. But she worked hard. I was never hungry. I always had clean clothes that fit me, and warm jackets when the season warranted.

"My mom always gave us the 'cut the shit' look." He shared, smiling his thanks to the waitress who brought our food.

"Maybe it's a single mom thing." I suggested, "You know since it's only them they don't have the time to volley an argument between two parents and a kid. So instead they develop an automatic tell that you are pushing them to their limit."

Vaughn ran his thumb along his lip again and regarded me with the strangest look. I thought he was going to say something, at least it had felt like he was going to say something, but he never did. The silence hung, slightly awkward between us. Our forks clanked against the authentic stoneware, the hum of conversation from the other tables blanketed us in a bubble of self-conscious silence.

"It's been a while since." Vaughn cleared the rest of his drink before continuing, "You know, dating. Or taking a beautiful woman out on a date."

An unsure half smile slid onto his face which drew a matching smile from my own, coupled with an unexpected blush as the result of the compliment. He thinks I'm beautiful. My stomach flip-flopped with the compliment, lighting me from the inside out.

"Work keep you busy?"

I asked, hopeful he would shed some light on what he was doing in Kansas City. He nodded, cutting his chicken. Clearly not planning to expand.

"I miss being busy with work."

I hated uncomfortable silence, so if he was going to back seat the conversation, I would drive.

"It's so ironic, you know? When you're at work, exhausted because you are working so many hours you tell yourself how wonderful it would be if you didn't have to do the whole nine to five grind every day. But then when you're at home not doing the whole full-time job thing, you're bored out of your freaking mind."

"I hear you. I wonder if when I'm finished with this case if I'm actually going to be able to step back and slow down. I'm so used to living and breathing field work for so many years, I can't picture not having a case occupying my thoughts day in and day out."

I wouldn't need to pull his story from him after all it appeared. I needed to ask questions sporadically and hopefully, I would have enough to puzzle together my new neighbor.

"Have you been working on your case long?"

"I know what you're doing Ms. Saint."

That smirk came back- the one that was slightly lopsided, and made me feel like I was riding a roller coaster. I could only widen my eyes with surprise at being called out, not able to think of diversion fast enough for his instincts.

"I'm assigned to Kansas City on a case I have worked for a

very, very long time. It has taken me all over the United States, and I'm hoping this will be the last stop. I want it to end here."

His mouth frowned into the bow his words arrowed from, proclaiming quite clearly his disinterest in discussing it further.

"There are so many more interesting topics we could be discussing."

He cut another piece of his chicken, pushed some of the rice and sauce on the fork before floating it towards my lips.

"Taste this, please. Tell me this isn't divine."

I took the pro-offered bite, savoring the cumin and cilantro I associated with so many different aspects of my own childhood.

"Mmm."

Vaughn's fingers traced my lips, startling me out of my remembrances.

"You had a little piece of rice that escaped"

He held up the offending object. Like he needed to prove to me there was a verifiable reason his fingers touched my lips.

"Good, right?"

I nodded.

"You mentioned something about the Garcia's abuelita earlier. Did she make this for you when she watched you?"

He signaled our waitress over and ordered a second mojito for himself pointing at my glass in question. What the hell, I reasoned, I wasn't driving. A little embarrassing to be a two-drink drunk these days.

"Yes, in fact, I was thinking about her a minute ago. But it isn't just her that used to cook for me. We spent a long time in Miami than we did in a lot of the other cities we lived in. I think I was actually there for two full school years."

I could hear my voice drift off as my mind carried me back to my days in Miami. The heat was always my strongest memory from there.

"We had lived in a two flat in Coral Gables."

I told Vaughn, picturing the tacky faded salmon-colored

building with the laundry lines running from the back windows down into the alley that was our 'backyard.'

"My mom worked two jobs while we lived there, so I didn't get to see her a lot. She got up real early in the morning to work at a cigar factory, you know hand-rolling cigars? I used to love the way she smelled when she would come home. Then after working at the factory, she would go and work as a seamstress at The Biltmore. Since she wasn't home a lot, Mrs. Garcia kept an eye on me, since Diego and Juan were probably the closest things I had to friends."

"So you were born in California, but moved to Miami?"

I nodded, playing with the straw on my drink. There were other cities in between but I don't think I needed to add in every detail of my nomadic life.

"Yes... California, Miami, Texas, New Orleans, Indiana, and Illinois. Oh, and Oklahoma was in there somewhere too I believe."

"How come you guys moved around so much?" Vaughn asked, sticking his credit card in the billfold.

"That would be a question that died with my Mother."

I didn't mean for it to sound as bitter as I felt it did. Honestly, though, I had no idea why we moved so much.

"She never gave much of an explanation to my questions. It wasn't like she was working for the military or some fancy corpo-ration where they transferred every so often. It seemed like every time I would settle in somewhere--get used to the ebb and flow of my days and make friends, I would wake up one morning and she was packing up our things again. On to the next city or a 'new adventure' as she liked to call it."

He caught me watching him finish out the check and explained, "It's so gorgeous outside, I thought we could walk along the river?"

"Technically, it's a creek, not a river. But the McMansions that border the creek do have quite a nice walking path."

He stood and took my hand, bracing me at the elbow without making any mention of the fact I was slow to catch my bearings.

He waited patiently; smiling down at me while the room stopped shifting. Having his face to focus on, while the world tilted helped to make vertigo pass quicker.

"I'm okay," I whispered, trying to collect myself before people started to stare.

"I know you are," he stated, matching my pitch, "but in case you aren't, I have you."

He guided my hand into the bend in his arm. Of course, I couldn't help but notice the very solid bulge of muscles obscured by his garnet striped shirt.

"I can't believe I forgot you are in heels."

He peeked down at my shoes as we walked the block towards the creek path.

"We can go back if you'd like. There's a fabulous café a couple of doors down that serves the best cappuccino."

Sure, my feet were a bit wobbly, but I for one was not ready for the date to end. Even if he had offered coffee at some shop a few doors down, what would there be left to do after coffee? I would walk up and down the creek, if it killed me, simply so I could try to learn a bit more about my elusive neighbor.

26

VAUGHN

I am seriously off my game. Not that I had any game of late. But my God could I possibly make this date suck any more than it already did? I wondered if she felt as awkward as I did, grasping for things to talk about. There is so much I wanted to know about her, but at the same time, I know conversations like that--the general getting to know you back and forth that is commonplace with first dates, requires a bit of give and take.

I could feel her assessing gaze on me every time I asked her a question. I would become transfixed with the tiny flecks of gold in her eyes as she narrowed them in my direction. If brains made sounds when they processed and ruminated over incoming information hers would have been buzzing and whirring at light speed.

I know she had dozens of questions she wanted to ask me, but I had dozen's to ask her too. Aside from her secret second language, there are simpler questions I wanted answers to. Why had she moved around so much as a kid? What is her favorite food? What kind of music did she listen to? When she is sad what cheers her up? Then there are things Vaughn the Agent wants to ask too--like why is she no one's charity case? Who is Isaac and why didn't she trust him?

"So, how did you end up working for a football team?"

I ventured as we meandered down the street towards the river's path.

I could feel her shoulder press harder against mine as she pulled them up in a shrug before answering my question.

"I worked for the football team in college as part of my internship during my undergrad and stayed on through graduate school. After working there I got an itch for Sports Marketing and one of my mentor's at school found out about this job, wrote me a glowing recommendation, hounded them incessantly until they granted me an interview. If not for Coach Turner I probably wouldn't have ever been considered for the job.

"Coach Turner... as in Ron Turner?"

It blew my mind how she casually mentioned people who most football fans would be drooling over the opportunity to shake these people's hands let alone have personal relationships with all of them.

"Yes. You know him too?"

I about went ass over feet into the river. Coach Turner, as in Ron Turner, former coach of the Chicago Bear's, Ron Turner.

"Um, no. I know of him since I watch football every Sunday like most men in this country, but I'm not on his Christmas card list, no."

I won a giggle. In the twilight, it's hard to see much of her face, but I could faintly detect a self-conscious smile and a slight flush in her cheeks.

"Okay, sorry that is a ridiculous statement. Sometimes I forget not everyone lives in the same world as I do."

She turned her face into my bicep, hiding her embarrassment, her giggle getting lost in my shirt. While it is still technically summer, the evening had cooled, and I could feel a slight chill on her cheeks when they turned into my skin.

"Should we grab a coffee somewhere?" I offered, hoping we could find a Starbucks to grab a cup quickly and keep walking versus sitting somewhere. I liked being out here in the quiet.

"I'm fine unless you wanted something."

"Your cheeks are cold."

Cradling them in my hands had been a mistake. She looked up at me with those big hazel-gold eyes, laughter causing them to glint in the almost darkness, her full lips pulled into a gorgeous smile. What man do you know who would be able to resist? Cammie is a siren on a normal day, but at that moment she was Calypso--the queen of seduction--and she didn't realize how tempting she is, Her beauty while relaxed and laughing turned my gut with desire..

Despite the chill in the air and the cold of her cheeks, her lips were impossibly warm. The first pass of my lips against hers Wasnt enough to quell the song of desire running through me. The second pass took that small spark of warmth and ignited it into a bonfire. I needed to back away; otherwise, the Hyatt up the street would be renting by the hour.

"Wanna head back?"

She pulled away, breathless and smiling.

My brain seemed to have lost the ability to compute. It didn't dawn on me until after my objection we walk just a little bit longer, that she didn't want to end the date, I'm pretty sure based on her affected breathing and the caress to my arm, she suggested taking things further. Way to fumble at the ten-yard line.

Southern Vaughn howled at my stupidity. Tempted as I was to pivot and head back to the car, the fight with Parker resurfaced at that moment. Fucking Parker. Leave it to him to find a way to insert himself when he isn't here. Thanks for the pitcher of ice water in my veins. asshole.

"Tell you what," I suggested, summoning all of my strength to avoid sounding disappointed or frustrated. "I feel like playing a game."

"A game?" She parroted.

I could hear it in her voice. The suggestion is juvenile. I probably reminded her of the clumsy fumblings of her fourteen-year-old self getting felt up by some pimple-faced idiot behind the school.

"I want to know things."

I guided her down a secondary path, one that would take us closer to the river's edge, where I spotted a few benches.

"I want to know things."

She replied, disengaging from my side and practically floating onto the bench and crossing her legs.

"Great, then my game will be perfect."

I hoped.

"Twenty questions. Answers can't be longer than three words."

I sat down next to her, pulling her close to my side again. Which, not to sound like a complete pussy--she fit quite nicely there. She melded perfectly against my side. These gorgeous lamps dotted the river bank, casting a yellow-gold hue around the bench where we sat. At least she seemed entertained by my idea and not annoyed.

"Fine. I start."

She leaned closer to me, hypnotizing me once again with the scent of rain, mixed with the amber fragrance of her perfume.

"At your next birthday, you will be?"

"Drunk."

I wanted to put a star on my chest every time I won a laugh from her. I'd walk around like an Army General, my chest decorated with various patches signifying the different ways I won them out of her.

"I meant how old will you be."

"Not my fault you weren't specific enough. My turn."

"Cheater."

"Not so. You asked a question and I answered it in under three words."

She crossed her arms and pouted like an imperious toddler. Would it make me sound emasculated if I said it looked adorable? Because it made me want to take out my phone, snap a picture of it and use it as her contact shot.

"I call foul."

"You have nineteen more questions, I guess next time you'll be more specific in your questioning."

When I ran my hand along her knee, an unconscious act meant to comfort her, I realized she didn't have stockings on. Her gorgeous, tanned legs, were bare to my explorations.

"I'm at a bit of an advantage since I already know you are twenty-nine and will turn thirty next month. Which makes you my Libra twin. So, I guess I won't have to waste any of my questions on how old you are. I know on October the Fourth you will be the big three oh, and you'll probably be drunk like I will be on mine."

"You should get a three-question deduction, and an extra five question penalty for being a snoop."

"I'm not a snoop if I have your file from the break-in."

"Using cop techniques aren't fair. It's cheating."

"It's not cheating. It's using the information made available to me."

She's actually mad. I thought we were still joking around, but I glanced down at her, and the laughter died on my lips. I had never misread a situation so badly.

"I'll be thirty-eight."

Some of the fight evaporated from her pouty frown and squinted eyes.

"Better."

"What would make it best?"

"Five free questions."

"Two."

"Three."

"Seriously?"

Her lips spread, revealing her perfect teeth, "You cheat you pay the penalty."

"Since my surrender seems to be needed in order to win that gorgeous smile of yours, I wave my white flag. Three questions."

"Favorite movie."

"Mr. Smith Goes to Washington."

"Never seen it."

"It's great. Anything by Capra actually could probably go in my favorites column."

"I don't know who Capra is?"

"It's a Wonderful Life?"

"Nope."

"Seriously? It's like synonymous with Christmas in America?"

"Nope never seen it."

"Oh my God. Prepare yourself to be schooled."

When she looked up at me, the moon reflected off her eyes, causing them to shine.

"What do you want Mary? The moon? Just say the word and I'll tie a lasso around it and pull it down."

Her nose crinkled and her eyebrows drew into a confused frown.

"What?"

"It's a line. Probably the second most famous line in It's A Wonderful Life."

"What's the first most famous?"

"Every time a bell rings, an angel gets its wings."

The frown morphed into a scowl, yanking a laugh right out of me.

"We'll Netflix it, it will make sense."

Despite wanting to continue sitting and laughing with her, I could feel her trembling as she sat next to me. Reluctantly, I stood, helping her to her feet. Her body swayed as she adjusted to the new position, causing her body to fall into mine. Her lips brushed against my pulse point before settling into the crook of my neck. On instinct my hand came up to her head, and cradled her there, enjoying the feel of her nestled there.

"I like you right here."

Her arms snaked through mine and around to my back, holding her even tighter against me. I tried to be a gentleman. With every ounce of control I had, I willed my hands to stay up in the safe zone and not take the journey down the dip in her spine and over the swell of her ass. My Benedict Arnold hands, however, turn coated--siding with the dark side of my ever-swelling desire. Either Cammie didn't have any panties on or she was in a thong. Whichever the case, my roaming hands, and aforementioned desire appreciated.

"Benjamin." The tips of her hair tickled the backs of my hand, warming my blood and sending the most delicious of sensations through my bloodstream. Her throaty affected whisper did things to my brain, turning it into a jumbled mess allowing desire to win over my gentlemanly struggle.

In heels, we stood eye to eye. I met her lips with the slightest dip of my neck. With a gentle pull of her hips, the part of her desire lined up perfectly against the swell of mine. Maybe not proper behavior for our first official date. I reasoned the month we'd been neighbors and the weeks we were friends extended our courtship. And, Not to mention the kiss from the evening previous. I wanted her in the biblical sense. Anyone with eyes would know this fact any time she is within a few feet of me.

"Usually if a woman is calling me Benjamin, it's my mother and I'm in trouble."

The pink in her cheeks had little to do with the chill in the air or the blush of her makeup.

"What should I call you then?"

"Actually, I kind of like hearing my full name in your voice."

"What does everyone else call you?"

"Vaughn." I shrugged.

I couldn't remember the last time someone had addressed me by my first name. Other than my Mom...or my sister. Noah, when he was still alive had. My friends from undergrad, but it had been a while since I saw any of them.

"Some people call me Ben."

"Ben."

My name came out of her mouth like a caress. Like champagne sipped from a glass, and rolled around her tongue for extended enjoyment.

"Benjamin." She continued, her eyebrows scrunching and rising as her lips wrapped around the syllables of my name.

"Benjam--" I pulled her mouth against mine, my tongue meeting hers mid-phrase, tasting my name on her.

"You can call me whatever you want."

Everything about her is soft: her throaty whisper, the smooth skin on her legs, her mane of hair currently tangled between my fingers. The way her body pressed against mine, her soft breasts against my hard ones, her stomach molded against mine, the soft yet firm bounce of her rear.

"So," I cleared my throat trying to get a reign on my lascivious thoughts, "if you came over on a Saturday morning to watch football, what shirt would you be sporting?"

"I think I answered that question already."

Had she? I didn't remember asking her. I replayed our conversation in my head and couldn't remember her mentioning what college she went to.

"I told you my college mentor is Ron Turner. Mr. 'I'm such a big fan of his' doesn't know what college he worked for?"

Still, I fumbled, lost.

"I went to Illinois." She laughed, pulling my arm into the cradle of both of hers, hanging on as we walked back to the car.

"Ah, that explains the vitriolic outburst."

"Vitriolic outburst? Oh, you mean against the over-rated Ohio State University?"

"Over-rated? Need I remind you who won the National Championship last year?"

"What do you care if I don't like the Buckeyes, you went to Georgetown."

Damn she busted me. I had forgotten I had told her.

"I went to Georgetown for my Master's. OSU is my Alma Mater."

"Of course you did. That's just my luck."

172

"Don't be a hater." I opened the car door, helping her inside. "We're both part of the Big Ten, we can coexist in peace."

"Any other school. Any one. Indiana. Penn State. Michigan. Hell, Purdue is more tolerable. But Ohio State?"

"You do realize your shit team hasn't been competitive for like ten years."

"Wow, unnecessary. I think that is a hit to the dangling fruit, to borrow a phrase from a good friend of mine."

"Oooh, I'm a 'good friend?' I'll try not to show my hurt feelings. Do you kiss all your good friends like that?"

"Well, if you want to be upgraded from good friend, you'll need to earn it."

"I'll earn it, and then some sweetheart. Extra Credit should be my middle name."

If the slight pink on her cheeks earlier had been a blush then the magenta--almost red flush--that went clear up to her ears needed a completely new category. One that hasn't been invented yet. I tried to catch her gaze, but she hyper-focused on her nail polish. Her mouth set in an imbalanced smirk.

Before I started the car and headed towards our collective homes, where the night could go any number of ways, I wanted to hold on to the magic just the smallest fraction longer. I loved the feeling of hanging in this in-between place, where dancing around the inevitable was sweet torture.

Cammie's neck is graceful like a ballerina's, a perfect slope connecting to a well-defined décolletage. If my mind traveled down to a more sexual path, it would be the first place I would want to suck and bite. For the moment though, in the quiet warmth of my car, I simply wanted to experience the feel of that slope, and the rumble of satisfaction traveling up her throat when my lips met hers again.

27

Camille

I'm drunk on Agent Vaughn. Benjamin. Damn. I needed to work on that. It seemed too strange to be calling him Ben or Benjamin when everyone else called him Agent Vaughn. And by everyone else, I meant Officer Parker.

Now is not the time to be thinking of Officer Parker.

The evening with Ben was nothing short of amazing. I couldn't remember a time I enjoyed myself so completely, while also feeling so totally at ease. Even with the stuttered bits of conversation where nerves got in the way, I never felt uncomfortable or uneasy. It has been the perfect date. Icing on top? The warmth of Ben's body as it held mine, be it his hand, or his arm, cradled into his side, or in his lap pressed against him as I am right now.

How on earth did I get to this position? A moment ago we were simply kissing--again. I couldn't get enough of the kissing. The kissing morphed into a make-out session in the driver's seat of his car. Thank God he'd exchanged the little Aveo for a beefier Yukon.

Speaking of beefier, there wasn't anything left to the imagination in Ben's lap, tucked perfectly between my legs. In a thong with no pantyhose on, I would embarrass myself if we went any further.

"Cammie." He groaned against my lips, "we need to slow this down."

His hips lifted off the seat, grinding along my own throbbing need. I answered his suggestion, bearing down against him. Pushing myself along his ever-hardening ridge. Bliss rocketed in waves through my whole body.

"I don't want to slow down Ben."

His hands found their way underneath my dress, grabbing on to my hips and pulling me down harder against him.

"I don't want to fuck you in a car Cammie."

His lips left tattoos of his interest all over my neck. Sucking at my pulse point appeared to be a hotline straight to my groin.

"You deserve hours of attention."

At that moment I didn't want hours. I wanted about thirty more seconds of him not changing a thing he did.

"Don't stop Ben. Right there."

I was lightheaded. I prayed I wouldn't pass out before I cashed in on all this effort. Almost there. If I could catch my breath I could last for the final few thrusts.

"Cammie." He groaned, pushing his head against the headrest.

"Ben. Please. Don't stop. Right--"

With an inhuman, guttural moan I fell, washed away on a cloud of bliss that made my whole body melt into a useless pile of goo. I couldn't shift over to my seat if I wanted to. Which, I didn't. I wanted to lay there, cradled albeit awkwardly, against Ben's chest, as the muscles in my body continued to softly pulse.

Neither of us spoke. Hypnotized by our rapid but slowly exaltations. We fogged up the windows. While nearing the end it remained in the high sixties/low seventies outside. We fogged up the windows like a couple of horny teenagers. A giggle escaped my lips, and the magic shell shattered.

Ben's eyes opened, his normally stormy blue eyes looking almost sapphire in the lap lit reflections.

"What?"

I loved that lopsided smirk. Wait. Loved? What the fuck is wrong with me. It is a smirk. A cute smirk. A smirk I enjoyed eliciting from him. Could one love an idiosyncrasy without being 'in love?' because I most certainly was not in love? That would be ridiculous.

"We fogged up the windows."

I drew a smilie face into the fog, content to remain cradled against his chest, even if my legs were starting to shake with the effort of remaining open while my upper body origami-ed into the small space between the armrest and Ben.

VAUGHN

I came in my pants. Cammie grinding against me, pleading for me not to stop, watching her come apart, caused me to come in my fucking pants like a thirteen-year-old. I didn't mean to.

When I told her she should have someone spend hours taking care of her, it wasn't bullshit. Losing ourselves in the front seat of a car, like a desperate horny teenager did not sit well with me. At all. I ran a hand down my face, trying to calm my erratic pulse and quiet the storm for two seconds. I needed to figure out a way to salvage this date and prevent it from going south.

"Quite an unexpected ending."

Cammie pushed off me, straddling my hips while she tucked her breasts back into her dress. I don't remember taking them out. I have to admit that I'm more than a little disappointed I didn't get a peek while semi-coherent. Later I keep telling myself. I'm determined that there will be a next time.

"Sorry to have um, created a mess."

She motioned towards the dark spot in the general area of where I blew my load. I realized, however, that I was damp on the inside and the outside.

"I think that both of us created that mess."

I sheepishly admitted, garnering a shocked gasp from Cammie as that little fact settled into her psyche.

"Thankfully I'm wearing black pants, and we are about to head home. Unless of course, you'd like to go paint the town red."

Thrown back in entertained delight is nearly as gorgeous as she'd looked a moment ago moaning in apogee.

"Sure! Let's go, Midnight Bowling. Perhaps a bit of laser tag?"

"You know, I wouldn't be the only one embarrassed in a black-lit room. They'll find a mess on your dress as well."

"So, I don't want this to be awkward."

She settled into her seat, strapping herself in.

"While unexpected, I obviously enjoyed myself."

Her blush returned, as did the shy half smile. Lower Vaughn rebounded with a vengeance. The load in my pants painfully yanked each hair out one by one. If not for that, I couldn't almost convince myself we'd yet to have any fun based on the burgeoning interest I sported.

"I know that this question is usually a veiled invitation to come back and have sex, but would you be interested in coming back to my place? I have Capra's entire movie collection. I really want to hang out with you some more."

"That would be great."

Her fingernails tickled up my thigh. A familiar gesture, not sexual in nature at all, my body didn't care. Despite being almost thirty-eight, I'd found a fountain of youth. I can't remember the last time I possessed instantaneous recovery time.

"We should probably, you know, clean up a bit before settling in for the movie."

She laughed, turning her face into my shoulder.

"Probably the best suggestion I've heard all day Ms. Saint."

I threw the car in park and cut the engine, jumping out fast enough to intercept my lovely date before she attempted to jump from my behemoth of a vehicle on her own.

With her curled against my side, we meandered up the sidewalk towards our apartments. It isn't until his voice cut through my smittened haze I realized someone paced the length of our patio.

"Vaughn, nice of you to finally arrive home. I've been calling you for an hour."

Unintentionally I jumped away from Cammie, so totally shocked at seeing Carter standing in front of my home.

"Carter, it's the middle of the night, the hell are you doing here?"

Technically, it's just past eleven. And if Carter is at my doorstep, I'm in a world of shit. I honestly didn't know where my fucking cell phone is. I couldn't feel it in my pocket and at that moment I couldn't remember if I brought it with me on our date.

"A word Vaughn. Say goodnight to the lady."

I turned to face Cammie, thousands of questions ricocheting around in her mind based on the fathomless look in her eyes.

"I'm so sorry sweetheart. I guess I need a rain check on the movie night."

I held her face in my hands, trying to show her how sincere my apology is by look and intonation alone. I placed a subtle kiss on her cheek, whispering, "Forgive me?" before pulling away.

After helping her up the stairs, and making sure she got in her house okay, I said goodbye with a promise to call her later.

"What's this about Carter?"

Carter stormed into my house, forgoing any formalities and launching full tilt into the tirade I'm assuming gained steam while he cooled his heels on my porch.

"What the fuck Vaughn. First, you disrespect me by cutting me off this afternoon and leaving without so much as an explanation. Then you don't answer your phone despite me calling you at least five times. Now I show up at your place, worried that they got to you too, only to discover you aren't here. Instead, you are out greasing your stick in some local honeypot"

I wanted to punch him. Despite him being the head guy in Kansas City, and technically my interim supervisor, I wanted to

179

punch him until he took it back. But there were other more pressing questions that my inner agent honed in on.

"What do you mean they got to me too?"

"Someone got to Wexler." He stated, collapsing into a chair in my living room, burying his head in his hands. "I got the call around eight. They think it is Jefe's men."

I didn't know Wexler. We'd never met. He was the inside narc here in K.C.

"Are we sure it's Jefe? There are dozens of rings here in the city."

"Not a hundred percent, no. But we're pretty sure. We need to get to HQ. I'm calling everyone in, even the UCs. Something's going on, and we need all of our resources together in one room to figure out a game plan."

If he is pulling under covers from their operations this is heavy shit. Like the Agents we were trained to be, we needed to put our emotions on pause and hold off on mourning the death of one of our own until the immediate threat is gone. While time is of the essence returning to the main office, I needed to get out of my cum soaked pants, otherwise, there is a possibility it could be days before I got out of them again.

"I just want to grab a bag, I'll meet up with you downtown."

WE WERE ON A GAG ORDER. I looked at the same people across the table from where I sat for almost twelve hours. We went over every piece of evidence, hearsay, and intel we obtained, and no one could figure out how Wexler was exposed To add insult to injury, this caught us with our pants around our ankles, no pun intended.

"Has anyone heard from Butler?" I asked, grinding the haze from my eyes.

Twenty four hours straight I'd been up; I shouldn't be so close to exhaustion already.

"Lisner and Dukard should be here at oh eight hundred. Butler from what I understand is on vacation."

One of the guys responded I think his name is Haines.

"Vacation? How the fuck is that asshole on vacation? We're in the middle of a case?"

"It's the CIA man, they do whatever the fuck they want."

I have three different requests into Butler, and he goes on vacation? How the fuck does that happen? There has to be more to the story than that. He didn't seem like the kind of guy who slacked off and pushed his responsibilities on other people. I didn't want to believe that a CIA Agent could get as high-ranking as he is, only to coast once he got there.

"Carter any word from KCPD?"

"I have the police reports from the detectives on the scene. I don't know what else you expect from them."

Those files were tattooed on my eyelids, I looked at them so often. Wexler wasn't just deep; he was a sleeper. He only checked in occasionally via a cryptic messaging system. His apartment was wired and bugged, same with his car. There wasn't any video of a struggle in his home or his car. The last audio obtained from his car, he spoke in Spanish to someone named Juan--which more than likely was a fake name. Juan told him Chuchi needed to meet with him at the warehouse where KCPD and KCFD would later be called for a five-alarm fire. His charred remains would be discovered amid the rubble, his car still parked outside.

Chuchi is El Jefe's Tricero, which is why we were all presently sitting behind locked doors trying to dig out from underneath the shit pile.

"Obviously they knew he is a narc."

Haines chimed in, going through a file again.

"They usually don't burn Narcs though- they cut their tongues out."

"If they knew he is a narc then burning him to death is sending us a message of some sort."

I needed Butler. Where the fuck is Butler. It didn't make sense.

Even if the guy is on vacation, big shit like this went down and the agency didn't give a flying fuck if you were out in the middle of nowhere on a fishing boat. They'd send a 'copter in to haul your ass back to HQ and credit you the time to be taken at a later date.

"Carter, can we get Officer Parker in here? He has a few suspicions in regards to the goings on - out on the street."

29

Camille

I didn't wait by the phone or pace my living room waiting for him to come back. Not consciously anyway. Sensible me knew whoever "Carter" is, he is higher raking than Ben. Ben had gone from relaxed to tense in a nanosecond. Within five minutes of going into Ben's condo, they left again. I went to bed assuming I wouldn't hear from him until the following day.

The following morning, Janet arrived, we went to occupational therapy, had lunch, watched a couple of episodes of Gilmore Girls--and still nothing. I had sent him a couple of text messages--nothing earth-shattering, just a 'had fun last night' and no reply.

"You're a million miles away."

Janet pulled me from my daydreams. We had discovered the charitable people who had refurnished my house, had also provided me with patio furniture. Presently we sat in said furniture, looking at the small pond and jogging trail. Every time a male form appeared over the tiny hill, I hoped it would be Vaughn running towards us. Totally ridiculous, I know, especially since I know he is off working.

"Sorry, I'm lost in my own thoughts."

"Were you thinking about the fun you had on last night's

date? I bet you thought I forgot. I'm waiting patiently, hoping you'll bring it up so I don't sound nosy. Someone is awfully tight-lipped, though. Did I miss the walk of shame this morning?"

Janet laughed at her own joke, tickled she is hip on the lingo.

"Is that what they do in your cock books Janet? Sleep together on the first date and then slink away the next morning?"

"Oh no, in my 'cock books' they wake up to a screaming orgasm and repeat the night before. Sometimes twice. And then usually they decide to say 'fuck responsibilities' and spend all day doing it.

As if that actually happens in real life. Eventually, he can't get it up anymore. Even if you're young, and well--limber."

"La La La La La--I'm not listening!"

I covered my ears trying to erase from my mind any mental pictures and sounds associated with Janet's narrative.

"Janet, considering you're a mother you sure have a dirty mouth."

"Oh, that's not the only thing dirty honey."

I walked right into that one.

"I swear sometimes I wonder whether or not you are saying these things for shock, or if you really are a dirty old lady."

"Hey--watch the old bit. There are only twelve years separating us."

"Helloooo!"

We heard from around the corner.

Janet rocketed to her feet, calling "We're around back!"

Moments later Parker appeared, bearing gifts of donuts and coffee. In the midst of my excitement, I remembered he fought with Vaughn the night before.

"Peter."

I hoped the look I cut him was imperious enough.

"Agent Parker, how are you today? Care to join us in getting a little vitamin B?"

Janet pushed out of the Adirondack chair, signaling for Peter to take a seat.

Odd that Parker wore his dress uniform. He was quite debonair in his shiny shoes and brass decorations.

Despite the fight in me desperate to be unleashed in a fit of self-righteousness, something about the set of his mouth and the slump of his shoulders gave me pause.

"Thanks for the donuts and coffee."

I smiled, accepting the proffered cup. You know the fastest and best access to my heart.

Peter did a poor job of hiding a smirk behind his coffee, watching me as he did so. I wasn't supposed to know the two of them had been fighting over me the evening previous. He probably didn't know it was loud enough for me to hear.

"How was your date?" He asked, pulling the donuts from the bag and distributing them to Janet and me.

"You know, I'm dying to know the same thing! That boy is a looker, isn't he?"

"Janet! As if a man is going to admit another man is attractive. I swear she forgets with whom she is talking sometimes."

"Well, I'm just saying. Officer Parker is spoken for, with an assumedly gorgeous wife at home. I'm sure he can comment on the positive attributes of his friend and partner without feeling emasculated."

"We're not partners."

Peter refused to make eye contact with either of us, choosing instead to flip the tab of his coffee lid against his thumb.

"Agent Vaughn is a bit higher ranking than I am."

"Friends then." Janet laughed, swiping her hand in the air as if shooing away a fly.

"Our date was fine."

I didn't want to get into details with either of them. Janet, I probably would share a bit more if Peter hadn't been there, but since I already knew what camp he sat in, I planned to be the Fort Knox of information.

"Fine? Just fine? Oh, honey, you do not look like that and have a *just fine* date."

"Janet! Oh my god!"

She shrugged over a sip of coffee completely oblivious to the fact her comments were mortifying.

"Since when are you a fan of Agent Vaughn?" Parker asked, "Last I checked you were raking him over the coals for scratching up the stairwell."

"Oh Officer Parker," she threw her head back and laughed like she was sitting front row at some high priced comedy club, "that was weeks ago! Besides, if anyone can make this one smile and blush the way he does--he must be good people."

"Is that so?"

I could feel Parker's focus shift to me, but I didn't want to make eye contact with him.

"Does he make you smile and blush Cammie?"

I snuck a look at Peter, and wouldn't you know he stared right at me, waiting to meet my gaze. He cocked his head; his worry-lined eyes taking a long pass over my face. I could feel him assessing me with each second that ticked by. Whatever he looked for, he appeared satisfied.

"You know, my hands are a sticky mess from this donut. I'm gonna go wash them. Are you okay out here Cammie? Is there anything I can get you while I'm inside?"

I shook my head, no, not backing away from the stare down with Parker. The melodic ping from my iPhone nearly blasted me out of my skin. I damn near dropped the link in an attempt to grab it from the table.

Mina: I miss your face! Let's hang out soon!

"Not who you expected it to be?" Parker asked. I'm assuming the disappointment I felt read all over my face.

"What do I owe the pleasure of your company today Peter?"

I plastered on a smile I didn't feel, pretending to be unaffected by the lack of messaging from Ben.

"Just dropping in, paying a visit to my friend."

He put too much stress on the word friend. As if suddenly the fact that we were friends is in question.

"I'm glad you came by." I lied. "You look really nice today. What's with the fancy clothes?"

"Someone got killed in the line of duty yesterday. I'm about to swing by the house to grab Nancy before going to a small get together for the fallen's family."

"Oh Peter, I'm so sorry! That's terrible!"

He nodded taking a long pull from his coffee.

"We're friends right Cammie?"

Peter stared at his feet, the cup of coffee cradled between his hands.

"Of course Peter. I don't know what I would do without all of your help these past two months."

I remembered how annoyed with him I had been, and despite him being fairly subdued because of the circumstances; I didn't want to miss the opportunity to discuss it with him.

"But, just because we are friends Peter, doesn't mean you have the right to meddle in my life. I appreciate you are looking out for me. I really do. But I'm a big girl. If Agent Vaughn wants to ask me out for dinner, that's my business, not yours."

His head snapped up in a millisecond. The formerly subdued aura replaced by indignation.

"Cammie, do you know anything about him? I'm trying to look out for you. He has temporary tattooed on his body. How do you know you aren't some passing fancy? Something to keep him entertained while he's in town?"

"Look, Peter, I appreciate all you do for me. I didn't ask for your opinion though. Whether Vaughn is here for ten minutes or ten years--that's my prerogative."

"I don't want to see you get hurt."

I could sense the strain in his voice while he tried to keep his outburst in check.

"Peter, whether I get hurt or not, it's my decision, isn't it? Dating Agent Vaughn is my choice, is it not? I'm going into this situation with my eyes wide open. Who knows what will happen. Besides, it was dinner, Peter. That's all."

"The way you jumped when the text came in--"

"Officer Parker, I believe I said my peace on the subject."

"Cammie..."

I felt kind of bad pulling the formalities card. However, I'm in the right. We'd only been friends a couple of months. I never met his wife. We didn't hang out. We didn't do lunch, or go to the movies, or do whatever friends of the opposite sex did together.

He came over to my house checked up on me, and sometimes would catch the tail end of a movie I watched and ate dinner with me. He is firmly in acquaintance territory. And acquaintances had no right to overstep their boundaries so thoroughly.

"Peter, it was nice to see you. Thank you for stopping by. I appreciate the donuts."

I rose from my chair, willing my vertigo to remain in check, and hugged him goodbye despite the more pressing desire to push him away and point a the stairs like one would a wayward dog.

"Cammie, I'm just worried--" He said over his shoulder.

You would think I sentenced him to the guillotine the way he dramatically descended my steps.

"Considering all you are dealing with between the attack, and now I hear you and Danny broke up, it's a lot of stress to go through. A new love interest might not be the smartest thing to pursue right now."

"I'm sorry about the loss of your friend Peter. My condolences to their family."

Janet must have been watching from the window above the kitchen sink, as she arrived just as Peter headed towards the front of the house.

"Everything alright Cam?"

"Yep, Officer Parker realized he had somewhere more pressing to be. No big deal."

I forced a smile on my face and waved goodbye to Peter before he disappeared from our vision.

"Okay, now you can cut the shit. What the hell is this about? I practically choked on the tension between the two of you."

I collapsed back into the chair with a heavy sigh, grabbing my donut and picking it apart.

"Well, let's just say he is not thrilled with the idea of Ben and I dating."

"It's one date."

"I know."

Surpassing annoyed, not even my Fluffy Fresh donut could appease me. Even watching the bikers circle the path didn't settle my dis-ease.

"Do you think he's right Janet?"

"Right about what? Who to date? Who is he to you? Last time I checked, his name ain't Saint! Ha! I'm a poet, and didn't know it."

"Janet you realize that's only funny when four-year-olds say it."

Despite my proclamation, I couldn't help but giggle.

She dumped the remaining packets of cream into her coffee, smirking at my chagrined reaction.

"It is funny and you know it. Ain't a Saint? The double meaning alone is enough to warrant a giggle. And in regards to neighborhood Officer Friendly, he's not your Daddy or your brother. Even if he is, it's not his life. If you want to date Ben, who cares what he thinks. Or anyone for that matter."

"What if he's right though? I haven't heard from Ben at all. Maybe he is looking for something super casual."

"I didn't realize you were looking for engagement rings and promises of forever. Yesterday you said it was 'just dinner' with the hottie neighbor."

"Isn't the purpose of dating to figure out whether or not someone has staying power, to settle down with and be 'the one?'"

"You're still young hon. No one says you have to settle down tomorrow and start popping out kids. What did Agent Vaughn say when you went out?"

"He said he didn't know how long he'd be in Missouri, and

despite Peter's complaints, he liked me and wanted to spend time with me."

Janet slapped her thigh, the echo resonating in the air like a gavel on a judge's podium.

"Well, that settles the matter. There's no need to be hemming and hawing over anything. You like Ben, Ben likes you. Just have fun, and let time settle the rest. Did you enjoy yourself?"

The feel of his long fingers wrapped around my hips pulling me against him was the first image to come to mind.

"Oh, my heavens! Would you look at that blush."

Janet's face is so close to mine I could smell the minty essence of her gum.

"Camille Saint! It looks like someone did the walk of shame after all!"

"We walked, quite proudly, hand in hand, back to our respective apartments after a wonderful date, thank you very much."

"Then what happened?"

I could only shrug.

"Some burly angry looking guy waited for Ben when we walked up. Ben apologized, said he had to leave, and he would talk to me later."

"Maybe he hasn't had a chance to call. Didn't Officer Parker say someone got killed last night?"

And isn't that a kick in the gut? If it were me and I had gone out on a date with someone, and it ended the way Ben and my date had, and I got to work only to discover someone died? I would at the very least shoot a text message off to said person to let them know I am okay.

"Yeah, he did. I thought I would have a text by now."

"Well," Janet followed my gaze to the jogging path as if she too were to see Agent Vaughn getting some exercise.

"It's entirely possible he hasn't been able to find the time. He isn't home. His little shitbox Aveo isn't parked outside. If someone from his job visited his home, it must be bad. I don't think any supervisors would ever come to my home unless it was urgent."

Hopefully, she is right. She had to be right. Ben had said he had a good time. We shared things. Delicious things. Naughty even. Definitely amazing. Certainly, if we lived next to each other, and he had to face me every single day, I wouldn't be his booty call, right?

30

VAUGHN

I took to naming each muscle as it tweaked and pulled. I graduated from manic focus to precipice of crashing. No amount of coffee, exercise, or fresh air would help. The free fall into the exhaustion was imminent if I didn't get some fucking shuteye. Even thirty minutes would bring some relief.

Just wishing for some secret sleep reminded me the story I told Cammie. My mind split. I both wondered if I could hide in the bathroom, and remembered I was supposed to call her.

Shit. SCIF had been instituted until they could finish investigating the downed officer. I was in a communications blackout. I couldn't reach out to Cammie. My cell phone, along with everyone else's --any device actually, were being scanned for data breaches. It is a standard protocol during SCIF especially when relocated to the Inner Data Center of the facility.

I placed Carter by voice alone. He paced in one of the closets they called offices. He and Hendricks engaged in a sparring match. Knowing he'd be occupied for a few minutes, I chanced sneaking out of the IDC. Lacey's office was directly outside the doors.

"Agent Vaughn!"

Lacey looked mortified to see me. I broke serious protocol

right now. If Carter found, my ass would be slung up from the nearest tree.

"You know you're under SCIF right now right?"

I held up my hands showing her I didn't possess anything that would be a breach.

"I need your help for two seconds. I promise I'm back downstairs like nothing happened. I've been here for almost forty hours, I need one favor... pretty please?"

I prayed my face looked as sincere as I actually was and she didn't think I was trying to win her over with a fake one. I took her silence as permission to continue. Grabbing a pen and scribbling as fast as I could while still making my handwriting legible to the average person, I talked as I wrote, in an attempt to speed up the process.

"I would appreciate total discretion with this favor." She immediately started to balk, "I mean, I'm a private person..."

I handed her the note as I continued to explain, and pulled my wallet out of my pocket, finding a hundred dollar bill and handing it to her.

"If you could send the prettiest flowers you can find to the address on this note, along with the apology written there, I would consider myself in your debt."

Lacey took the proffered note and cash, a soft smile accompanying the slight flush on her cheeks.

"Agent Vaughn a romantic? I never would've guessed."

"They're just flowers, Lacey. I was in the middle of dinner with a very lovely woman when my evening got cut short. I haven't been able to even text an explanation. Will you help me?"

"Sure Agent Vaughn."

Lacey delicately folded the note around the hundred dollar bill and placed both in the bag that sat directly behind her, "One question though, are you sure you want to sign these flowers Benjamin?"

I did it without thinking. But honestly who sends fucking flowers and signs them with their last name? Was it that strange?

"Thank you for your help Lacey." I smiled, refusing to take the bait. "I appreciate it."

~

"VAUGHN!"

I heard from behind me as I pushed through the metal doors leading to the IDC. It would figure my dumb fucking luck I would get caught when trying to do something honorable.

"Look, it was just for a second," I began to explain, turning around to face the voice that busted me. "Jesus Christ Parker, I can't put into words how relieved I am to see you."

Parker jogged the final few steps to catch up to me, the strangest look on his face.

"So, we're okay then?"

That's right. We'd had words. God that seemed like eons ago.

"Now isn't the time for pissing contests and hurt feelings."

I tried to rally while also providing myself a caveat in case once the shock of the unfolding events wore off I was in fact still pissed at him.

"Right."

He said, removing his hat and running his hand across his bald head.

I didn't want to be caught out in the hallways by anyone else, so I practically ran back to our main hub, with Parker trying valiantly to keep up in his shiny shoes. Standard issue dress shoes were slippery as fuck, especially since the average officer only brought them out for two reasons, promotions and funerals. Considering we were all on lockdown, I knew it was the latter that warranted dusting off the dressie.

"Look, I asked for you specifically," I began stopping in front of the wall of Intel we assembled.

"Beat cops aren't usually privy to this kind of information. Let's just call me Gepetto for all the strings that needed to be pulled. I assume the flaming hoops you jumped through upstairs was no picnic either. Take a look at the timeline and these images. Do you recognize any of these guys?"

Despite labeling him as a Barney Fife, Parker was a good cop. His instincts would put him in a detective's chair if he chose that route. While he walked the perimeter of the room, absorbing the information we compiled, referencing his own notebook, I saw his wheels turn.

"Did you ever get the audio you were looking for?" He asked, looking up from his notebook.

"One of the files," I grabbed my laptop off the conference table and moved to an open chair closer to where Parker stood.

"I'm still waiting for one more. I recorded my conversation with Cammie about her break-in," internally I fought with whether or not to reveal all of this to him, considering we went toe to toe about her safety. I watched Parker's face waiting for some kind of break in his stoic expression. Nothing came, so I continued.

"There is a technique called Therapeutic Suggestion..."

"Where the target is put into a state of relaxation similar to hypnosis, but where the conscious mind is still active and func- tioning, at a rate similar to the twilight state."

Parker finished for me. The smirk on his face told me he was more than enjoying the fact he surprised me.

"Yes. Anyhow when I discussed the break-in with Cammie, I thought utilizing Therapeutic Suggestion might be helpful in gaining access to the blocks in her memory. But in that state, she couldn't remember much. However, during her session, Cammie spoke Spanish to me. Twice. She also mumbled something I couldn't hear and hoped we would be able to access with better technology. I'm still waiting for it."

He nodded, lost in his own thoughts as he continued around the room. I called up the piece of audio I did have back from my friends at the CIA and played it for Parker.

"Do you speak Spanish?" I asked.

"No, I mean I took it as a requirement in high school but I think at this point all I can do is count and swear."

I handed him the translation so he could follow along while the recording played back between Jefe's three mercados. The translation was pretty spot on, but I guess I probably should have expected the CIA had people who specialized in the various dialects and knew the differences between Mexican Spanish and Colombian Spanish. Parker looked at his files from August 3rd and 4th when this chatter occurred. Once again we surveyed the various disturbances and arrests t. There were plenty of robberies and petty theft, B & E's and the like, but each was tossed aside because either the perps didn't match the descriptions, or they didn't fit the timeline. Except one.

"I don't understand the significance, but Cammie's break-in and abduction match the timeline." I looked at the files again, not able to come to grips with how or why Cammie could possibly fit into this thing.

"Do you have her hospital files?" I asked.

"No, we don't get access to those. She's protected under HIPPA."

"Nothing?" I asked, making a note to subpoena the hospital.

"Not even the standard drug screen? She was almost an abductee, didn't they screen her to make sure she wasn't roofied?"

"Probably, but that isn't anything shared with us. That's part of her medical file. Why do you need to know ?"

"Is it possible Cammie is a dealer? Or working the streets for Jefe? She doesn't seem the type but little surprises me these days."

"You can't honestly be saying that Vaughn. You, who supposedly like her enough to date her is going to start questioning whether or not she's an addict or a dealer? I don't get you."

I was fucking exhausted. Did I honestly think she was either? Hell no. But I needed to rule every possible angle out because none of this was making sense. At all.

"Of course not."

I grabbed the file and flipped through it for the millionth time.

It refused to provide the information I needed. The sketch of the perp that tried to kidnap Cammie was in the file. I pulled out the picture, laying it out in front of the two of us.

"Do you know what Isaac looks like?" I asked, staring down at the picture.

"I think she would if it was Isaac coming up behind her. I mean, he's one of her boyfriend's best friends."

"Ex-Boyfriend."

I corrected without thinking. Parker grunted at my correction. Whatever. So maybe I was becoming a bit territorial, but with a woman like Cammie, who wouldn't be.

"Are there any pictures of him? Or any information?" Parker asked, pulling out his notepad. "His name is Isaac Ramirez..."

"He's already being pulled in for questioning. I think Hendricks said something about KCPD bringing him in."

Parker nodded, looking at the files a bit more.

"Can we get you in there for questioning?"

I knew the answer was probably no. He was a beat cop, not a detective. Cops needed to put in their time before becoming a detective. Those guys are territorial around their perceived underlings.

"I couldn't walk in there, no."

"What if I got Carter to lean on your boss? If he has anything to do with this, we would need that information.

You know the case, you know what we're looking for."

"I'm assuming the detectives questioning him will know also."

"I want you in there."

I didn't know how much pull I had. Why the sudden urgency? I was blaming it on exhaustion. But I had a hunch. Or a feeling. Who the fuck knew. I preferred to err on the side of caution in regards to Cammie than ignore it completely.

"Carter."

I saw him coming out of the office where his powwow recessed.

"This here's Parker, KCPD. He was OOS at an attack of a

woman back in August and looking at this file, there might be a connection. I'm not a hundred percent sure, but close. I want him in on the interro. Do you think you could lean on PD?"

Carter glanced at the file I handed to him, not looking convinced.

"This Isaac Ramirez they are bringing in for questioning? Ramirez is a friend of the woman who was attacked right around the time of the Jefe chatter. I think Parker should be in there."

"Vaughn, I can't get involved in local hierarchies."

"Carter. Look. I wouldn't make a big deal of it if I didn't think the two were connected. Parker here knows the case. Knows more than the detectives will. Will know what kind of questions the detectives should be asking."

I feared the cheap fiberboard table Carter balanced his upper body on would succumb to the pressure of him leaning on it. It took immense effort to remain focused on our conversation instead of watching in concern as the legs wobbled under his weight.

"I'm sure the Agency will be briefing the detectives on what information they need without my involvement."

He tossed the file back on to the table and sauntered away. I wanted to push. I wanted to get in his face, We'd all been awake for almost two straight days. I knew pushing would be a bad decision.

"Vaughn, it's not a big deal. I know the interrogating detectives. They're good guys."

My head spun, the buzz in my ears became too much to tolerate. My eyes burned with the ever-present desire to lie down and submit to the call of sleep. Seeing I was on the losing end of the argument, I gave up with a shrug.

"Does she know what's going on?" Peter's voice dropped a notch in volume. He stood so close to me I could smell the vanilla cream in his coffee.

"Not that I know of. I mean, she knows we keep questioning

her about her break in but other than that I don't think she thinks much of it. Remember she thinks we're both cops."

"No, I mean... Carter pulled you mid-date. Did you call her? Text her"

I was doing a good job of holding my guilt at bay. At Parker's question, it floated back into my conscious thought. Hell floated was the wrong word. The guilt announced itself with the pomp and circumstance of a king entering his court. Ice-cold shame snaked its way through my system.

"We've been on total communications lockdown." I tried to explain, but since Parker already thought I was an asshole and a tail chaser I assumed it fell on dead ears.

"Just before you came in I snuck upstairs and asked Carter's assistant to send some flowers for me.

Unfortunately, it's all I can do right now."

Parker nodded, taking a long sip from his coffee cup.

"Look I know we've been dancing around what happened between us, for the sake of the case. And I'm not commenting on anything else that went down. But, I think she might be wondering why you didn't call."

"You've seen her?"

"Well, for all of five minutes before she read me the riot act and kicked me out of her house."

Laughter was not welcome in a SCIF room. It was a place for serious business and grim faces. It was a place of whispering unless we were all meeting together. It said 'this shit is intense.' So for me, of all people, to burst out laughing? Especially since Carter practically installed a Nanny Cam on my ass-- I would be his dinner when he cornered me to chew me out.

"She did what?" I tried to stifle my outburst.

"Yeah. I knew it was coming. She always has this look ..."

"Oh God, don't get me started on the look!"

Thinking about it made my insides ripple--a combination of guilt and a feeling I couldn't describe. I think I missed her. At least it cut the tension between Parker and I. Like actually cut the tension. Not just us pretending the tension didn't exist.

"She knows you're in the middle of a case."

He told me, trying to cover his mumblings with his coffee mug.

"I told her about the funeral, she's a smart enough girl to put two and two together."

"Vaughn!"

Fucking Carter. Apparently, he didn't need to abide by the inside voice rule like the rest of us diligently followed. Both Parker and I snapped to attention.

"Pack up your shit. You're on a flight out at oh two thirty."

31

~Camille~

I t had been a week. An entire week. Of nothing. No Vaughn. No Parker. I climbed the walls. I sent texts to both of them. I called both of them. No response all week. My anxiety inched up from annoyed to concerned to worried and now I', beside myself.

Every cop car I saw on the street, I craned my neck to see if it is one of them. Anytime the news reported on the police, I worried someone would announce their names.

Vaughn sent me flowers the previous week. Gorgeous flowers. The kind you take pictures of and upload to Facebook. And the note. Jesus the note about killed me.

> "Go easy on the lipstick, 'cause you're gonna get
> kissed.' Forgive me? I'll make it up to you.
> Promise. Benjamin."

I read and re-read that note so many times the ink started to wear off the cardboard. Originally I thought he was being forward. After showing the note to Janet, she said it was a quote from *It's a Wonderful Life*.

She tried convincing me to watch it with her, begged actually. But I declined. After so much build-up, the only person I wanted to experience it with is Ben. Well, I did. Before going out of mind with worry. A full week later the elation from the gesture wore off a long time ago.

Piling on to my malaise, my doctor felt between my continued vertigo and the slight delay in my memory retention I couldn't be cleared from the medical assistance. Janet and I were still attached at the hip for at least four weeks.

I handled my date just fine! Other than having the tiniest bit of balance issues I thought I did great. My words were back. I communicated in full sentences. So what if I experienced dark period around the time of my attack. I argued PTSD but they didn't take too kindly to that.

Weekly hypnosis sessions were now on the docket. Like having to be trucked to occupational therapy isn't enough. I wanted Vaughn. I wanted to tell him about this, so he could suggest we work together. Like we did before. The last thing I wanted to be subjected to is a headshrinker once a week.

"We don't burden other people with our problems, Camille."

I could see my mother, arms folded, rag in hand, hair tied back in her hairnet still from working at the factory, railing at me from where I sat at the kitchen table. She had been called into school because of an exercise in class where we had to talk about our parents.

I did my presentation on my Mom. When I made no mention of a Dad it brought up questions. I started crying when someone asked why. The teacher decided for my own emotional health, I should see the school counselor so I could deal with his abandonment.

"If you have a problem, you deal with it. People don't need to know your business. Does a hole in a dam get filled because there are a dozen people watching it? No. So what makes you think

*sharing your problems with others will make them
any better?"*

"Still upset about your appointment?"

Janet brought me a cup of coffee and the homemade donuts
we'd made from a recipe off Pinterest.

"I don't know what I'm upset about."

The list is long. *Upset* isn't really the word. A storm of different
emotions fluttered through me. Upset barely scratched the surface.

More than that though I'm mad. Mad at my dumb brain and
body. Mad that Ben doesn't have the decency to text. Mad I
worried when they didn't deserve my attention. Even madder still
at Parker because apparently, he had decided to walk away like
everyone else when the going got rough.

"Do you think Parker upset? I mean, about our fight? Do you
think I was so mean to him that he cut contact?"

I am a hug convert. Prior to Janet's arrival, physical contact
with strangers made me uneasy. She is soft in all the best places.
Like a mom should be. She doled out her hugs so charitably, it is
near impossible to inoculate yourself against their charm. In the
absence of my own Mom, Janet unknowingly became a perfect
stand-in. Regardless if she got paid to spend time with me.

"You don't honestly believe that, do you? There's a lot of bad
stuff going on right now. All these cops showing up dead? And
those gun battles! Heavens, did you hear about the one down by
the casino? A cop isn't safe anymore these days."

"I'm so worried Janet. He isn't calling me back or responding
to my text messages. Vaughn either. Every time they report something else in the news my heart stops. I'm afraid it will be one of
them next."

We tried going on a walk around the neighborhood, watching
Dance Moms on TV, playing a game of cards, Janet tried valiantly
to get me out of the funk I'm in. At six she ceded defeat for the
day, packing up her things and preparing to head home.

"Great Caesar's Ghost! Cammie is going to be beside herself!"

I heard Janet practically shouting from my foyer. In less time than it took me to stand, Parker, stood in my doorway.

"You... where the f--OH MY GOD--I've been so worried!"

I launched out of my seat on the couch. Full on flew into his arms before gravity caught up with me and I collapsed against his chest.

"I've been so worried!"

I didn't want or expect them to show. The pure relief at seeing my friend opened a maelstrom of emotions inside my chest. Despite having words the last time we talked, relief is the only emotion I focused on.

"You have no idea," I chortled, trying with desperation to hold back tears, "I'm so fucking glad to see you."

"Vaughn is on communications lockdown." He explained holding me in a fierce hug, "I was too. I'm sorry you worried. "

Janet shooed us both to the dining room table, bringing out the rest of our homemade donuts.

"I wish I could stay and hear the story but my natives are restless at home. I'm so glad you are okay Officer Parker. We've been so worried."

"I could barely get a message to my wife."

He continued, watching Janet's shadowed figure descend the outside stairs.

"Everything happened so fast. With everything going on, and our officers getting killed... There's so much security right now. I just got my cell phone back an hour ago. I saw all of your messages, and wanted to come over in person."

"Everyone is okay?"

I asked, trying not to make it too obvious.

"Vaughn is fine. He's been sent to track down a bad guy. I don't know much more than that. He isn't allowed to have his phone with him. Know he is beating himself up over how your date ended"

Parker continued, surprisingly generous with his information.

"Look, I'm sorry I stuck my nose where it didn't belong. I can't help feeling a little protective of you."

"I'm sorry too Peter."

I tried to swallow the emotions avalanching through me, "all this week... when I thought you were dea--hurt... I kept replaying our fight over and again in my head. I was so worried I'd never get to tell you how badly I felt."

"It's in the past now."

He winked at me with that stupid childish smirk I didn't realize until that moment I had missed.

"So what's new with you? Anything?"

I gave him the run down from the doctor. He liked the idea of hypnosis better than I did, pointing out how well the session with Vaughn went. I didn't know it was public knowledge.

"How do you know about that?"

"Cam, we're on the same case." His ears got all red, the blush of embarrassment climbing steadily up to his bald head.

"It's still unsolved unless we can get something concrete. Which is why I think full hypnosis is a great idea. Maybe you're intentionally blocking things out you don't even realize. Like the bad dreams you had which you don't remember."

I never considered I somehow impeded the progression of a case with my inability to remember things. In fact, I forgot there is a case pending. I had assumed they gave up because of how little they had to go on.

"Cam, can I ask you a question?"

Our conversation had lulled into silence, both content to simply sit and look out the window at the kids trying to enjoy the last vestiges of warm weather. Time moved at warp speed. We were only a couple of days away from October.

"It's not about Ben is it?"

It had been a joke. I tried to make light of something clearly the giant elephant in the room. Apparently, it was still too soon since he smarted at my comment.

"No. I wondered what happened to Danny."

It seemed so long ago now. Despite it happening a week ago give or take a couple days. Gosh, time went so fast, and yet slowly at the same time.

"He sent me an 'it's not me, it's you' over text message."

I thought I'd been over it. Danny hadn't been on my mind in at least a week. As soon as I voiced the words though, I got angry all over again.

"He needed to handle things back in Columbia. My situation was too much to handle."

He nodded in understanding, apparently satisfied with the answer.

"Has he called or texted since you broke up?"

I tried not to guffaw right in his face. Had I heard from Danny? That would be a bit hard since he blocked my phone number.

"No, unfortunately, Danny isn't interested in communicating anymore."

He gave me the strangest look. I didn't feel like expanding. It still hurt he blocked my number. But I needed to move past it. Danny is in my past. Totally and completely in my rear-view mirror.

"Do you keep in contact with any of his friends?"

"Danny and I didn't socialize much with his friends. Other than Isaac who lives here in Kansas City. His other friends are in Columbia. I wasn't privy to Danny's life in Columbia. Most of our relationship happened while he interned for the team. We never spent any time at Mizzou. "

"Is Isaac the guy he went to watch the fight with?"

Wow. That fight. The one that spawned my fight with Danny. Seemed like eons ago. I guess I should send Danny a thank you note. If it weren't for him, who knows what would have happened with Agent Vaughn.

"Yes, that's Isaac."

"Has Issac reached out since you broke up with Danny? Did Danny ask him to come and check on you?"

His ears were red again, same with half his face. He did that thing where he soothed his discomfort by rubbing his head like a genie's lamp.

"No Isaac doesn't like me much. I never found out why. Considering that, I can't imagine my health ranks high on his list of concerns."

He nodded again, remaining stoically silent. I turned on the television. It lost its luster after weeks at home. The weird silence hanging in the air was borderline uncomfortable though.

"If you see him, like if you run into him at the Walmart or something, can you do me a favor and not engage with him? Don't wave or smile at him, or try to initiate a conversation with him okay?"

Isaac, like Danny, had been nowhere on my radar. But when a cop asks you to stay away from someone? It put my spidey sense on high alert.

"Is something going on with Isaac?"

"I can't say anything Cam, just promise me, okay?"

What could I do except agree?

32

VAUGHN

When Carter told me to pack my shit, to get my ass on a flight at two in the morning, honest to God I thought I had been fired. He'd been less than congenial since this whole situation went down, We're in a grim world of hurt around here, and my fear was I pushed too far. Of course in my head, I knew that it would take a whole hell of a lot more than that to be pulled off a case. On instinct, I immediately thought the plane would be dropping my ass back in D.C..

Maybe D.C. was better. Instead, I am in the lovely city of Minot, North Dakota. Why you ask? What connection does Minot have to the Jefe case? No fucking clue. Apparently, some little hayseed just getting their feet wet in the world of fighting baddies heard from a friend who heard it from Ferris at the Thirty-One Favors last night that Jefe was about to make a big move in North Dakota.

They decided not to ask me, the Jefe expert. Hell the expert in all Central and South America drug chains. If they asked, I could have told them, fuck no Jefe isn't in North Da-Fucking-Kota. That's Meth territory. Not coke.

But what do I know? It's only been my job to track him down

for the last seven fucking years. Three of those solely focused on him.

So here I am, in some shit hole motel. More than likely contracting scabies from this piece of shit bed. While I wait it out with a bunch of blowhards that I don't know.

Worse than that, I didn't get a chance to go home and pack. The town had a twenty-four hour Walmart, so none of us will be subjected to cleaning our drawers in the motel sink with hand soap.

The supposed trade is going down tomorrow night. I hoped this would be a get in and get out type of deal. We were still on communications lockdown. They gave me a burner phone. One to be used only for business. I couldn't risk calling Cammie from the motel phone because it could compromise this useless mission.

I feared I'd used the last bit of her patience. And, I worried about her to no end. What else could I do locked in a motel all day long?

Parker promised he would let Cammie know the first chance he got. If she is mad at him too though, there isn't a guarantee she'll take his phone call or answer the door. God, I'm completely useless. No wonder so many DEA are single. This constant concern and worry were too fucking much.

At least there is a bed, even if the cleanliness of the sheets is to be determined, and the all clear to sleep.

33

Camille

"You know what we should do?"

Mina stopped over after work and made a surprise appearance, she'd come bearing gifts of greasy burgers and fries from HiBoy Diner- which was this shit hole in the wall drive-thru near the stadium. While it was my usual type of evening--hanging out at home, trying to keep myself entertained within the confines of my apartment, Mina couldn't sit still for more than a few minutes at a time.

It was strange how after all these years I lived in Kansas City, an attack and resulting head injury gave me not one, but two friends, and a friend with benefits.

"Take a walk around the neighborhood and work off this food? I swear I'm going to have to buy all new clothes. I'm afraid to try on my business suits, I can feel I've put on too much weight to fit into them anymore."

"Shut up, you look fine and you know it. I saw you rocking out in a bikini two weeks ago. And no, walking around the park is for old ladies. I think we should go dancing."

"Mina, I can't dance. I can barely stand without getting dizzy."

"Okay, then let's get all dressed up and go to a club. No

dancing necessary. We'll sit in a booth and look pretty while the boys buy us drinks."

"I'm sorry I'm not very fun. You know I can't drink."

"So we'll get all dressed up, have a change of scenery for the night, and we'll drink virgin margaritas instead."

It sounded like fun. It was better than being a forever prisoner at my house. One can only keep themselves entertained at home and running a few errands Janet and I were able to do, for a limited time. My date with Vaughn was the best day I experienced in a long time. Thinking about it, I wondered if it was the date, or because I freed myself from medical prison for the night.

"I can see you thinking about it..." Mina teased, throwing a pillow in my direction, "you're smiling which means you like my idea!"

She was up off my couch and in my bedroom closet faster than I could voice any type of disagreement.

"I'll drive." She called from my bedroom.

From the muffled sound of her voice, I knew she was in deep in my walk-in closet.

"There's this new club down by the River called Fuego, I heard about it from some of the players. It's mainly a whiskey-sipping club, with a couple of local lounge acts. Really swank. High brow. The perfect place for me to bag a rich husband."

Mina emerged from my bedroom weighed down with nearly every dress in my closet. Held against her body, she examined each while continuing to extol the benefits of the jazzy whiskey lounge. Her curves were Jessica Rabbit to my Shakira.

"Okay up. Off the sofa and in the shower."

Apparently satisfied with my collection of clothes, she shooed me into my bathroom. While I showered, she laid out the makeup and styling tools needed to make me Cinderella. I stifled the tiny voice of concern telling me not to go clubbing. Vaughn and I went out without incidence. Nothing happened then. I drank that night. I couldn't be a hermit forever.

~

FUEGO WAS everything that Mina promised and then some. Housed in a warehouse right off the river, it exuded a speakeasy kind of feel. Dark Walnut woods on the bars, burgundy walls, rich velvet horseshoe booths, some woman who looked like a younger version of Lena Horne, decked in sparkles, sang about how her man did her wrong.

It was quiet and subdued in an Oxonian library kind of way. It oozed with wealth and opulence. We were able to sit at our table and enjoy the music and have a conversation without being ogled and approached by twenty-year-old meatheads with false bravado and a fake I.D.

"Check out that drink of water at your two o'clock."

Mina nodded at an imposing man dressed all in black, leaning against the bar like it owed him something, his eyes never stopping long to focus on any one thing.

"God, his arms are bigger than my thighs."

I chuckled, watching Mina attempt to solicit his attention with an exaggerated grab at her straw, She wrapped her cherry red lips around her straw just as he passed by.

"He saw me."

She told me, putting down her snifter in exchange for her water goblet, hiding her comments behind a sip.

"Looks like you struck out."

I watched while she feigned her disinterest.

"He's watching the door."

"Oh no, he saw. He lifted his eyebrow when our eyes met."

How a lifted eyebrow expressed interest was beyond me. My experience is minimal. Mina reigns supreme in male-female flirtations.

"So, where's your hunky boyfriend, speaking of gorgeous men."

Mina tossed her hair over her shoulder, her earrings tinkling with the sudden movement. The deep purple dress she chose hugged her everywhere it should. It looked a million times better on her than it ever did on me.

"He's on assignment."

I tried not to sound disappointed. I didn't know where our relationship stood. Intellectually I felt silly for being upset.

"Do you consider someone a boyfriend if you never had a conversation about it?"

"You guys are dating."

"We went on a date."

"You slept together."

"We had a hot make-out session that ended...well. We have not slept together though."

"He sent you flowers."

"Because he felt guilty for having to cut our date short."

"Whatever, I say he's definitely in the 'someone special' category, label or no label."

The man of Mina's attentions passed us as he began to prowl the length of the club. He was a Grecian statue personified. Even in his dark t-shirt and trousers, I could see every ridge and contour of his body. The ripples moved beneath his shirt like a summer tide going to shore, and the focused non-smile he wore while he moved about the room. The term panty dropper was invented for men like him.

"Mmm, coffee with a hint of cream, just how I like them."

Mina mused following her interest around the room.

"Mina, I swear, I can't take you anywhere."

"That man is gorgeous and you know it. Those muscles. Damn, they put the fantasies with your Secret Agent man to shame! He could do more than tie me up and tie me down. He'd full on throw me against the wall and fuck me standing."

We drank thirty-dollar whiskey. We didn't pay for it. Our football-playing friends called ahead asking for the red carpet treatment. We received it in spades. Thanks to Mina's dirty mouth and dirtier thoughts, said thirty dollar whiskey pooled between the mountain of tits I had as a result of the push-up bra.

"I cant take you anywhere," Mina laughed, trying to help me mop up quickly before anyone noticed.

"I was thinking the same thing! Your mind is so dirty I'm pretty sure there should be a hazmat sticker slapped across it."

The object of her affection made his rounds and was circling back towards us.

"Ladies."

He nodded and smiled at us, the intent to continue on evident in his gait and forward propulsion.

"Where's the fire cutie?"

The grooves in the man's forearms when he crossed his arms over his chest--as he was doing --were wide enough to put the Grand Canyon to shame. If most well-built men had pythons for arms, his were anacondas.

"No fire."

The stoic set of his mouth finally separated into a smirk.

"Why not cool your heels for a bit."

"As much as I'd love to take you up on that offer, I have work to do."

Mina's eyebrows rose in surprise, I guess she didn't realize he worked there.

"I see. In that case, we need two more Laprohaigs. Pass that along to the bartender."

"Please excuse my friend," I inserted an apology.

"She isn't used to the punch whiskey packs."

The man in black didn't take his eyes off Mina. Despite her dismissal of him, he stood sentry at our booth. His eyebrow lifted in entertainment.

"It's no bother."

He lifted his finger at the bartender, and moments later two more tumblers appeared.

"How unusual to see two women, as beautiful as you are, gracing a place like this with your presence. Are you meeting your boyfriends here?"

"That's an awfully sexist observation."

Apparently, the whiskey did more than punch me.

"How do you figure?"

He cut me with a look of genuine confusion, which apparently entertained me more than it should as a giggle bubbled up unbidden.

"Well, you assume because we're in this club, sipping on whiskey, we couldn't be anything other than a man's arm candy. Maybe we came in here, seeking the quiet solitude a place like this provides. Sometimes women prefer to enjoy a night painting the town red without being slobbered over at the meat market nightclubs."

"Or perhaps I was trying to figure whether or not I would need to assist you in keeping away the droolers and the slobberers while visiting our establishment."

He countered, nodding his thanks to the waiter depositing our refills. The man in black waved his hand across our table, which was the universal signal for no charge on the drinks.

"We're on a house tab," Mina inserted.

"Then I guess I just saved the house sixty dollars." The man shot replied back.

"You got a name, Mr. Man of Steel?"

Mina's appreciation of the man's physique tickled him. I watched the seconds of indecision to stay and chat or continue on. He swung into our booth with catlike grace.

"Butler."

Even his fingers looked muscular. How does one develop muscles in their fingers? I became transfixed with his muscles. No man should be that built. Even a simple gesture like extending his hand highlighted peeks and ridges that didn't seem capable on a human body. He definitely isn't gross like Arnold Schwarzenagger, Mr. Olympia, oiled and bulky way. Sure the shoulder muscles beneath his t-shirt looked like they gave birth to little baby muscles--but it worked for him.

"Is that what you do?" I asked, unable to hide my curiosity, "keep unaccompanied women safe?"

"For now."

"And what about later?"

Mina looked at Butler so sincerely. Usually, she is such a ball buster. She dismissed him minutes earlier, yet now something sparked between them. Not sexual tension. At least I didn't think it was. Something in the air shifted, though. Butler didn't answer. Instead, he swung back out of our booth, surveying the room once again.

"Well, with all those muscles I can see why they hired you."

When he laughed, he fully committed. Butler didn't snicker or chuckle. He threw his head back and laughed. In the subdued silence of the club it stuck out, but that we entertained him felt nice.

"Well ladies, it was very nice talking to you. I need to get back to what I was doing."

"Thanks for the drink Butler," Mina called to his passing form.

"Oh my God."

We were two whiskey's in a piece, Little Lena Horne finished her set and now some woman who wanted to be Adele was at the piano desperately attempting *Someone Like You*. Keyword: attempting. Mina also attempted to continue whatever eye fuck she engaged in with Butler.

Each time he passed, she wrapped her cherry red lips around that black straw and pulled deep. Even I got the innuendo. She wasn't outwardly concerned with being too overt. He appreciated the act since his meander past our table increased in frequency to every few minutes.

"What?"

Mina's eyes reluctantly pulled away from tracking her man of mystery around the room and refocused--with some effort--back on me.

"That's so strange," I said more to myself than to her.

"What is?"

She followed my eye line to the front door where the very person Officer Parker and I discussed not more than a week ago stood.

"Isaac is here."

Mina leaned over the table, practically falling out the booth as she ogled. It was such a long time since seeing Isaac. Most of Danny's interactions with him happened on his own.

I never told Danny he couldn't hang out with his friend. We'd never gotten into any kind of fight. Or engaged in melodramatic 'him or me' crap new girlfriends sometimes do. Issac never acted outwardly aggressive, but when we socialized together, his dislike for me was obvious.

"Who knew he could afford to be in a place like this?"

He looked pretty good by Mina's kind of standards. He was in a well-tailored sports coat, over a shirt that was at least of the Nordstrom variety paired with a nice pair of jeans and shiny shoes. He certainly isn't slumming it by any standard.

"I wonder what he's doing here," I said again more to myself than out loud, but Mina was insistent on being part of my inner musings.

"Well, he's having a drink like most people here. Hmm, maybe I underestimated him."

"You didn't think he was cute a year ago."

"True. But he seems to have grown up a bit."

"Honestly Mina. My cop friend told me he's bad news."

Okay, those weren't his exact words. But I'm certain it was the subtext of the discussion.

"Really? What could a little pipsqueak like that possibly have to make him bad news?"

Except even from where we sat he didn't look like a pipsqueak anymore. He filled his suit nicely. Not that he spent hours at the gym but he certainly was lithe.

"Oh shit! He saw us!"

Mina fell into the cushions of the booth, bouncing off and

rolling underneath the table. If he hadn't, she certainly drew the attention of everyone in the bar. Including Isaac, and wanna-be Adele up on the keys. I refused to look up. If I made eye contact with him, he would think I wanted to talk to him. And, I didn't.

"So you must be feeling better if you're up and about."

I sensed his presence seconds before he spoke. Being around him never raised the hair on my arms before. Or twisted my gut. I blamed Parker. He made me afraid without giving me the reason why.

When I finally did make eye contact with Isaac, there was something different about him. I couldn't place it. Up close he looked less imposing. He wore his hair the same as he had, was a bit gangly still, and pinned me with the same tiny coffee bean colored eyes.

He was Danny's friend, but that he knew I had been in the hospital surprised me.

"Isaac. Hi. How are you?"

I tried to keep the conversation general and prayed he would move along after some uncomfortable small talk.

"Danny know you're out here on display?"

He didn't look at me while he talked. His eyes skated the room. Never stopping for too long on any one thing. If the mention of Danny didn't set my hackles pointing, his passive-aggressive dismissal certainly did.

"Desde que tú y Danny son amigos tope seguramente se dieron la noticia"

Mina spat.

I looked at her for a translation that didn't come.

"Puta."

Issac flicked her off, walking away without any further comment.

Puta, I knew.

I didn't need a translation for that one.

"I simply told him to ask Danny why you were out on display."

"I highly doubt it was that innocent."

"I may have implied they have a sexual relationship in a not nice way." She shrugged with a smile.

I looked at my phone. It was eleven. Not usually the time people our age called it a night. They'd be making it to the club about now.

"You want to leave don't you?" Mina asked reading my mind.

We took an Uber Black to the club instead of driving. Mainly because Mina insinuated she planned on getting laid that night. Uber would be easier for us to go our separate ways. Neither of us wanted the uncomfortable 'who is riding with whom' at the end of the night.

"Come on, I'll leave too. Danny's needle-dick little friend killed my buzz."

I gathered our purses while Mina took a tip over to the bartender with our thanks. I could feel Isaac watching me from the table in the corner. There was no hostility in his look but it was definitely not an impassive stare of idle curiosity either.

"Is there somewhere I can take you, ladies?"

Butler intercepted us at the front door, holding it open before following us out.

"We're heading home." I smiled my thanks at the chivalric gesture, buttoning up my coat as Mina and I were met by the shocking disparity in temperature from the warmth of the bar.

"It will take you forever to get a cab around here." He pressed.

"We're getting an Uber." Mina held up her cell phone, the app already pulled up on the screen.

"Consider my offer an extension of the VIP services you received inside." Butler smiled, pointing his key fob at an oversized black SUV parked illegally in front of the club.

Mina didn't bother to throw a questioning look my way to see if it was okay, instead allowing herself to be escorted by Butler to the behemoth of a vehicle, and assisted into the front seat. What option did I have?

The bar was only a few blocks from my condo. The entire ride home I chastised myself for being one of those dumb girls who got into cars with complete strangers. The ones who think 'oh, I'm only a few blocks away from home,' and then you saw their heart-broken parents crying and pleading on the ten o'clock news. 911 was pre-dialed on my phone. My thumb at the ready in case anything crazy went down. Seeing Isaac freaked me out. I'm sure Butler was on the up and up, but after all that happened over the past two months, I was stupid for being so gullible.

Mina carried the conversation for the entirety of the ride home. I don't think I contributed one syllable to the discussion, stuck instead inside my head screaming at myself for accepting a ride from this stranger.

"Cam... we're here!"

Mina snapped her fingers in front of my face trying to bring me out of my daydreaming.

"Sorry- I don't know where I went."

I guess whiskey probably isn't the wisest thing to drink when imbibing in alcohol was an activity few and far between these days.

"I'll walk you upstairs before taking off."

Mina offered, extending her hand to help me out of the backseat.

Butler undid his seatbelt as well. Apparently intent on making sure both of us got to our destinations safely.

"Well, aren't you a sight for sore eyes."

The words, spoken by a voice I ached to hear again, caressed me like a feather. Giddy joy overflowed from every pore.

"Vaughn!"

He stood at his door as if he too were arriving home. A black duffel bag strung over one shoulder, and a bouquet of flowers in the other. I launched straight out of my shoes, diving into him, and yanking him towards me. The duffel bag fell to the concrete with a dull thud. The flowers which were in his hand were now pressed in against my back. The annoyance and anger that bubbled and spit over the past week disappeared beneath a wave of relief.

34

VAUGHN

I don't advise visiting Minot, North Dakota. There isn't much there. Except fucking snow. Why bother tooting my own horn. You know I was right. There is absolutely no damn reason at all for me to be there. I won't waste my breath telling you I knew from the get-go Jefe had no reason what so ever to be in Minot.

I could fucking spit and hit terra firma in Saskatchewan or Manitoba, depending on which way the wind blew. Jefe didn't deal in Canadian. Maybe he did. It isn't my job to care about what happened with our neighbors to the north. They had people just like me working in their own country to keep the baddies out.

Two days after landing in Minot, and more than likely contract scabies and bedbugs, it was determined Jefe had no dealings in North Dakota. Carter naturally heard an earful from me. He, hand to God, uttered the words 'You're right Vaughn,'

Why then did it take me another week to get home? Because it's fucking North Dakota and one long arc of piss away from a country that produces some of the best winter sports athletes in the world. Why do they do that? Because of fucking snow. Lots and lots of goddamned white shit. It literally vomits out of the sky

221

in mass quantities measured in feet. Three feet to be exact. In the midst of that being cleaned up, we got showered with another twelve.

The entire town shut down. Food wouldn't deliver. We certainly had no way to get to the Walmart. Not like anyone would be there working.

That left the vending machine. Do you know how bad a person smells after eating that crap for a week? Now multiply it by four and lock it up in a dump of a hotel. Take away air circulation, add in a questionable cleaning regiment and you have some semblance of understanding what I dealt with. I'm shocked Cammie isn't looking up at me right now accusing me of smelling like a four-day-old fart.

Speaking of Cammie. I fucking missed her. When did this happen? When did I become that guy?

I hadn't seen my mother or my sister for a year and I didn't feel like this thinking about them. I couldn't make it back from KCI fast enough. And yes, I had gotten massive shit from Tom, Dick, and Curly for the crappy flowers I grabbed from some terminal vendor on the way to the parking garage.

"I've been so worried."

Her arms snaked around me and filled me with some flowery stuff I'm not even going to put pen to paper over. I already feel like half my balls are missing talking about what I already have. It was nice though, okay? It is an awesome feeling having someone express that much excitement at seeing me standing in my doorway, unshaven, exhausted, smelling questionable. Still running to me as if I were Santa Claus on Christmas Morning.

Then I saw him ambling up the staircase holding hands with Mina. What the fuck?

He saw me too. The look of recognition flitted across his face before he could school his features. In that brief span of time, I could see the same question I had just expressed, only he sucked at hiding it.

"This is Butler, he works at Fuego and offered to give us a ride home so we didn't need to wait for an Uber."

Cammie nodded over her shoulder at the pair, seeing I stared at them and not at her.

"How chivalrous."

Agents don't squirm. Regardless if they are FBI, CIA, DEA, Homeland--you never lost your cool. You never showed anything other than passive interest. But I knew on the inside Butler had to be squirming like a rabbit caught on a fence line. If I feared the hot water I'd face for my romantic interest, surely he had to be equally concerned. Especially since he is supposed to be on vacation.

"Have you ever been to Fuego?"

Butler asked me, extending his hand in mock greeting.

"It's a great place for people watching. A nice break from the usual."

"The place is great!"

Mina agreed, sidling closer to Butler broadcasting her interest--in my opinion about as subtly as a breaking news update.

"It's really swank."

"Mina stopped by for a visit."

Cammie squeezed me pulling my focus back to her.

"The players put us on a list. We got the royal treatment."

God did she look beautiful. She wore a hot red number offering up her tits like gifts to the gods. It hugged her in all the right places. She wore flats, but even so, the shape of her calves was accentuated by the dress that ended before her knees. Her makeup looked mysterious and sexy as hell. Dark smoky eyes lined to make the shape look almost cat-like. Her pouty red lips. Holy hell where I imagined those lips.

"It's a quiet place."

Butler continued, ending my appreciation of Cammie.

"Right on the river. Not surprising it would be a fan of Chiefs."

We'd both been trained in all kinds of communication and

subversive techniques. Despite Cammie and Mina contributing to the conversation as if we were honestly talking about the club and its attributes, I knew gave me much more.

On some subconscious level, I had never put two and two together, at that moment I realized Jefe might be batting us like little dipshit mice. Jefe's literal translation meant Chief.

"Will you be there tomorrow?" I asked Butler, cradling Cammie at my side.

"Should be." He replied, turning towards the stairs, Mina following close behind.

"Maybe I'll stop by."

Butler nodded before turning to head back down the way he came--assumably to continue his evening with Mina. Who was I to judge? I was about to do the same with the gorgeous woman cradled against my chest.

"Are those for me?" She pointed to the flowers now broken and smashed in their cheap cellophane wrapper.

"I bought them on my way home." I explained, "I didn't realize the time until I pulled up. I figured I would give them to you in the morning."

If I had my wits about me, I probably would have suggested that. I should have told her I was exhausted and wanted to shower, eat some real food and collapse into bed.

I would have remembered my house actually belonged to the Agency and my den is full of confidential casework. It would have dawned on me my rule had always been to fuck women in their homes, not mine. But Cammie isn't any woman. She definitely isn't *just a fuck*, and there is nothing else I wanted than to spend time with her. I was so relieved to be home. Excited to see Cammie again.

If we're being honest I was mostly thinking with my dick. The woman looked like a habanera mated with a firecracker and produced Cammie in that dress. When she followed me into my apartment I didn't even think twice about. I simply held open the door and allowed her in.

"You look beat."

I was. And I desperately wanted a shower.

"Beat is too soft a word for how I feel."

I could feel her following my movements as I stashed my coat and bag in the closet before moving about my living room depositing the various items in my hands.

She stood, gathering her purse and coat getting ready to do the one thing I didn't want her to do.

"I need some food and a shower."

I placed my hand on hers to stop her from leaving. That one point of contact, three fingers on my hand which caressed the satin of her wrist, rocketed a thrill of desire straight through me.

"Please stay."

I forced out around the lump in my throat. I took her by the hand and lead her to my couch.

"Give me like five minutes, please?"

I never begged. I wasn't a beggar. What did it matter if we ended up doing any of this the following day?

"Go on, I can wait. I'm so glad to see you back home again."

She pointed the remote at the television, pretending to be engrossed in finding something to watch.

As badly as I wanted to luxuriate in the warm water that didn't smell like eggs, the fabulous water pressure, and the simple pleasure of being clean, I didn't want to stretch the patience of the woman who had already spooled enough patience on me to knit a sweater.

35

Camille

Vaughn had very little in his cupboards by way of food. Even less in his refrigerator. I hadn't seen him in two weeks and based on the stale air in his apartment he hadn't been in here either.

Anything in his fridge, with the exception of the beer and condiments, was no good anymore. The best I could offer him was some chicken noodle soup and a can of biscuits I found. Hopefully, that would at least temporarily satisfy his hunger.

Just being in Vaughn's presence left me vibrating from the inside out. I felt as if I mainlined espresso. I was jittery and warm, full of unexpressed energy. When his fingers had caressed my wrist I thought I was going to jump out of my own skin.

It was at least a week since I revisited images of our make out session post date. As soon as we came in contact the only things my brain served me were bite-sized images of his mouth on my breasts, his warm, panted breath moaning out his satisfaction in my ear, his fingertips digging in to my hips with purpose, dragging me against the piece of his body that made me explode with ferocity.

Left with nothing to do, and worked up to the point of frustration merely by my own wayward thoughts, inspiration hit me. I'm certain my mother in heaven jumped in front of the Virgin Mary and covered her eyes.

"I made you dinner."

I could barely hear my own voice over the sound of the running water. The sounds of Vaughn's hands gathering soap stopped completely, so I assumed he heard me. I'm not a forward person. Not like this.

I blamed the whiskey. And Mina's bad influence. He saw my breasts last time. Almost had sex already, so I wasn't throwing spaghetti at the wall with my actions. There was obvious interest from both parties.

"Cammie?"

Vaughn looked so boyishly adorable with soap covering his hair and dripping down his face. His hands jerked as he tried to clear his sight line.

Despite the steam in the bathroom, the heat coming from Vaughn's body and the water behind him, that slight in-between of cool air and damp body sent a shiver up my spine.

"What are you doing?"

He asked, staring at my naked form, his eyes going no lower than my own. He looked absolutely confused at my presence. Like he'd fallen asleep and was dreaming this interaction.

"I came to tell you dinner's ready."

I stood, naked, in Vaughn's shower... and all he did was stare. Not at the good parts either. His eyes cemented to my own. He refused to allow his eyes to dare move to uncharted territory.

Did I totally misread this situation? Was I a complete idiot throwing myself at someone who perhaps grew tired of the girl who couldn't stand on her own two feet most of the time? Maybe dry humping him to my own climax turned him off from furthering our relationship.

He sent flowers, I told myself. Since arriving home he didn't even kiss me, though. He brought flowers home with him. They had been in his hand when we walked up. .Aside from my own affected breathing and the soft plops of the water as it rolled off Vaughn's body and swan dove into the drain, there isn't much else being said. Except of course for the entire conversation ping-ponging in my head.

The steam surrounding us clung to the scent of his body wash. An implacable scent that smelled fresh without distinctly reminding me of one specific smell. Without direct access to the water, a shiver began deep in my bones, chilling me from the inside out. Multiplying the chill of embarrassment that sunk into my psyche.

"Sorry, I..."

What exactly could I say? I totally misread the situation. Or, I thought you might enjoy a more sensual hello? I sucked at this. My chances of rebounding and not being labeled as a clingy weird girl were following Vaughn's discarded water straight down the drain. I shoved at the glass door, unable to make a graceful exit since the dumb thing didn't want to cooperate with me.

"I um... you're food is on the stove whenever you're hungry..."

The latch finally cooperated with a whoosh of the cold air.

"Cammie," his hand was on my own, pulling the door closed again. Just that act sent a wave of longing through me. It broke against my body like a tempest explodes against the shore.

My body followed his directive back into the shower, beneath the spray of water that both warmed my skin and heated my core. He placed his hands on my shoulders, The skin beneath his palms jumped and twitched as if being slowly roasted beneath a flame. I fought desperately to keep my arms at my sides. To keep an impassive look on my face so as not to show how deeply he affected me by a few simple gestures.

In case he was about to tell me I overstepped. That I should grab a towel and dry off, and go back to my house. I didn't want him to know that my insides twisted with anticipation, desperate to welcome him deep inside my core.

36

VAUGHN

I needed a minute to collect my thoughts. One minute I'm in my bathroom about to take a few strokes to try and calm the wayward thoughts, and the next Cammie's sexy body and demure insecurity grab me by the balls like she was a soldier at Normandy Beach on D-Day.

It had been a total gut shot seeing her. I don't think I'd ever seen her in anything other than sweats. Well, our date she wore a dress. Then, however, she exuded class and elegance.

That red dress? Jesus, Mary, and Joseph, that dress. It isn't even those luscious breasts. despite being served up and begging to be feasted on. The way the satin of the dress floated over her rump in the most delectable way isn't the focus of my white-hot desire either. Though that satin swam over her ass like even it knew she was too hot and it feared being burned. Cammie is the entire package.

It is evident that her friend played dress-up doll with Cammie. With her eyes linked in smoke and her lips painted cherry red, she screamed sexpot. Don't get me started on her mane of hair. Wild and proud like a lion standing on a cliff overlooking the Serengeti.

Her honeyed mane kinked and twisted around her face and across her shoulders almost as much as my own insides twisted with lust.

I needed that shower to call the dogs back and tamp down my desire. With as hard as I was, I wouldn't be able to enjoy just spending some time with her. It was late. I was exhausted. I earnestly wanted to explain to her, however, why I left so suddenly. And, apologize for being silent.

Then. a siren slunk into my shower, twisting me in her seductions and drowning me where I stood. Even more shocking was the similar situation I just imagined moments before she walked in. A delicious fantasy that bubbled up in the midst of my attempts to remove those wayward thoughts from my head, to begin with.

Her eyebrows had set into a wrinkled V to match the pouty set in her mouth. If not for the hopeful expectation in those amber eyes, I would have assumed she was angry at me. Before my eyes, the water chipped away at her sexy exterior revealing the vulnerable woman beneath.

"I missed you."

There were a thousand things I had thought to say. A smart assed comment about letting in the cold air. Asking why a man can't enjoy a little privacy. A flippant comment about following directions. Any number of jokes that sounded totally stupid in my head. e

As soon as she looked at me, it was the only thing that made sense. The only thing necessary. I barely got those words out before my hand made the decision for the rest of my body and yanked her against my mouth assisting the water's attempts to return the demure beauty to her original state.

Each time we kissed, her body went soft in the best way. Like, the way I made her feel, just by that solo action, took the steel out of her body. She needed to wrap her arms around my neck because her bones had been replaced with butter. Her fingers tickled into the matted hair at the back of my neck, slinking around and up, splaying across my skull, holding me in place while she attacked my mouth with equal vigor.

Gone was the softness of that initial melding. It morphed from a slow exploratory journey of reawakening desires to getting sucked away with the inertia of a nuclear bomb. All of the oxygen in the room disappeared. Only to be fed back into the other with enough static heat to catapult its eventual combustion.

With the lithe grace of a ballerina, she lifted onto her toes and lowered back down again when the effort became too much. Until she released a guttural moan, I didn't realize the motivation for her rolling on her toes.

We were naked. Obviously, since people in showers tend to not wear clothes. In that nakedness, however, smashed against my body, the rounded globes of her breasts mashed against my chest, the parts that separated us as male and female lined up perfectly.

It was late. I'm tired. My brain isn't fully functioning. You know all the man-haters out there will say that the blood I needed to think had flown south.

As that half muffled moan vibrated against my mouth in concert with her rolling up on to her toes, it finally dawned on me. The last thing I wanted was to fuck her in a shower. Maybe eventually. I hadn't seen her in almost two weeks. Our date had been a bust. would do everything I possibly could to ensure our first time together is a bit more civilized.

37

Camille

I guess he's interested after all. Really interested based on the hardness that rubbed in all the right ways against me. Touching him, in his nakedness, his body truly is a work of art. Where Mina's present boy-toy is power and intimidation, Vaughn is silent strength.

Just by the way his clothes clung to him, you could tell his physical form would be chiseled perfection. He has peaks and ridges hinting at his perfect beneath his clothes. When I snuggled into his chest, or wrap my arms around his bicep, I get a taste of the package Vaughn presents. But standing there in front of me, with not an ounce of insecurity on his face? Like he knew what he offered is incomparable.

When he is completely unguarded, like when I stepped into his shower, he had this silent strength that is difficult to describe. There is no cocky smirk or the playful glint in his eye which he sported like a comfortable pair of gym shoes. He simply broadcast resolute strength.

I couldn't tell you if it was the way he wiped water from his eyes, or how his hair was a shaggy mess from weeks on assignment--maybe it way the way he said my name and asked me to stay with a single word. Regardless, as soon as his lips slammed against mine, I was awash in my own animalistic need.

Walking naked into a man's shower is an open invitation to be fucked standing up, but the rate at which my body went from simmer to boil shocked me. Just a few passes of his lips, and a couple of strokes against the hardness smashed between the two of us, and I already am a handful of well-positioned strokes away from completion.

As if attuned to my body like a conductor knew his orchestra, Vaughn had me seated on the shower bench and positioned between my spread legs long moments before my brain caught up to the party. It wasn't until the sensation of that first pass of his tongue; warm and wet, suggesting instead of demanding, that conscious thought and corporeal feeling burst in a detonation of atoms like thunder meeting lightning. My whole body was alight. It floated on air that crackled and spit with the suggestion of the downpour on the horizon.

"Ben..." He corrected.

Did I call his name? I must have. Words were becoming difficult to summon, so I hoped the groan that broke sounded apologetic enough.

I couldn't hold still and not because he placed me on that small bench, slick with soap and warm water. Rather, having a man like Agent Vaughn...Benjamin...Ben, whatever... having him powerful and assured as he is, takes a knee to focus only on my own pleasure? It is too much.

The scruff on his cheeks, still a little soapy abraded my thighs. Delight rippled through me from the point of contact down to my curling toes and all the way up to the hair on my head. Vaughn's tongue morphed from gentle lapping to languid strokes teasing me up the short summit to my impending orgasm burned as bright as a high noon sun in summer time.

I desperately wanted to come. But, desperately wanted to fight it. To sit on this precipice a little longer. To float in the in between.

I wanted to ride the razor's edge for as long as I could possibly tolerate.

As much as my mind insisted we hold pat, the lower half of my body did not get that memo. It spread its arms wide and fell backward right into that pleasured abyss.

VAUGHN

Cammie is a goddess. She is sensual like an amber scented bubble bath and comforting like the ten-year-old sweat-shirt you wear on weekends. She is an amalgamation of classy yet totally erotic at the same time. The fact that she blushed like a virgin from me going down on her is too much for my hormone-addled brain to compute. If it weren't for my own need demanding I pay attention to it, I would have done it again just to see if that embarrassed, hazy delight stayed plastered on her face.

She accepted my hand leaning into me while she tried to gain her bearings. While she floated in that dream-like state, I washed the remnants of her makeup from her face, trying to tamp down the riot of tenderness that pushed against my rib cage when she turned her face into my hands and sighed in contentment. This is a situation I've never been in before. I don't make it to the shower portion of festivities with most ladies. I couldn't help but feel a bit knotted as to how we avoided a dirty shower fuck fest in favor of laying her out on my bed and treating her the way she should be.

"Ben."

I don't think my name has ever sounded as good as it does coming from her lips. Especially in that gasped whisper that echoed and bounced off the tiles of the shower. Every inch of her skin is covered in goosebumps. Caused either by my fingers running through her hair and down the arch in her spine, or perhaps left over from my oral attentions.

She followed me out of the shower, that rosy blush on her cheeks returning when I ran a towel over her skin to dry her off. The steam from her skin carried the combined scents of her own rain and eucalyptus smell combined with the fresh scent of the soap I used on her. It is intoxicating.

Cammie ghosted into my bedroom, wordlessly dropping the towel I wrapped her in, the golden flecks in her eyes catching the slivered light shining in from the living room.

"Kiss me?"

Like she even needed to ask. It is the one thing I thought about on never-ending repeat. The towel that wrapped around my waist slid down my hips and hit the floor with a wet thump. As if realizing at that moment exactly what had been momentarily hidden behind that towel, Cammie's fingers traced over my abs inching towards the one part of my body so desperate for her touch it bounced and shifted in an effort to quicken the process.

In that hemisphere of wonder, where panted breaths and sensitized skin, giddy with need smoldered, the seconds trickled lazily by. I floated in sweet agony while her fingers explored my body.

She had my toes curling in anticipation for that first stroke. Would she be gentle? Allowing my length and its heat to trace over the entirety of her palm before taking a timid hold and a tender pull. Or would she grab and yank, twisting in such a way it would mirror the way my insides churned for her? Would she wait to see if I'd show her how I liked it, or decide for herself?

Finally, her nails tickled through my pubic hair, her fingers creating a V around the root of my cock, before cradling my whole package in the warm softness of her palm. Whether it was a firm or soft grip I couldn't tell you because as soon as her hand wrapped around me, I was gone.

Lust knocked me out cold with a fierce right hook, painting

stars in front of my face knocking me off-balance. A breeze from the air conditioner could have blown into my room and I would have fallen over, spread on my bed at her mercy. Caressing became groping as both of us, desperate to feed the raging hunger, couldn't stave off the inevitable. With grace I didn't realize I possessed, she was in my arms and we were pirouetting onto the bed behind me. The pair of us, loose limbs and firing libidos, climbed against each other, searching for that perfect fit.

"Condom."

I couldn't believe I even remembered, being as cotton headed as I am in the moment. Cammie leaned up on her elbows, her heaving breasts illustrating how affected her breathing had become, distracting me momentarily from my task.

Finding a box of condoms in your bedside table probably isn't an appropriate time to be sending up gratitude to higher powers, but there was maybe a ten percent chance I actually had any form of protection in this house. It is well established this is a temporary residence, and my dry spell was long. However, I had won the preparedness lottery and I wasn't going to ruin the good karma by not acknowledging my luck.

Her gaze followed my hand, her lip sawing between her teeth as she watched me cover myself for her. I wanted to be everywhere at once. I wanted to be on top of her and behind her, over her and under her, licking and sucking, biting, pulling, pushing, pounding. I wanted it all and am at a loss as to how to satisfy each of those battling desires while also making sure she enjoyed herself as much as I knew I would.

I knelt at the end of my bed, cradling her foot in my palm, kissing each toe, the instep, eventually making my way up to the definition in her calf I had been desperate to worship.

"I wanted to kneel at your feet and worship these works of art the second you pointed your toe to show off your shoes."

I admitted, allowing my lips to pass over the ridges that defined the various muscles in her leg. She squirmed a bit, giggling at the tickle that my scruff covered jaw.

"I haven't been able to stop thinking about you."

I sucked at the back of her knee, loving the way she squirmed and sighed.

"Knowing that I would be coming back to you kept me from going crazy this week."

Her skin is so soft, still warm and sweet smelling from the shower. Her legs demurely closed, blocking my view from her most private parts, despite having just seen them in all of their glory in the shower. Just thinking about our shower activities had me pushing her knees apart to tease her a second time.

"Oh, Ben," her thighs mittened against my ears, her hips both jolting towards and wriggling away from my focused attention.

"Ben, you don't have to."

She practically whined. Diligently pushing onward, her pleas to cease falling on my deaf (and covered) ears, soon her protestations were simply monosyllabic vocalizations so nonsensical that I figured she must have given up the fight. Her fingers tickled through my hair, shooting hot need through my body.

I paused my journey towards her mouth with a brief stop to the rosy pucker of her nipples, twirling each around my tongue while Cammie continued to bow and bend beneath me, whimpering my name and piercing my skin with the fingernails that tickled down my back. I'm about to reach the inevitable boiling point, and I hadn't even made it to the actual act yet.

Tracking her jaw with my lips, I fed her the remnants of her own passion, enjoying the subtle tastes that danced across our dueling tongues. Like a flower arching towards the warmth of the morning sun, that first push into her snug depths radiated molten heat straight up my spine, igniting dynamite in my bloodstream.

I couldn't get enough of her. Drunk on passion, gluttonously feeding on her. Sucking at her neck with the desperation of a thirsty vampire, pulling at her nipples like a starved child, cradling her in my arms as if I feared she would float away. Her panted breath in my ear, the pleading appeals of ...there... yes...more...keep going.

She is so unrestrained in her passions, and because of it, I acted only to ensure her satisfaction. Her detonation strangled me, constricting and pulling the orgasm out of me with such ferocity that my eyes clouded and my ears failed to deliver any further stimuli to my brain. Powerless to do anything other than marinate in the rapture that pulsed through my body, I was practically yogic in my held position.

Camille

I ached everywhere. A good ache. The ache you only read about. It existed. It pulsed through me in time with my quickening heartbeat as I reflected on the night before.

Vaughn lay next to me, his arm cradling the pillow his head rested on, his mouth twitching ever so often while he slept. Almost ten in the morning. I rarely slept this late. On the weekdays Janet arrived at eight, and I got up way before she arrived. And now that I am a bit more self-sufficient, she just checked in on the weekends usually by nine to make sure everything is okay. Shit. She is probably out of her head with worry.

I needed to locate my phone. Did I even bring my purse in with me last night? Other than the remembrances of Ben going down on me, the near nuclear sex, and falling asleep cradled against him, the rest of the night is a blur. I felt the bed dip, and a warm, heavy arm encircled around my waist, simultaneous to a scruff-laden jaw tickling against my neck. The combined sensations caused me to arch in pleasure, bringing me in direct contact with Ben's version of a good morning.

"Good morning."

His gravel voice tickled against my ear.

"It is a very good morning."

My hips of their own accord arched once again, feeling the length of him against my naked buttocks.

"If you keep that up and it's gonna be an even better morning."

He teased, cradling my hip in his large palm, countering against my wiggle.

I remembered Janet telling me about her dirty sex books and the morning after sex that they all apparently had and I couldn't help but giggle.

"I must be off my game if you're laughing at me."

Vaughn's lips tracked down my neck, leaving a wet trail that cooled against my skin while my insides began to smolder.

"I'm not laughing at you."

I tried to turn around but his hand on my hip stilled me before snaking around and tickling up my thigh, guiding it back and over his own.

"I am laughing at something Janet said."

Words had already become hard to form. He had done little more than tickle across my thigh and position me for his explorations. People really did this? Had sex at night and again in the morning. It is a totally foreign concept to me. But, who am I to complain? Vaughn's other hand slid underneath my neck, and tracked down my collarbone to my breasts, twisting and plucking each nipple individually until they both were turgid peaks begging for his attention.

"You're quite ambidextrous."

I impressed myself with the ability to form words. My vision had gone fuzzy at the corners. When Vaughn's thumb began circling my clit, his fingers scissoring me open, sliding along my lips before embedding themselves inside me, the world went white. His hands were everywhere, creating a symphony of feeling throughout my body. So many stimuli my addled brain couldn't figure out which to focus on.

"So beautiful." Vaughn cooed in my ear.

"I could stare at that blissful look all day long."

Blissful? I didn't feel blissful. I felt rabid with hunger. Desperate to reach the summit that his fingers and lips and tongue were pushing me towards at a glacial and torturous pace. Every time I moved in counterpoint to his attention he slowed his ministrations even further, keeping me from climbing at the pace I preferred.

"Ben."

I'm not above whining. Or begging. Is that what he wanted? Did he need me to beg because I'd totally be down

for begging.

"Please Ben. Don't stop. There. More. Please, Ben more."

Nope even that didn't work. His thumb circled my clit like the second hand on a clock while the fingers inside me pulsed with equal torment.

His push into me is sweet agony. He fed me one inch at a time, pulling out before sliding back in.

"Cammie."

He tucked his face into my neck. His lips left wet kisses at my pulse point. I'm certain he could feel my pulse pushing against my skin. It felt as if every ounce of blood in my body desperately wanted to be freed from that one vein. The warm breath of his panted delight, the abrading scruff against my cheek, his talented hands manically touching every part of my body while his cock caressed my insides. It is a maelstrom of pleasure that threatened to drown me it is so consuming. How could one man, possessing only two hands, one mouth, and one cock elicit such intense, agonizing rapture?

"My God Cammie. I'm not going to be able to hold off much longer."

He waited for me? Wow. He waited, for me. That realization sent my body into a flurry of convulsions so sharp and prismatic it stole sight and sound from me as it ripped through my body.

"Holy fuck." Ben groaned as his pace stuttered, hips and groin smashed against my haunches. The force of his thrusting practically rolling me over onto my stomach.

Breathless, beyond sated, still hazy and starry-eyed I could only lay cradled in his arms while my body tried to reassemble itself after being absolutely shattered. In my haze I could hear my phone going off, the dulcet tone revealing Janet's phone call by sound alone. She is probably worried sick. It's after eleven and she hans't heard from me since yesterday, but my limbs refused to cooperate when I tried to remove myself from my the warm comfort of Ben's arms.

"Ugh."

The only word that I could form.

Ben's haze filled gaze came into focus, his mouth puckered in a questioning frown.

"I hope that isn't a summation of your thoughts of the morning's activities."

That lopsided smirk surfaced across his face, but hidden beneath is a shadow of a question.

"My phone. That's Janet calling." I tried to explain. "I can't move."

With a passing kiss against the swell of my breast, he slipped from the bed, his naked well-defined ass bouncing as he jogged towards his living room in the direction of my ringing phone. It stopped ringing before he slid back into bed, the warmth of his body covering me better than a blanket could.

"Good Lord."

She had started her check in texts at seven thirty, and preceded to text me every half hour until about ten when she'd started with the phone calls.

Ben read the text messages over my shoulder, laughing before planting kisses on my arm, making his way up to my neck.

"She's just making sure you're okay, you can't fault her for wanting to make sure you're safe."

Janet barely said hello before I cut her off, "Helicopter doesn't begin to encompass my description for you."

"Cammie! Thank God! I was just on my way to your house to check on you."

"Janet, it's Saturday, enjoy your weekend. I'm fine."

"I was worried."

"Oh, is that what the eleven text messages and three voicemails were for?"

With a last parting kiss on my back, drawing embarrassing purr from my throat, Ben exited the bed,

slipped into a pair of sweatpants, and grabbed his own phone from it's charging dock on his dresser.

"What is that?" Janet asked.

Nothing got past that woman.

"Are you okay? Are you hurt? Feeling sick? Should I call a doctor?"

"Oh my God Janet. I'm fine. Totally fine."

"You made a noise."

"Janet."

"Where are you? Are you still with Mina?"

My face felt hot. Am I blushing? Holy shit, I am.

"No, I'm home."

Technically I am near-ish my home... close enough.

"You sound strange."

"I'm in bed."

"It's almost noon, are you sure you don't want me to come by? Do you need me to refill your Antivert? I could have sworn you had enough to get you through the weekend. Did you take your medicine?"

While the flood of concern had its charm, it also leads to explanations I didn't want to give but it looked like I wouldn't have much of a choice.

"Oh my God Janet. I'm fine. I'm with Ben."

There was a torturously long pause. I could practically tell how many seconds ticked by just by counting how many breaths I took waiting for Janet to process that information.

"*With Ben*, with Ben?"

VAUGHN

She is fucking adorable. The way her face is turned into my pillow, her legs kicking beneath the blanket, a quiet squeak in her voice. I barely listened to her conversation with Janet, but I did hear her admit she was with me. Which lead to a whole lot of "ohmigod Janet"s and some giggling.

Just watching her from my living room where I hastily shot off replies to emails and text messages made me hard all over again. I came fifteen minutes earlier. I couldn't remember when my rebound time was almost instantaneous. I needed to focus on my work. Having her twisting and turning beneath my sheets, her scent hanging in the air is a horrible tease distracting me from things needing my attention.

"JANET!" Cammie's incredulous squeak bounced off the walls, drawing me away once again from the text message from Butler I tried reading.

"You're TERRIBLE."

I wanted to know what Janet said that could elicit that kind of reaction from Cammie. They were talking about me, obviously. But was it a good "he's the best lay I've ever had" kind of discussion?

Butler: 1300. Fuego. Developments.

A new message dropped into my phone while distracted by Cammie's conversation. A little before noon gave me enough time to shower and get myself together. I needed to find a way to gracefully end our time together.

I didn't want to. I would rather get a root canal with no novocaine. The thought of spending an hour out of my house instead of in bed with Cammie seemed torturous. Isn't that a kick in the balls?

I'm supposed to be the job. Not smitten with a neighbor in a city I didn't reside in.

While I responded to Butler, Cammie exited my bed and presently danced in place while she chatted on the phone. She never mentioned she is a dancer.

Her gaze looked out to the park below while she chatted with Janet, the t-shirt I wore the night before hanging past the swell of her ass. Every so often she would rest her foot against her knee in a perfect triangle before stretching it. Perfectly pointed toes out behind her, then to the side, and back again before returning to her flamingo pose.

Her phone call ended as I came into the room, the dazzling smile she shot in my direction stopped me in my tracks.

"She worried because I never checked in with her last night."

An eye roll accompanied the dramatic flip of her phone onto the bed before she joined me in the middle of the bedroom. "So ..."

The word drawn out and sing-songy. I knew it held the obvious question of where we went from here. It is a position I never found myself in. Women never came to my house, so it was easy for me to slip out of bed and tiptoe out of their houses never to be seen again.

This is different. She is different. And I have not one iota of a clue as to what to do now.

"So." I replied back, pulling her against my chest. "How does brunch sound?"

Those were not the words that my brain formed. I was supposed to tell her I had work to do. I was supposed to be suggesting we get together later because I had a meeting to attend to. Where the fuck did this suggestion of brunch come from? I'm not a brunch guy. I didn't do brunch. Where does one even get brunch?

FUEGO *WAS* QUITE the swanky establishment. While not the place I could picture Cammie and Mina painting the town at, it had a certain relaxed coolness about it that did speak to the elegance Cammie exuded with little effort.

There is an underground garage where deliveries came and went, and that is where I was instructed to park so as not to draw any attention of passersby.

"Vaughn." Butler's gruff voice greeted me, my eyes still trying to adjust to the dimly lit interior after the sunshine of the afternoon.

"So you're not on vacation after all."

By grip alone, Butler communicated his lack of agreement for the cover the agency provided regarding is absence.

"After listening to the audio you sent us from your mark's hypnosis I decided to look into this Isaac fellow."

My mark. Cammie isn't a mark, she is my girlf--fuck. Did that thought seriously surface in my head?

We took a seat in one of the horseshoe booths surrounding the stage, where his files were spread out. My own laptop case similarly overflowing. I pored over my own files infinitely while stuck in that motel room.

"We've been curious about Isaac as well. But we ran his record and it's clean. Not as much as a speeding ticket."

"He got into it with Jasmine and her friend last night."

Butler is on a first formal name basis with Cammie's friend now? Interesting. Taking her home clearly wasn't only a safety measure--though intellectually I knew that last night. Surprising all the same.

"Oh? Got into it how?"

I tried to ignore the custodial surge that stormed through my being at the thought anyone 'got into it' with Cammie. I didn't want to entertain the subtextual implications these feelings might signify. Not now anyway.

"It wasn't until later in the evening, when Jasmine and I were at my place she gave me the play by play. Apparently Isaac and Mina's friend..."

"Cammie."

Butler raised his eyebrows but continued, "Apparently Cammie and Isaac never got along. Cammie according to Mina doesn't know why Isaac has such hostility for her. It's been that way since she and Danny started dating."

Cammie mentioned it in her session with me. Something about him being a hustler or something similar.

"Do you have the transcript from her session?"

It provided little insight I didn't know already. The session was practically memorized I'd listened to the one on my cell phone so frequently.

"What about the indiscernible audio?"

"HQ has been working on it. They have processed and repro-cessed the audio over and again trying to get it. Obviously recording on an iPhone isn't ideal for these types of things."

Like I didn't hear that a thousand times. Honestly, though, the government can find a hidden twinkie in the back pocket of a man walking in a crowd down Madison Ave at rush hour from space but didn't have the technology to filter grainy audio from a cell phone? Please. We had the technology, I know we did. It is more BS red tape. If it is at HQ though, it meant Butler believed it pertained to our case.

"Wait... HQ as in DC?"

Butler nodded, grim-faced and stoic. From the pile of manila folders strewn across the tabletop, he produced on filled with photos and pulled them out.

"Isaac seems to be running with some interesting people." He began, pulling a picture of him talking to our recently deceased undercover.

"What the hell?"

"He appears to be one of Jefe's men. I don't think he is anyone of importance. Maybe an errand boy. Perhaps some kind of liaison. That's why I'm here. Isaac and his group hang out here nearly every night. Granted it's a popular establishment, most of the athletes for the various sports teams hang here, a few local celebrities." Butler continued, though I only half listened. Isaac is one of Jefe's men? Isaac knew Cammie. Cammie said she always had a bad feeling about him. What did Cammie have to do with the Jefe case? Maybe it is coincidental. She happened to know someone who is mixed with some bad people. It happened all the time. People were friends with people they would never expect to be involved in illegal things.

"Where's this Isaac guy now?"

"Being questioned."

Being questioned? What the fuck? Why is this the first I am hearing about it? Jefe is my fucking case and the CIA grabs someone for questioning pertaining to my case? Not.fucking.happening.

"Let's go." I grabbed my keys and collected my bag, trying valiantly to tamp down the hot rage threatening to boil over.

"Vaughn. This isn't your deal."

"Like hell, it isn't!" Okay, I said I tried to tamp down my rage. It isn't really Butler's fault, and hindsight should have reminded me the guy probably outweighed me by at least a hundred pounds of pure muscle.

This situation may be the only time I am actually grateful Carter is on my speed dial.

"Vaughn. Back from Minot?"

"Carter. Why the fuck is The Agency infringing on my investigation? They have a suspect in custody, and I wasn't so much as notified. This is my case, Carter. My.fucking.case. I was brought here specifically to take care of this fucking case. So tell me then why I need to hear from an Agency man they have one of Jefe's men in their custody for questioning since this morning. Fix this!"

I disconnected before he had a chance to respond. Also in hindsight again not a smart move. Carter technically is my superior, he gave orders not me.

"Let's go," I told Butler again, seeing his stuff still strewn across the booth. He stood, those python arms crossed over his chest, that twitched in some testosterone filled show of masculine superiority.

"Vaughn, there's nowhere to go."

"Bullshit Butler. This is my case and I have every right to be present at any and all interrogations regarding Jefe. Either I go to the Agency on my own and raise holy hell, or we go together."

Camille

Floating. That was a good word. I am positively floating. And not because in the past twenty-four hours I had not one, not two, but a handful of the most explosive and utterly satisfying orgasms I ever had.

Benjamin.

God even his name made me shiver. Memories of last night and this morning played on never-ending repeat in my head. Not just the sexy ones either. The way he pulled me close while we cuddled in his bed. The way he smiled at me and extended his hand when we walked into the twenty-four-hour diner down the street. The way he deferred to me when ordering before placing his own. He was a gentleman to the nth degree.

Our breakfast, while uneventful, had been such a pleasant deviation from the normal my life became. We were two people hanging out a greasy spoon, laughing and chatting over nothing, but my god it was something to me. He never even looked at his phone once while we ate, instead focusing his attention completely on our conversations. It wasn't until we left he informed me he needed to head to work on a promise to come over when finished.

"Helllooooo!"

Mina called at my patio door. Only the screen covered the entrance. I wanted to air out my condo, so left it open most of the day. While I could only last on my feet for short periods before getting woozy, I buzzed with unspent energy. I spent my day directing my energy into a cleaning kick. Okay, I vacuumed straightened my living room and lit a candle. But still. For me, it was a lot. If Ben came over later, I wanted it to smell fresh and clean and not a cave where someone holed up for some time.

"Look at what the cat dragged in. How's it hanging?"

If the oversized sunglasses and disheveled appearance weren't a billboard to her enormous hangover, the grunted greeting as she passed by certainly was.

"I am never drinking again."

She flopped onto my sofa, leaning her head against the pillows and covered her face.

"So much hurt."

"Did you just get up?"

The clock over my fireplace said it was past two.

"I've been up for a while. Butler had to work this afternoon. Why a bodyguard has to be back at work now when the clubs don't even open until eight or nine is beyond me"

I handed her a bottle of water, which she accepted and cleared in three huge gulps.

"I haven't been this hung-over in god knows how long."

Mina wore a pair of sweatpants which looked way too big for her frame, and a t-shirt from some place called the Salty Dog.

"Oh my god...you spent the night at his place didn't you?"

With a huff she raised her head enough to meet my gaze, a cat ate the canary smile spread across her face.

"Obviously. Why else would I mention he is working?"

"You're wearing his clothes."

"It was better than putting on a fuck me dress in the middle of the afternoon. I don't need an uber driver judging me."

"Wait, uber driver?"

"Yes. My car is downstairs."

She pulled my crumpled dress from her bag, plopping it onto my coffee table.

"I can dry clean it if you want me to."

"Did you Monika Lewinsky my dress?"

"Eww. Seriously Cammie. That's something I would say. And no. It's just wrinkled."

We sat in relative silence. The ticking clock and ambient noise from the park the only sounds filling the room. She opened the second bottle of water, loudly gulping it down. I checked my phone--again--to see if maybe Vaughn sent me a message. He hadn't. Not that I was expecting it. I refused to be like that. To be the one who can't go an hour without wondering if he was thinking about me.

Though, maybe I was because I'm tempted to send one to say hi. I didn't. Because he said he'd talk to me when he got home. I refused to be the clingly girl.

"So..." Mina began turning her body enough she could face me without having to lift her head.

"You and Vaughn?"

"So," I countered, "You and Butler?"

We both laughed, simultaneously proclaiming, "You first!"

"Butler." Mina offered. "Delicious."

"That's all I get?"

"What else needs to be said?"

"It's obvious he's delicious, we established it at the club last night."

Mina picked at her the bottle of water in her lap, a flush creeping up her neck and coloring her cheeks.

"Holy shit Mina, you're so red!"

"The things that man is capable of."

Her face broke into a wide smile before burying it in my sofa cushion.

"Holy fuck."

"So, was it like a one night stand kind of thing or ... how did you leave things?"

Mina tapped the water bottle against her leg, biting her lip as she considered what she was going to say.

"You know, I wouldn't say no. I'd be down, I mean like legitimately going out, on a date."

"Wow. Is Mina going to date a commoner? Someone without a six-figure income and a five-year plan?"

"Whatever." She rolled her eyes at me, slapping at my shoulder.

"So how did you leave things this morning?"

She shrugged and blushed, "He told me he was sorry but he needed to go to work, he left me some breakfast in his kitchen and he would call me later if it was okay."

Mina's phone pinged from within her purse--the sound eliciting a reaction from her I would have never expected.

"Not him."

She sighed chucking the offending object back into her bag.

"Oh my God. This is not me. I'm not the 'I can't wait to hear from him' girl."

"Ha, I was thinking the same thing!"

Now it was my turn to jump when the ping of my phone sounded. Unfortunately, it was Janet and not the one person I wanted to hear from.

> *Janet: So are you still reenacting scenes from my 'dirty porn books'?*
> *Cammie: OMG Janet. Too much. Seriously. Hahaha*
> *Cammie: I'm at home, Mina came over*
> *Janet: Did you take your medicine?*
> *Cammie: You know Janet, I am a responsible adult. I pay bills, take my car in for oil changes, go to the dentist every six months.*
> *Janet: I know. I'm making sure my favorite patient is a-okay. You know I worry about you on the weekends.*

She really needed to stop saying stuff like that. Not because I didn't appreciate it. I did, more than I could probably accurately put into words. Janet very quickly became someone I depended on. Not just physically. Not in the aspects of patient and caretaker, but as a friend, a confidant, a stand-in Mom.

It was why she needed to stop. Soon I wouldn't need to be taken care of. I would get better. Go back to work. Be a normal functioning human. Which meant Janet would move on to someone else. I didn't want to think about how badly that goodbye would hurt.

"Vaughn? Not fair!"

Still laid out on my couch, incapable of doing more than lifting her head, Mina shoved at my thigh with her foot.

"Nope. Just Janet."

I sighed, mirroring Mina's positioning.

"We're pathetic."

She laughed, snuggling deeper into my sofa, propping her head on the palm of her hand so she could continue to focus on me without having to strain to hold her head up.

"Completely."

"Let's do something today."

Despite the suggestion of activity, Mina didn't make any movement from my sofa.

"Like what? You seem pretty laid out."

"Meh, I'll rebound. Want to go shopping?"

"Seriously Mina? I'm broke."

"Hmm. Movie?"

The look I shot her I'm assuming gave her a similar response. I couldn't wait to go back to work. For no other reason than to finally be able to start paying back all of the people who helped the last two month. The discretionary income for movies and takeout wouldn't hurt either.

"Come on."

Mina shot off the sofa with more energy than I thought she could possess given the moaning and groaning she engaged in.

"My treat. We're doing a movie marathon. The salty popcorn will do our hangovers well. And the hours spent in a dark room with our phones off will distract us from how badly we want to hear from our men."

I couldn't argue. I sent a text message to Janet so she knew if I didn't respond it wasn't because I was dead, and followed Mina out to her car for an afternoon vegging in front of a super-sized movie screen.

VAUGHN

I s there anyone at any of the agencies who don't have their heads up their ass? How many times did I have to stress the importance of this case and witnesses to said case before the light bulb went on?

Fucking CIA. Since when does the CIA get involved in drug cases? Jefe is mine. Anything pertaining to Jefe? Mine as well.

We all sat down at some overpriced restaurant with linen table clothes and fancy garlic infused butter shaped like swans, drinking iced tea, disingenuously laughing at banal jokes. That supposedly is how you whisper sweet nothings in their ear while we jerked them off and made them think we wanted them. So why then are they cock blocking me?

What a fucking waste of time. Just as I told Carter. He got an earful from me on my way to the Agency. He is currently voicing his displeasure all over Kansas City' over being left out of key pieces of information.

We assembled at CIA HQ, dispatched in various capacities, circling like vultures waiting for the kill. Hopefully, despite the fumbles, we're closing in on Jefe. We had Isaac, whom we all suspected to be an inline into Jefe's organization.

It is no surprise to anyone that Isaac refused to cooperate. Insisting he had nothing to do with the cartel. Of course by the time I arrived he lawyered up and is being managed by a bevy of suits. Count on the CIA to fumble a pass at the ten-yard line.

At least Butler had the decency to appear contrite. When we arrived, Butler learned that my audio had been cleaned and would arrive shortly. If Isaac isn't going to be any help, perhaps my recording of Cammie might be. The connection to Isaac is evident. But we had no idea if it is of significance or simply from knowing Danny.

Danny would be questioned as well. Not because he is a suspect, but his association with Isaac, meant he too needed to be questioned.

The afternoon had been such a royal waste of fucking time. Now after seven, we practically had nothing to show for it.

"I said we weren't to be interrupted Dukard." Butler snapped as the door to the room we claimed pushed open.

"Guys--you need to hear this."

Some lower-level agency guy poked his head in, clearly intimidated by Butler's bite.

Hell, if I was on the receiving end of Butler's ire, I'd probably be intimidated too. We already well established that the guy could probably bend a semi-truck in half with his fingers.

"What is it?"

The heaved sigh from Butler evidence that he too had come to the end of his patience. Briefly, I entertained the notion that he desperately wanted to return to his new romantic interest.

"Chatter on the eleven seventeen."

I didn't know what eleven seventeen meant. Agency mumbo jumbo. Whatever it stood for, it's important enough to rocket Butler into action. He flew out the door hot on the heels of Dukard, momentarily forgetting me.

"Jefe."

That one word out of Butler's mouth got me moving double time.

"They've switched channels and are using more in-depth forms of cryptology, but it's definitely them, it came up on voice match."

The Agency's inner sanctum bent and wove in the most confusing serpentine patterns. I would never be able to find my way back. There isn't even a dignified shot of a former president hanging from a wall to give me a navigational reference point.

How the fuck they managed to not get lost every day they traversed these halls is beyond me.

Dukard pushed through a Plexiglas door, the seal on the door whooshing as we entered. The surveillance room had floor to ceiling TVs on one wall and an extensive collection of audio and surveillance equipment on the other.

There had to be at least fifteen people monitoring various screens based on a cursory headcount.

"It started about five minutes ago."

Dukard continued, pointing at a group of young men, all dressed in unremarkable white shirts and black pants, seated along a bank of TV screens with the tell-tale peaks and valleys of audio wave files, headphones covering each of their ears. None even broke their concentration for a second to acknowledge our presence.

Dukard reached over one of the men. Though he couldn't be more than a few years out of school. He appeared nonplussed that Dukard intruded in his personal space. The kid's focus is laser locked. His eyes never left his screen, typing his transcription as conversation fed into his headphones. With the press of a button, the room began to broadcast what I assumed is the same thing the kid listened to. The men spoke in a very archaic dialect of Colombian Spanish. There is no doubt these are Jefe's men.

"Yes. Diverted."

One of the men said. By voice, it sounded like Omar, Jefe's Segundo.

"What is diverted?"

I asked Dukard, as if he would know. Since the guy with the cans on his head wouldn't be able to hear me.

"Ask him what is diverted."

Dukard put his fingers to his lips like I am some fucking kindergartner asking for a second cookie. Butler shoved a tablet into my hand just as I wound up to mouth off and tell Dukard where he could shove that finger.

The tablet scrolled the translations as they fed into the system, taking the can-kid's shorthand and turning it into standard English.

I scrolled through the conversation that occurred prior to us arriving. There isn't anything there of note. Dancer. Roses. River. The number eight. And now diverted. What.the.fuck.

"Butler any of these codes mean anything to you?"

There is a white board across the room from where we stood. I wrote each of the words out, trying to find any semblance of pattern or clue to what they said.

"Did they mentioned a dancer before? Does Fuego have strippers? Maybe they're talking about the waitresses? Dukard, call KCPD tell them to send an unmarked to Fuego and watch the docks.

Maybe they're doing some kind of handoff tonight."

It is reaching at best, but it would at least cover a base just in case.

"It seems too obvious."

I said more to myself than to the others.

"Fuego is probably the diversion."

Butler joined me at the whiteboard, trying to make sense of the various phrases being thrown out from the Segundo and whomever he was speaking to.

"Probably. I figured getting PD there would at least cover that base."

"Dancer. Roses. River. Eight."

Butler repeated the words over and again as if chanting them like some kind of fucking yogi leading us all in a meditative exercise.

"There's gotta be more. We're missing something right in front of us."

"This is the diversion."

Butler stated again, running his hand across his chin in frustration. He looked down at the tablet in his hand, more words running past the screen.

"Watch. Coming. Dancer. No. Eight."

He called out as the words scrolled past. The chatter stopped, just the popping of the audio could be heard in the room.

My bones vibrated. Panic coursed through my body. Something is going down. Right now, something is happening. Because we spent so long measuring our dicks and wrapping ourselves in red tape, Jefe would slip through our mother fucking fingers. Again.

I never felt more helpless and frustrated in all of my years working at the DEA. Butler's jaw worked the piece of gum he chewed in triple time. Dukard paced the length of his room, his head down, hands on his hips. The silence from surveillance taunted all of us with the absence of activity.

"Did you try eleven nineteen?"

Butler asked Dukard before tapping on the shoulder of another headphone wearing guy.

"I want all of you scanning every thirty seconds. Whatever you hear report it. I don't care if it's Aunt Fanny calling her daughter to inform her that her bunions are back. Any and everything on any channel you scan gets logged. Got it?"

The room burst into a flurry of activity, all of the seated men furiously typing, scanning, adjusting, calling out random words and phrases they heard on the channels they eavesdropped on.

"Butler this is a waste of time. They should only be listening for Spanish calls."

"Did you ever think that's how they keep getting the drop on us?"

He asked, not taking his eyes off his tablet.

"You know the theory of hiding in plain sight? Maybe the diversion is the convo in Spanish. Maybe while we're waiting for the Spanish to pick up again on eleven seventeen, they're having a conversation about--who the fuck knows--soccer scores on another channel."

I couldn't argue with that logic and hung back in the shadows watching them all shout out various words and phrases. A woman, dressed similarly to all of the men in the room, pushed through the doors walking with a determined but excited stomp towards Butler.

"You need to come with me. HQ just returned the audio file you are looking for."

He pointed to me and thumbed towards the door, and we both followed the tawny-haired young lady down another maze of hallways to yet another surveillance room that looked exactly like the one we had just left.

"This just came down." She explained, "I figured you don't have your phone with you in surveillance. Seemed like a better idea to just play it for you."

With the push of a button, Cammie's voice filled the room. Just hearing it sent a warm wave of longing through me. I loved the sound of her voice. Barbed wire coated in honey. Such a delicious combination of hard and smooth. When it is tinged with sleep as it is in the recording, it made me ache, in the sexual sense.

We listened to the back and forth between the two of us. She talked about the break-in. The destruction of everything in her house. Danny. The argument. It was coming. My body twisted as adrenaline coursed through it, heightened and alert. Anticipating one grainy, and undistinguishable phrase. We were there. The moment we had all waited for. Hopefully, it is something worthwhile. I'd be shit on if ridiculous and inconsequential came out. Butler and I both would be in a world of hurt for sending it all the way up the chain and wasting resources for no reason.

"tenemos a Jefe" *We have her, Jefe.*

Good God. Cammie! In reality, the pair of us moved into action in mere seconds, but in my head, it felt like we some kind of matrix-like alternate reality where everything gaped in nightmare-like sluggishness. I bolted towards the door and took off blindly down the hallway, desperate to find the room that housed my cell phone.

Tell Jefe we have her. Why did Jefe want Cammie? Never mind the case for a minute--that I would digest once I could be assured of her safety. I couldn't do that without my goddamned phone. We had to surrender them when we entered the inner sanctum of the Agency.

I could hear Butler behind me shouting out directives to people we passed. Maybe he is shouting them at me. Actually, he probably is shouting them at me since I didn't see anyone else in the hallways I blindly ran up and down.

His meaty hand pinched against my collarbone, yanking me to a full stop.

"Vaughn."

My whole body shook against his grip. I could see his mouth moving. Could tell words formed and voiced, but nothing processed.

"Snap the fuck out of it man."

"Cammie."

The only word I could say, and the only one that mattered.

"Where is she?"

He asked, walking ahead. I followed. He knew these halls better than me. Taking off in blind panic obviously didn't help me locate anything of value.

"At home, I think? I need my phone. Where the fuck did they take my phone?"

We pushed through yet another set of doors into a massive room filled with DEA and CIA. Carter stood with Hendricks, hands on his hips, looking at a screen projecting data.

"We have a link."

Butler announced to the room as we entered.

"We need full dispatch to Nine Carrington Court Two A. Cans and songs. SWAT. Everything we've got."

"I need a phone. Someone give me a fucking phone."

I didn't know her phone number. How the fuck did I not know her phone number? We'd been talking for weeks. She had been in my bed last night. Yet I didn't know her number. My files are somewhere in the office Butler and I had used.

"Someone put me through to KCPD."

At the very least I could get a hold of Parker. Surely Parker had her phone number. If nothing else he could get to her immediately.

"Butler, get KCPD to radio Parker. Tell him he needs to get to Cammie's house immediately."

I didn't give anyone time to relay information before I too was out the door. I followed the agents scrambling towards the garage, planning to steal a ride from one of them. Butler hadn't been fucking around with his directive. I watched in silent awe as the SWAT tank rumbled out of the garage. Followed by a line of blue and whites, SUVs, and the DEA Van. We each took a different route towards Cammie's house. Some had sirens blaring, others stealthily wound down back roads to ensure coverage for every avenue out of her house.

What kind of asshole didn't even know the number of the woman he slept with? I felt nauseous at my inability to warn her. I had sworn an oath--in its variation--to serve and protect. Yet I couldn't protect the one person, who by association alone, should be protected more than anyone else. This is why Agents are single.

Camille

Mina and I actually ended up seeing two movies. Upon Mina's insistence, after watching some sappy Nicholas Sparks movie that had both of us ugly crying by the end, she had insisted she couldn't go home with a sad movie hangover on top of her actual hangover. We had snuck in--her idea, not mine--to some ridiculous comedy with Melissa McCarthy. Five hours later, full of calorie-laden popcorn and hopped up on what essentially amounted to an entire two liter of pop, we headed back to my house.

"Nothing from Butler."

As soon as we were out of the theater, the first thing Mina did was check her phone. Damn, she had it bad.

"Anything?"

"Nope. Just a missed called from Peter."

I tossed my phone back in my purse, and followed Mina out to her car, regretting immediately bypassing the bathroom.

"How does a five minute trip around the corner feel like thirty when you have to use the bathroom?"

I whined attempting to distract myself by the pressure on my bladder rocketing me into complete discomfort.

"How does someone your size consume a vat of soda the size of your head?"

Mina laughed, pulling into the entrance of my development. I barely said a proper goodbye before I made my way inside, as quick as a vertigo addled shut could.

It was gloriously sunny outside when we left that afternoon. It never dawned on me to turn any lights on. A fact I realized while I fumbled for my keys and placed my lock by feel alone. Thanking whatever god looked after girls with full bladders, I pushed my way inside. I didn't bother with the lights since it would have taken too many precious seconds. And the having light to peeing my pants ratio favored the latter.

The warmth soaked through my shorts and trickled down my thighs registered before the shooting pain in my scalp. The abject terror of being yanked backward by my ponytail didn't register at first either. A man held me down. A very large man with rough hands. He reeked of an indescribable foulness akin to garlic and salami.

Was I screaming? Sound ricocheted off the walls. It sounded like me. But, I couldn't tell if it actually was.

I fought hard to stay in the moment. I focused on the houndstooth pattern of the shoe that held me down. The bite of the rope binding my wrists burned. My muscles screamed with pain as I twisted and turned against my aggressor. I used that pain to prevent myself from passing out.

I'm going to die.

That thought I tried to ignore.

Found – The Jefe Cartel Book 2 is finished and with my editor.

I hope to have it released Late May or Early June! Stalk me on all social platforms for more information about book two! <u>Sign up for my newsletter</u> – because I'll be putting out a call for Betas real soon!

Keep turning for a sneak peek at Book 2!

Did you enjoy the book? Please help Independent Authors such as this one spread the word about their books by leaving a review on Goodreads as well as at your place of purchase. This book is lendable, so go on and share this with a friend!

WILLOW'S MEA CULPA

~

Just like any movie these days—you have to sit through the credits before I show you some leg.

Thank you first and foremost to you my reader of this book (If you've made it and are still reading you're an even bigger rock star!). Thank you for picking up my book. For helping me keep my dream alive. Thank you even more if you leave a review and tell your friends to read this. We'll be besties. 👯

When I first started out writing, I was unemployed, my husband and I had just spent a small fortune on IVF, we were out of money and I said "I'm going to write. The money I make on my books will fund our adoption." So that is what these books are (slowly) funding. My dream of being a mom. Again, thank you for doing your part in helping me fulfill the most paramount of dreams and goals.

A huge thank you goes out to Deb my favorite Beta on the planet. If it weren't for her, this book may not have ever gotten finished. I started this book probably 18 months ago (maybe longer) and she received it piecemeal as I wrote it. Then, I cliff hung her with no resolution because, life. She deserves the world for being patient, being a cheerleader, being my pace keeper---all the good things. I love the shit out of you.

Of course, now she up and got engaged, and is in the midst of planning her wedding so who knows how much of her time I will have for the rest of this series.

You should sign up for my newsletter; I might be looking for a replacement. I kid. I kid.

My life has gone through some crazy changes over the past couple of years. I'm no longer repping the 312. I mean I'll always be Chicago at heart, but now I'm hanging out in the mountainous vista they call the desert southwest.

I had to say goodbye to my favorite Starbucks crew - Store # 13437—RESPECT – since part of this book was written in "my spot" you still deserve a little BOB love. Starbucks just isn't the same out here, and everyone is all "OMG Dutch Bros."

I've taken to writing at Panera on Sunday mornings. If you ever want to see little old church ladies get stabby AF …innocently sit in "their" spot on a Sunday morning.

To the **Jets** and the **Sharks** of the Sunday morning church crew (I used to refer to them as Crips and Bloods, but we're sorta close to L.A. so...) —I'm so honored to have finally been welcomed into your circle of friendship.

As per usual with my books, I took a LOT of creative liberties:

To the Kansas City Chiefs, you'll probably never know that Cammie worked for you, but –fist bump- for being a hell of an organization. I'm sure Arrowhead Stadium is quite safe, and the owner of the football club more than likely knows the names of all of his employees.

To the DEA, CIA or any other "Agency" that I mention in this book. Figment of my imagination. Those Internet searches… book research. I make light but they keep the bad guys out and protect my ability to write whatever the heck comes to my head without fear. So, even if Vaughn is a potty-mouthed unabashed challenge to the hierarchy no disrespect is intended.

To Minot North Dakota- I've literally never been there. I had a boss a long time ago who lived there briefly and would tell us stories. I abhor snow and cold so I more than likely won't ever visit. I'm sure it's lovely, and more than likely even gallons of snow wouldn't cause your town to shut down—since you get snow so often its old hat to you guys.

To the city of Columbia and Colombia the country. I tried really hard to make sure I spelled each correctly as I referenced them. I went back with a fine toothed comb like a million times. If by chance there is one straggler that is misspelled, please accept my most sincere apologies.

To the twin Kansas Cities---Okay funny story. This one time I had a bachelorette party in Las Vegas. We spent the entire night out partying and didn't make it back to the hotel till close to six in the morning. I was a broke twenty year old at the time and flew Southwest to Vegas—the cheap "want to get away" flight that had layovers.

Fast forward to an hour or so later someone wakes up to go to the bathroom realizes we all passed out and needed to get to the airport post haste to make our flights. More than likely still drunk, I land in Kansas City to lay over for an hour before getting to Chicago. To this day—like fifteen years later—I have absolutely no idea if my layover was in Missouri or Kansas. None. The terminal was only five gates. There was a sandwich stand, bathrooms and that was about it. I was actually able to go outside and sit on a bench and smoke and call my Mom while I passed time. In my head, Im assuming this was Kansas because…well… Kansas. But it could have been Missouri. *shrugs *

Anyhow, tangent. Apologies. It's two in the morning and I've been putting finishing touches on this thing all day. I need to get it uploaded before Amazon banishes me to the red room of pain.

I'm sorry to the twin Kansas Cities. Someone who didn't have a drunken experience like mine more than likely can tell the difference between the two cities. (And if someone local cares to enlighten me, I'm all ears)

FOREVER GRATEFUL HASHTAG
BLESSED

~

I Couldn't Have Done it Without You

SO MANY THANK you's need to be said. THEN I'll shut up and give you a peek into the next book.

Having moved away from the Midwest, regional differences were really surprising. It is kind of unfriendly here.

It was a shock considering how many Midwesterners live here. Making friends has been kind of hard. People aren't interested in inviting new blood into their social circles.

Which is why I owe my thanks to my new tribe.

To Janet, Katie, Tracy, Christa, Dolores, Georgina, Karen, and even Brad! Thank you for welcoming me in and including me in your circle. Your friendship and enthusiastic support has meant the world to me. Having this tribe of amazing women (and man) have made the transition a little less lonely.

So, it should be said real quick, that I started this book a long time prior to moving. The "Janet" character had already been created and named. It wasn't until I was in edits that I realized I have a Janet in my new circle of friends and a Janet in my book. As wonderful as friend Janet is, book Janet and friend Janet are not the same. Just a serendipitous coincidence.

To my group of fist shakers—you know who you are. Your friendship and support, are just two of the many reasons why you guys are the very best bunch of See You Next Tuesdays anyone could ask for.

To at the ladies at the RWA (East and West), thank you for your support, advice, sympathetic ears and helpful tips. I am so glad to be part of both of your organizations.

And of course, it goes without saying that I am forever grateful to my family and friends, you are the best book pimpers and cheerleaders a girl could want!

FOUND: JEFE CARTEL BOOK 2

FOUND JEFE BOOK 2

Vaughn

HELPLESS. It wasn't an emotion I was used to feeling. I was the guy. The one who always had the solution. Brains or brawn. But I always had a way of solving things. Now I was the passenger in a car of someone I didn't even know, willing them to drive faster, push harder, run over people if he had to get there. I didn't have anyone to reach out to. No one that I could talk to that would tell me everything would be under control. No one to bark orders at if for no other reason then to make me *feel* like I was solving something. I didn't even have a goddamned phone. It was in the desk drawer of some asshole somewhere in the C.I.A.

I could only hope that Parker made it there in time. For the first time in the least sarcastic way possible I actually appealed to any higher power that would listen. I would unpack these emotions later. I would figure out why on earth I felt so strongly the urge to protect Cammie at a much later time. When I was sure she was safe. When I knew that no one could get to her. When the bad guys were put away. Right now, this fucker needed to move a whole lot fucking faster than he was.

FOUND: JEFE BOOK 2

Cammie

THERE WAS a funny smell in the room. Strange. Musty but damp at the same time. Bitter but sweet. It was dark. Or nearly dark. I realized my eyes had been closed and were just slowly coming into focus. Somewhere in the room someone was crying quietly.

"Hello?"

My voice sounded strangely disconnected. The crying stopped.

"Is someone else there?"

I continued, feeling around my body.

The ground was cold and covered in small stones. Where the fuck was I?

"Hello?" A timid female voice called back.

"Is someone else in here too?"

She sounded as far away as a voice could feel while being in the same proximity.

"My name is Cammie."

I told the voice in the darkness.

"Cammie Saint. I'm from Kansas City, Missouri. Do you know where we are?"

The girl began to cry harder than she had before. Inconsolable tears that echoed off the walls and daggered into my psyche. I never heard anyone cry like that before. As if they witnessed the end of the world.

"You are in a very bad place."

The voice told me.

"And most likely you're never getting out of here."

"cierra la boca, tu puta."

Something blunt banged against the wall—or a door. There was a door! Someone stood on the other side of that door.

I didn't have to hear the Spanish being spoken to know what had happened.

He'd found me.

HAIL TO THE CHIEF

Made in the USA
Middletown, DE
06 February 2019